OVER 100
GREAT NOVELS
OF
EROTIC DOMINATION

If you like one you will probably like the rest

NEW TITLES EVERY MONTH

If you want to be on our confidential mailing list for our Readers' Club Magazine (with extracts from past and forthcoming titles) write to:

SILVER MOON READER SERVICES

The Shadowline Building
6 Wembley Street
Gainsborough
DN21 2AJ
United Kingdom
or
sales@babash.com

or telephone
01427 816710
(UK office hours only)

NEW AUTHORS WELCOME

Please send submissions to
Silver Moon Books Ltd.
PO Box 5663
Nottingham
NG3 6PJ
or
editor@babash.com

First published 2004 Silver Moon Books
ISBN 1-903687-55-1
© 2004 Giselle lorimer

Bound to Please

By

Giselle Lorimer

Also Giselle Lorimer
Enslaving Anna

Chapter One

Charlotte stirred lazily in her big four poster bed. The birds were singing their hearts out in the trees outside her window. She felt deliciously happy, and as she became fully awake she remembered why. Four whole glorious weeks, a full month of summer, with the grand old house all to herself.

Until last year she'd been living a hundred miles away, in her own smart little flat, paid for by her mother and Henry. But when she'd finished her college studies and walked right into a top job with Palmersons, Mummy had suggested she move back home. After all, the house had eight bedrooms, so there was plenty of space. And Henry's law firm was based in the same town as Palmersons, so she could get a lift in to work every morning...

She had known it wouldn't work, she was far too used to her freedom by now. But she couldn't afford to rent anywhere decent yet, and Henry wasn't about to shell out on a new flat for her when living at home made such good sense. No one got to be as rich as Uncle Henry by being spendthrift. Cue for nine months of being treated like a child, back under her mother's ever-watchful eye, and it had driven her almost crazy. And if that wasn't bad enough, there was trouble brewing between her and Uncle Henry, trouble she didn't want to admit to, not even to herself.

But yesterday the loving couple had headed off on a month-long cruise, and she was free. Really free; for the next two weeks she'd be enjoying her first ever annual leave.

She stretched luxuriantly and pushed the white linen covers down her body, one breast slipping out of the chiffon teddy she was wearing. She was perspiring slightly, it was already warm... another scorcher of a day on the way. She trailed her nails across her little pink nipple, watching it bunch into a tight, hard bud. Slipping her hand under the fine material, she stroked her naked pussy lips, enjoying the satin smooth feel of her newly denuded skin. The aged nurse at the laser salon had been a little surprised when Charlotte had explained she didn't just want the standard bikini line treatment. No, she wanted her labia completely hairless.

Until recently she hadn't known how exquisitely sensitive a woman's mons veneris becomes when totally depilated. She'd seen the porn of course, all those cheap, fake-blonde tarts with shaving rash; how common they looked. But she had always supposed it was just something girls did to please their boyfriends. And being avowedly virginal, why should she care what her pussy looked like? But one night she'd just been in the mood to experiment... twenty minutes later and she'd been stroking entirely naked nether lips for the first time since girlhood. And the sensation was so delectable that she knew at once she wanted her pussy totally hairless. She thought about getting it waxed, but that would have needed repeating every couple of months, what a bind! And then she had read about the new laser treatment, how quick and effective it was, and only a bit painful.

They'd told her she would need six sessions to eliminate the thick, dark, purplish-red curls that covered her pubic mound. The first two had been fine, it stung a bit as the laser trailed over her skin, but not unbearably. She was a little sore afterwards, but nothing major. But the hair had clung stubbornly to life, so at each session the nurse had had to increase the power of the laser. During the third session, Charlotte had gasped and twitched and only just been able to bear the pain. At the fourth session she'd cried, and been unable to stay completely still. And when it came to the fifth, the nurse had said she couldn't continue, for Charlotte bucked like a wounded animal when the laser blasted against her labia. The treatment wasn't intended for the full Brazilian look, said the nurse with a look of pinched disapproval, Charlotte would just have to have the usual short back and sides, like everyone else, she couldn't treat a patient who didn't stay still. Her lips were pressed together in a hard thin line that clearly said what she thought of the girl she was being paid to treat.

Charlotte, however, was a rather spoilt young lady and extremely used to getting her own way. She'd paid for her six sessions, she'd paid for naked nether lips, she was damn well going to get them. She raised her voice in fury, and the ensuing argument was so raucous, and potentially damaging to business for LaserLovely, that both the manager and the security guard had arrived in the treatment room to see what the fuss was about.

She wasn't quite sure whose idea it had been, that the two men should hold her, to steady and support her. Had it been the hag of a nurse, who really did want to see her suffer? Or one of the men, who had wanted to see her spread? Anyway, once suggested, she couldn't sensibly reject it. But when it came to it, the pain was so excruciating that Charlotte had needed more than steadying. And so it was that she experienced her fifth session of laser treatment immobilised upon the narrow hospital bed by two burly men, one stood on either side, her fragile wrists pinned down above her head, her ankles held high and back and widely spread, so that the nurse had unfettered access to the naked genitals of a patient who could no longer do more than wriggle in an unsuccessful attempt to evade the instrument of pain. Charlotte had started to scream, but that wouldn't have been good for business either, so they'd stopped for a moment, and she'd suffered them to gag her. After that she could only moan and quiver, as the nurse did as she'd requested. The pain had been terrible; if she hadn't been held immobile she'd have been out of the door and down the street, half-naked though she was. If she hadn't been gagged she'd have begged and pleaded with them to stop. Luckily however, the procedure was brief, and fifteen minutes later a shaken and bedraggled Charlotte had left the salon, never to return. No more hair grew back, she didn't need the final session; a fortunate outcome as she'd never have been able to face those two men again. For when it was over, and she lay back, sore and stunned, and they reluctantly released her ankles, she'd become aware that her spread and exposed pussy was visibly moist with sex juices, and that both pairs of trousers, close by her, close by her face, were bulging with erect cock. Perhaps then, the old nurse did her a favour: Charlotte would never know, but, once she'd been gagged, the vicious harridan had surreptitiously turned the intensity up to maximum, to punish the uppity little tart who'd come so close to losing her her job. As the maximum setting was usually reserved for tough bristles growing out of moles on old women's chins, or similarly tiny and insensitive areas, it was unsurprising that the pain was so intense when used on a young girl's most sensitive flesh.

Charlotte's pussy lips were swollen and red for the rest of the week, but she'd got what she wanted and, perhaps, also what she deserved.

Now she started to stroke her clit, already wet from the sight and feel of her own body. She got wet so very easily, she reflected. Men her own age sometimes asked if she was a lesbian, as she never responded to them. But she wasn't particularly interested in girls. She loved sex, was passionate about it, frigged herself at least twice a day. But alone, always alone. She liked to be in control, and she was scared of what might happen if she ever let a man into her bed. There was a darkness in her, she didn't understand it, and it frightened her. She shivered at the memory of those two men holding her open, their large, brutish hands wrapped tightly round her slender ankles, and her own aroused response.

She got out of bed, and, standing in front of the huge ormolu mirror, peeled off her flimsy clothes and let them fall to her feet.

She was a slight, slim figure, only about 5'2", with long, dark auburn hair that fell in rich waves over her silky shoulders. Her skin was pale, unfreckled and unblemished, like a smooth ripple of cream. Her legs were slender, her hips neat, her bottom... ...she was vain enough to turn to admire it... small and pert. Her breasts were stunning. They weren't actually very large, but as she was so tiny they jutted out in a manner that demanded attention. No man ever failed to appreciate Charlotte's breasts.

If she could have heard the whispered conversations that followed her around college, in any pub she happened to visit, even on the bus or at the supermarket, then she would have understood that men really did think it a dreadful waste of a gorgeous body that, as far as anyone knew, none of them had ever had their cock inside her.

She wondered what Henry would think of her body if he saw her naked. She sighed. Dangerous ground.

He hadn't appeared to take much notice of her until that day in his car, just two weeks ago. He had been driving her home from work. She was sitting, settled back comfortably in the Merc, idly daydreaming about sex. It was hot, too hot, it'd been hot for days. She was wearing a soft skirt of pale blue silk, under it her legs were bare; it was far too hot for stockings. She was clammy with the heat. She had glanced at Henry, about to ask him something, and saw that he was looking down towards her lap. Following his gaze she saw that the thin silk was sticking to her body, tracing the line of her thighs. And somehow it'd pulled tight over her pussy lips. You could even see the shape of her pussy lips through the fabric. And just where her lips parted the silk was darkened with moisture. She felt her heart beat faster.

She looked up, straight ahead, out of the window. They were stuck in a traffic jam. She made no sign that she was aware that her clothing was awry, no sign that she had seen him looking. She just stared out of the window, as though the back end of a Peugeot 206 was the most fascinating thing she'd seen in weeks. She could feel her breath quickening, and she knew her love juices were flowing freely now. She wondered if that betraying patch of dark moist silk was growing larger.

The problem was, she had fancied Henry since they had first met. It had been most unfortunate. She knew Mummy was dating a new man, knew in fact that Mummy was head over heels in love. They were due to be introduced at the weekend, Charlotte and Henry, the daughter and the new lover. Then a few days before she'd been in the city, at the theatre with an old school friend. In the interval they'd gone to the bar. As she stood, waiting to be served, she'd become conscious of the man next to her. Quite why he drew her attention she couldn't have said. He was much older than she was, old enough to be her father, she thought now, grimacing at the irony. But he was tall, and very handsome, in a silvery, distinguished-looking way. But it wasn't that. There was some air of power about him, something she couldn't identify. He wore the power so gracefully, the way a man who has always been privileged wears an expensive suit. So totally at ease that you don't notice the suit, it just adds dignity to the man it clothes. She had felt her sex juices start to flow as he brushed against her.

And then he was gone, and the moment was past.

Three days later she'd travelled home to meet Henry for the first time. She'd rung the bell chain and heard Mummy's voice in the hall, all happy and gay and in love. And she'd felt a surge of joy, because it was so good that her mother had a man to love, after all the years she'd been alone since Daddy had died, for although there had been boyfriends none of them seemed to last more than a few weeks. Then the door had swung open, and there was Mummy, smiling like a teenager and holding tight the arm of… Henry. The man in the theatre. The man who made her cunt squeeze with desire simply by brushing her arm.

He hadn't appeared to recognise her. Why should he, she thought with chagrin. She had very much wanted him to remember her. But every time she thought about him, she saw Mummy's smiling face, and she knew that it was a good thing that the intense attraction she'd felt had been entirely one-way.

Well, that's what she'd thought. Until that hot afternoon, sitting against the leather upholstery, her silk skirt sticking to her pussy and showing him what a hot little slut she really was, under the veneer of demure young lady. The *façade* of demure young lady.

She'd chanced a quick glance down. The patch of wet silk had indeed grown larger. Now it looked as though someone had pressed her dress up into her groin, for her labia were clear under the wet fabric. Parted lips, like a flower. He must be able to see that I am hairless, she thought, and the thought made her hungrier still.

She'd done something bad at that point. Up till then she'd been innocent, if a girl who gets wet just from brushing against a man can ever claim the term, 'innocent'. Well, let us say then, that until that point she'd been guiltless. She had done nothing to encourage him, it was hardly her fault if her pussy flowed with fuck juices so easily, no woman chooses to be born a natural whore. But then she did something very bad. She kept her eyes fixed on the cars ahead, and slowly, casually, rubbed her thigh with her right hand. As though she had a slight itch. Not even an itch, the merest tickle. Or just a need to touch herself. But as she rubbed her thigh, as the heel of her hand trailed up her leg, she let it catch the soft silk, so that the skirt was hiked up her thigh, revealing five more inches of her sweetly perfect leg.

The man next to her glanced at her face. She pretended not to see. She looked straight through the window, at that Peugeot 206, and her breath was shallow and rapid, and she desperately wanted him to reach over, to put his big hand on that naked thigh, slide up, pushing the silk out of his way and discovering her naked lips, her fuck honey,

11

and above all her burning clit, that throbbed and yearned for his touch, and her cunt, that yearned for his penetration. But it had to be him, she would never make the first move.

The Peugeot moved off, the jam dispersed. He didn't touch her, nor did he look at her for the rest of the journey.

Afterwards in her room she had frigged herself almost violently, then cried herself to sleep. The only man she had ever really wanted enough to take the risk with, and her mother was in love with him.

But the next morning she had again worn a thin silk skirt. Only this one was several inches shorter. She had been ashamed to do so, she knew she was behaving like a tart, but somehow she just couldn't help herself. Maybe it came of being little miss rich girl, little miss privileged, who had always been able to have just what she wanted. She'd been disappointed. He hadn't touched her. But he had looked. And after that she'd felt his eyes on her whenever they were alone together. Drinking her body in, savouring it, swallowing her whole. But when her mother was there he never gave her a second glance.

Thinking about Henry had made her wetter than ever. Her naked lips were glistening with her fuck juices. She moved to her dressing table, and opened the Faberge box.

Inside was a fine, black, tripartite cord. Two ends of it finished in small loops, the third in a larger loop, large enough to slip over one's hand. If anyone had been prying, nosing around her room, they would have had no idea as to the use Charlotte had for this simple device.

She moved back to the mirror, and slipped each tiny loop over her two sweet nipples. Then she drew the cords so the nooses tightened, ensnaring the delicate pink flesh. She pulled gently. The cords were properly attached, her breasts were tugged this way and that by the threads. Stepping forward, she looped the cord over a hook just above the mirror, then carefully slipped the free end around her wrist. Now she was ready to frig herself, in just the way she wanted.

Until this point the lovely girl's movements had all displayed complete decorum. Now, however, anyone watching could see what a wanton slut she actually was. She plunged three fingers of her left hand deep into her burning cunt, and started to pound into herself as roughly as any porn whore. With her right hand she rubbed her swollen and slippery clit. As she did this she squatted slightly, with spread legs... and the cord around her wrist grew tight.

She yelped in pain as her nipples and breasts were tugged high, as though tormented by a cruel lover. It was this, this passion for pain, that had made Charlotte so resolute in her decision to remain a virgin. No man could have slept with her without discovering what she really wanted in bed, and where would that path lead her? Charlotte dreaded to think what degradation she might suffer if anyone discovered who she really was, the pain slut behind the face of innocence. If she was to lose her virginity it could only be with a man she trusted completely. And she only knew one man like that.

Her full breasts jiggled painfully as she strummed her clit. Her poor abused nipples were scarlet and aching, and the heady mixture of pain and arousal made her moan and buck in total abandonment. Not a pleasure she could have indulged in with her mother at home; her screams of ecstasy echoed round the house.

Tom's cock was rock hard. As a window cleaner, he had seen many sights that still gave him pleasant memories.

He'd seen that blonde tart Shannon, barely out of school and getting it up two holes at once with her strapping, black neighbours turning her into a wild moaning animal. The men had noticed him, but they hadn't given a fuck, they just rammed her all the harder, enjoying the audience. Shannon hadn't noticed that she was being watched, but she understood soon enough when he showed her the pics he'd taken, and had most obligingly and meekly satisfied his needs, twice weekly for the next six months, until her family had moved away. She really hadn't wanted the rest of the town knowing what she'd been up to, she'd have spent twenty four seven on her back if it'd got out.

And he'd seen that nice widow, Sarah, on her knees sucking the biggest dick you ever could imagine, and taking it all the way in. Someone had certainly been giving her deepthroating lessons. It was the sight of Sarah with her mouth full of cock that had first inspired him to buy the camera.

And he'd seen that rich git old Mr. Benson, stuffing his ancient tool up the arse of the Thai girl he said was his wife, but whom everyone agreed he must've bought, as why else would a pretty girl in her twenties be partnered by an ugly old man?

But whilst all those had been pleasant perks in his working life, he'd never seen a sight that had made him so instantly rock hard as stuck-up Charlotte Summerfield without a stitch on her perfect little body, and when she started hammering her cunt and tormenting her own nipples as though parading herself for a porn show, he knew exactly what he was going to do. They all said she was a virgin. Well, not for much longer she wouldn't be.

He wanted to interrupt her before she orgasmed. He wanted her hot for him. He tapped on the window.

The girl looked round, her pretty mouth open in shock. God, that mouth will look so sweet full of my fat dick, he thought to himself. She turned away, struggling to remove the threads from her tits, and then started to pull a robe around her gorgeous lithe body.

"No," he said, his voice carrying clearly through the open window.

She looked up, furious, about to tell him just what she thought of him, but he just smiled and held up the camera.

Oh God, what a treat it was to see all the colour drain from her face as she understood. What a delicious moment of power! He knew for sure from that horrified expression that he had her exactly where he wanted her. The little bitch would do anything he asked in order to avoid those pics getting out. He was in for the ride of his life. The thought made him pause. He didn't want her just the once, and then it be a pleasant memory. He wanted possession. He wanted ownership. He wanted the goddamn movie rights... he chuckled to himself. There was money to be made from this little whore. And he knew just who he'd be needing as his business partners. He didn't mind sharing, he'd get a bigger helping himself that way. But if she guessed at what he was planning she'd never agree to it, pics or no pics, as all the town finding out about her depraved behaviour wouldn't be half so bad as what he had in mind. He had to handle this very carefully.

She was still staring at his camera, white as a sheet.

"This'd look pretty good on that big billboard outside Palmersons dontcha think?" he said to torment her further

He turned the camera so that she could see her own image, her spread legs, her cunt stuffed with most of her own hand. And those tormented nipples.

She flushed and glared at him. She was no fool, she knew she had to acquiesce.

"What do you want?" she asked, reluctantly.

"Go down and open the door," he replied, smiling in triumph.

Charlotte stumbled out of the room, shut the door behind her and leant heavily against it. She was shaking all over. With fear, of this horrible man. With arousal: she had been very close to orgasm when he had interrupted her. But also, with excitement. She knew what he wanted: she was going to get fucked. A man's cock was going to enter her, tearing her hymen and filling her up, the way she longed to be filled. She was scared but the fear was subsumed by the massive desire she felt to be fucked and fucked and fucked. And with no guilt, she really didn't have any choice in the matter, she was sure of that. And with a bit of luck he'd be rather rough with her too; after all, he already knew what she liked. And when it was over she could go back to her calm, safe, man-less existence, but with such glorious memories. It was perfect. He thought he had the better of her, but she was still in control.

Tom waited by the door. She was taking her time coming. Shit, what if she'd realised how foolish it was to trust him, to bargain with him, maybe she wasn't going to come down. But just then he heard soft footsteps behind the door, and moments later it opened.

She looked far cockier than he had expected, in fact she looked positively excited. Little whore. He knew exactly how to play her now.

God, what a beauty. Stunning. He felt his cock twitch and swell back to full hardness as his eyes trailed over her tits and belly. She'd look damn fine on film he thought, and suppressed a grin. He'd let her think they were making a straight swap.

"So then, I take it you don't think this'd make a pretty sight on that billboard?" he smirked at her.

"What do you want me to do?"

She was trying to sound reluctant, but her voice was breathy, eager.

"Oh, you don't have to do a thing, girl. All you have to do is lay right back on that big bed of yours, spread those pretty thighs, and make sure that if you open that pretty mouth it's only to take my cock inside… or maybe to say 'please' and 'thank you'. In return I'll delete those photos I've just taken. Though I have to say, seems like a crime to me; destroying works of art like that."

She didn't reply, just stood there, swallowing slightly and

looking up at him with such huge and suddenly helpless eyes that for a moment he considered letting her off as lightly as he'd just promised. But only for a moment. God that mouth would look good full of cock. He couldn't wait.

"Up you go then." He got hold of her shoulders and turned her around, then playfully slapped her ass, pushing her towards the stairs. " Lead the way, baby."

She dutifully climbed the stairs ahead of him. Her bottom was peachy perfect, round and sweet and smooth and silky. It would have been a crime indeed to let an ass as good as this one go unfucked, sheer waste of human resources. He smiled to himself. They had reached the landing, and she led him along a corridor, then stopped by a plain, oak door. She looked up at him again, and he could see she was getting scared now. She might be a slut who was secretly desperate to have eight inches up her pussy, but all the same, losing your virginity to a man who's just walked in from nowhere is a frightening prospect. And now they were so close to the bed reality was beginning to bite. She swallowed again.

"In you go." He deliberately kept his voice light, teasing. He wanted to soothe her, not scare her out of her wits. They'd be plenty of time for that, later. She gulped, and opened the door.

The room was beautiful, as he had glimpsed from outside the window. Light and airy, high white walls. The bed was perfect, an old four poster, classic. He sized up the possibilities. She stood close to him, like a little dog at heel, somehow needing the reassurance of his big body, even though it was his big body that would shortly be nailing her to the bed. It was a mute plea for kindness, he understood that. He ran his left palm down from her head, over her long hair, down the sexy curve of her back to the flare of her buttocks, still looking at the bed. She was trembling slightly, he could feel it.

"Right." He turned and looked her in the eyes. "Up you get, gorgeous. Are you flexible?"

She was on the bed, settling herself back with her head on the pillows. Oh, and the little beauty was even spreading without being told. It gave him a warm feeling to know she really did want him, whatever head games she might be playing in her own mind, this little lady really did want his meat hammering her.

"Yes. I do yoga."

"So… can you get your feet up by your ears?"

She could, and did. Oh, what a sight to behold! That sweet naked pussy raised and displayed, just for him. Nice.

"Right. So honey, this is what I'm going to do. I'm going to tie you like that, with your legs up high, because you look gorgeous like that and because I like fucking trussed birds. From what I saw earlier I think you'll like it too. You ok with that?"

He was being so normal, so like a regular boyfriend, that Charlotte had completely relaxed. OK, so he was rather common. He had rough, dirty hands and two day old stubble. And he was far older than any man she'd have chosen herself, he must be in his mid forties, more than twenty years older than she. And he was ugly, in fact he reminded her of a troll. But now he was being gentle and kindly, and she trusted him already. She nodded to say she was happy to be tied.

Tom bound her quickly, efficiently, using silk scarves from her own wardrobe to tie her ankles and wrists to the bed head. He'd done it enough times before, after all. He watched her face the whole time, looking for the change he knew would come when she was finally secure. He tied the last knot and smiled as she quivered with arousal. The sweet mouth came open in a small, silent gasp of excited pleasure and fear at her own helplessness. He looked at her cunt. Her fuck juices were coming so fast they were practically trickling from her virgin hole.

"One more thing. OK if I gag you? I think you'll enjoy it,

and I certainly will…"

Why does he keep asking if it's ok? thought Charlotte in frustration. Doesn't he realise that half the pleasure is in feeling powerless, totally under the control of a man?

Totally under the control of a man. Even thinking those words made her vagina clench in excited, hard contractions, wanting cock. She nodded urgently in reply. He took a few moments making the gag, raiding her undies drawer and stuffing a silk stocking with several pairs of panties, twisting and tying it to form a bundle that would really stuff her mouth but be quite safe. He tied it in place. It was a bit too tight, it was uncomfortable. Charlotte tried to say so but all that came out was a muffled "mmmm" noise. She tossed her head from side to side, hoping to shift the gag a little, but it was tied fast. She looked at him. The bastard! He was smiling at her. He knew damn well it was too tight, he'd done it on purpose. She bucked angrily on the bed and his grin widened. Then he moved to the scarves that tethered her limbs.

Oh, he's going to untie me, thought Charlotte, half relieved, half disappointed. But he wasn't. He retied each restraint, far tighter than before, pulling her so open it hurt.

"Mmmm!" Charlotte squeaked in angry protest. The man just smiled, and stroked her helpless breasts, teasing the nipples into hard jutting buds. Suddenly he clenched his hands around her tits so roughly it really hurt. Charlotte screamed but the gag reduced it to a whimper. She felt her pussy rush with a sudden wave of fuck juices: fuck-me-please, fuck-me-now, juices. Oh God. Oh God. What a fool she had been. What had she let herself in for? She twisted and wriggled but to no avail. Totally under the control of a man. Now it was real. The pain was real. And her arousal was just as real as she had always known, and feared, it would be. What would become of her now?

The man laughed at her, slapping her tits hard with the

flat of his hand so that they jiggled and shook. With great delicacy he dipped a finger in her cunt, brought it out, glistening, wet. He trailed the tip over her belly. She realised he was forming a letter: S. Her flat stomach quivered with desire at his touch. He dipped into her fuck hole a second time: L. And again: U. And finally T. Then he turned away from her, reached in his pocket and pulled out his mobile phone.

CHAPTER TWO

"Boss? Hi. Oh, I'm doing well. Very well, actually. I've got a rather nice package you might want to take a look at."

Tom held the phone over the slut's displayed pudenda and took a shot. Then another, holding it high at the end of the bed so that the boss could see exactly what was on offer. The whore was wriggling and mewing through her gag, but he didn't take any notice.

"Yes, nice isn't it? Yes. Want me to call up the guys and make a party of it? Uh huh. Yes. Maybe you should tell Stu and Rich to bring their gear? Yep. Too damned right!"

He laughed. "Want me to ask her?"

He turned and looked the girl right in the eyes, smirking with pleasure. "The boss wants to know is it ok if he brings a bunch of our mates around, and we all fuck you senseless?"

The girl tried to say "No!" but all that came out past the gag was a pathetic whimper.

Tom frowned in mock concern. "Hey boss, all she says is 'meeew'." He imitated her in a derisive fashion.

"Oh yes. You're right, sir. Oh, by the way, she likes pain. Yes! Yes, right in the act. Her nipples, all tied up with a cord. Yes, that's what I thought." He laughed nastily. See you soon then."

Tom turned back to the helpless virgin who would shortly be learning how to please and suffering for her art.

"He reminded me: silence means consent. So sweetheart, I think you've just consented to your first ever gang bang. What a way for a classy girl to lose her cherry! I'm quite surprised that you want it, I should think it's going to be a bit of an ordeal satisfying six burly men, especially when we take turns to ram our cocks up your virgin ass, but it's your choice, who am I to argue?"

He smiled at her, quite relaxed, very sure of himself, and reached forward to caress her breasts and thighs, watching her cunt as he did so.

"My, my, my, what a whore you are. The thought of six cocks and you're trickling fuck honey like a waterfall, you're so impatient. Well don't worry, baby doll. We'll stuff you good and proper, each and every one of us."

He got up, and walked towards the door, but paused.

"Oh sugarlips, I nearly forgot. I promised to delete those pics, didn't I?"

He reached for his camera, and pressed a few buttons.

"There you go. All gone. Uh, did I say? Stu and Rich, they'll be bringing some video cameras. It's alright if we film you getting fucked in all your holes, isn't it? You won't mind at all, will you? Good. Didn't think you would, I could tell right from the start that you are the sort of girl who likes to please."

And with that, he was gone.

Charlotte wriggled and writhed in her bonds. She was frightened, more frightened than she'd ever been before. She was scared of what these men might do to her, but more, she was scared of her own reaction. The thought of being tied into complete helplessness, and fucked, sodomised and tormented by a whole gang of men, had been her secret, darkest fantasy for years. Now her perverted dreams were about to become reality, and she could feel her body's wild response. Her vagina ached for possessing cocks, her nipples were taut at the prospect of abusive male hands. Tom was right: she was a whore. She had to get away. If she didn't, the consequences didn't bear thinking about.

She tugged at the restraining scarves in panic, and felt a sudden slackening in the silk that ensnared her right wrist. She pulled again. The knot came tight, but now the loop of silk was no longer biting into her flesh. She pulled with all her might, but her hand was too big to slip through. Curling her thumb in towards her palm, she tried again. The silk rubbed cruelly tight against her skin, so that her eyes pricked with tears, but she kept on pulling, more with the terror of a trapped animal than with planned intent.

Suddenly, her hand came free. At the same moment she heard the crunching of gravel as a car pulled into the driveway. She lay totally still, sweating with exertion and fright. Tom's footsteps through the hallway. The front door opening. Male voices. Then her heart contracted as another vehicle pulled up in front of the house.

She must work quickly. A wave of calm detachment rippled through her. She picked at the silk that strapped her left wrist. Little by little the knot loosened, then came completely open. Now her hands were free.

Spattering gravel as another car arrives. Sounds of ribald greeting, the words 'shag the bitch till she can hardly stand' float up the stairs. Deep laughing voices as they begin to climb. They are too close, she must bide her time.

With shaking hands, Charlotte ties slipknots in the free ends of the scarves that bound her, slips her wrists through her new-made nooses, pulls so they are tight and flops back on the bed, perspiration tricking down her forehead. Five men walk into the room.

The men were all dressed in working clothes. Greasy overalls, paint-splattered boiler suits. Big, coarse blokes, all over six foot tall. Rough, grimy hands. She trembled in terror.

They gathered round the bed, discussing her displayed flesh in the crudest terms. She felt like an animal being appraised at market. The hands reached out to stroke and inspect. Uninvited hands all over her breasts, her belly, her thighs. Fingers spreading her pussy lips, her intact hymen noted by the crowding heads, her clitoris poked and tweaked. Someone spat on his finger, then pressed it against her puckered asshole, pushing until she gave a little muffled cry as it slipped inside her. Her muscles gripped tight as he thrust it slowly and repeatedly, mimicking the movements of a cock. She tried to stay silent but couldn't help herself; she moaned in pleasure, it was such a new and deep sensation, as though the sexual heart of her nestled there and he was discovering it. They all laughed. He pulled the finger out and, despite herself, she sighed in disappointment.

"Nice tight hole!"

"Breaking this bitch in will be the best fun I've had in months."

"And she'll be a nice little earner; we'll get it all on film, sell it on the web, sell it down town... we'll make a mint."

"Best wait till the boss arrives, though. Don't think he'd be too impressed if we started without him."

"Of course. Let's just leave her here waiting for him and go get some snacks and drinks and settle in. I bet there's lots of posh grub in this house." The man was peering round the room, noting the fancy furnishings that spoke of money.

"OK if we make ourselves at home, sweetie?" as Tom spoke he reached forward and gave her left nipple a cruel twist. She yelped, but through the gag all that could be heard was a little "mmm!"

"I think that must've been a 'yes' lads. Let's go and take a look round our new, um, business premises, and see where Daddy keeps his beer, now we've got his daughter spread and ready for a little action."

The men left, variously stroking, pinching and slapping her trussed and naked body in parting. Her breasts wobbled and stung as one man aimed hard slaps at each in turn. The last to leave was Tom. He reached forward between the bedposts and cupped her silky pudenda in his big hand, so her pussy glowed under the warmth of his touch. She felt her fuck juices begin to flow, her cunt clench hard with its need to be filled. Delicious little tremors of sensation rippled through her so that when he took his hand away his palm was glistening with her honey. He smirked at the evidence of her arousal.

"Only a whore has a shaved twat." His accent was broad, ignorant, uneducated. "You've brought this on yourself, displaying your whore cunt to anyone who happened to look. I'll take your cherry, bitch, because I'm the one who reeled you in. Then I'll enjoy watching the rest of the gang, banging you the way you deserve. I'm especially looking forward to seeing you take the boss right up to the hilt. I might as well warn you, he's got nine inches of rock hard rod just waiting to nail you to the bed. And honey… he's not gentle. None of us are. But that'll be ok, because you like it to hurt, don't you, slut?" And with that he leant over her and pulled on her nipples, so steadily and hard that she wondered if he meant to lift her away from the bed. She cried out, and he let her fall back, her yelp of pain lost in the gag that stuffed her mouth. He was already walking out of the door, and he didn't turn. She realised, ruefully, that to him she was nothing more than a plaything.

When finally the door closed behind them Charlotte lay silent again, listening to their footfalls, down the stairs and into the hall. When she was sure they'd really gone she wriggled her wrists free and pulled the hateful gag from her mouth. Then she started to untie the bonds that held her ankles. It was slow work. Her fingers were stiff from the tying, and the silk had been knotted again and again.

Eventually she freed her right ankle. After that it was a little easier, as she was able to sit up, tethered only by the final bond that snared her left foot. She felt like a rabbit, gnawing its way to freedom from a trap, as she pulled and tugged and tore at the silk with her nails, finally dipping her head and biting at the fabric, so tightly had the knots been tied. It seemed to take an age, but at long last the material gave way and she was free.

She climbed down from the bed and almost fell, her legs were so stiff after being strapped up for so long. She staggered to the window.

Four vehicles were parked in the driveway. Tom's window cleaning van, a smart Porsche, a scruffy transit van and, a black motorbike. Then, as she watched, a bright yellow Lamborghini Gallardo sped up the drive, spattering gravel as it spun to a halt. She knew without being told that this car must belong to the man Tom had called 'the boss' At that moment a tall, dark figure opened the driver's door, and she ducked hurriedly out of sight as he glanced up towards her window. She anxiously watched him over the sill. He seemed to be looking right at her, as though he could see her, as though he could see right inside her. His gaze was strangely intense even at that distance, and little shivers rippled down her spine. There was no time to lose.

She crept to her door and listened. She could hear voices downstairs, but by the sound of it they were all in the lounge. She wrinkled her pretty nose at the thought of their big boots resting on Mummy's elegant new coffee table, their scruffy overalls against the sleek leather upholstery. Slowly, cautiously, she opened the door. The sound of voices was louder now, she could make out occasional words… fuck… suck my cock… whip the whore… merchandise. She shivered again, then drew a breath for courage and crept out onto the landing.

She tiptoed along the landing to the bathroom that faced the back of the house. She slipped through the door and pulled it to, behind her. It shut with a clunk and she held her breath, frightened that her captors might have heard. But there was no change in the sounds of merriment from downstairs. She stole to the window, and pulled it open.

A long bough of the old apple tree reached right to the window. It was far too close to the house, Daddy had wanted to cut it down. But she and Mummy were fond of it, so it had been allowed to remain. She climbed carefully out of the window and into its covering branches. This year's fruit were already swollen but not yet reddened, festooning the ancient branches like a dull, green necklace. When she brushed against them some fell to the ground, heavy thuds that sounded loud.

She realised at once that she'd been foolish. She should have stopped to dress, it would only have taken seconds to pull on jeans and a shirt. As the rough branches scratched against her bare breasts she wondered ruefully how she'd be able to get help without a stitch to cover her. But maybe she could hide in the woods until they had gone. The important thing was to get away.

She climbed down as quickly as she dared, trying not to mind the scratches that left her with specks of blood on her arms and thighs. When she was about ten foot from the ground the branches gave out, so she lowered herself, dangling high above the ground until she plucked up the nerve to let go. She fell heavily, but the ground was mossy and she wasn't hurt. She picked herself up and ran.

She ran full pelt across the manicured lawns and into the shrubbery, more excited now than fearful. The sun was hot on her naked back and buttocks. Ahead of her lay the grounds of the house, miles of land. It was mainly wooded, she knew it all like the back of her hand, she knew a hundred different hiding places, and there was no way they could find her. She was free!

She pushed away a strange feeling that lurked in some unsavoury corner of her mind. A feeling of intense disappointment, and the sort of resentment a child feels when her mother has confiscated some precious toy, declaring it 'dangerous'. She almost wished they would come after her. Tom was foul and the other men not much better, but there was something fascinating about that dark figure climbing out of his car. Who was he? What instinct had told him she was there, by the window? She slowed her pace a little.

Then, with a shock that cut right through her, she heard voices behind her, back towards the house. Shouting, angry. Then a low, urgent injunction: "Find her, girl. Go!"

Why had she been so foolish as to pause? She ran again, even faster than before. But now, behind her, she could hear something crashing through the bushes, some huge beast. She was terrified and ran like a hunted animal, her heart pounding, bushes and creepers catching and scratching and snaring her limbs, she ran heedless, her breath coming in urgent gasps. Whatever it was behind her drew closer. She turned to look back, and so she just saw the great German Shepherd as it leapt up at her, its paws on her shoulders, flattening her to the ground. It lay on top of her, a massive, solid weight of hot damp fur. She tried to wriggle out from underneath it, but the bitch dipped her head and carefully took the petrified girl's neck in her great jaws. Charlotte was so frightened she pissed herself.

She lay there, feeling the heat from her piss sink away into the cool earth, as the men's voices drew closer. It was almost with relief that she heard them approach; she just wanted the dog off her. Every now and then the bitch gave a low bark, to hurry her master to his quarry, but her jaws always returned to Charlotte's slim neck.

"Well done, Sheba!" Carl Bredon chuckled to himself to see the naked girl pinioned to the ground by his well-trained bitch. "Release!"

Reluctantly, Sheba got up. Bredon bent down and pulled the girl to her feet. She was shaking with fear and probably exhaustion, her body was slick with sweat. Sheba gave her leg a friendly lick and the girl squealed in panic and pressed right up against him, so desperate was she to evade the dog. He relaxed his grip on her arm to stroke her reassuringly and the little slut slipped from his grasp, leaping away from him like a gazelle chased by lions. This time he caught her himself, bringing her to an abrupt halt by sinking his fingers deep into her thick hair, quickly wrapping his other arm around her slender ones so that they were held fast behind her. Still she wriggled, though she must have known it was futile.

"Tom, undo Sheba's collar for me would you?"

Tom looked surprised, but did as he was bade, and held the collar out to the boss. But Carl didn't take it, just gestured towards the young girl pinned helpless in his arms and said, "Put it on this bitch, instead."

Tom chuckled and did so.

Charlotte felt the smooth leather fastened close around her neck. It had a strong, canine odour, and it was still warm from the animal. The man holding her released her hair to fumble in his pocket. Moments later he was clipping a heavy metal chain lead to her collar, watching her as he did so. He was dark, handsome, his mouth twisted in a cruel smile. Unlike the other men he was smartly dressed, in an expensive suit of dark worsted. Gold cufflinks glinted at his wrists.

Now he released his grip on her arms. He had her powerless, on a collar and lead like any other owned bitch. The cold, metal chain of the lead hung down against her breast.

She knew escape was now quite impossible, but she had the same instinct to flee as any wild animal bound for the first time. Her spirit had yet to be broken. As the man reached to fondle her breasts she tugged away. The chain came taut, and the man gave it an angry jerk, pulling her back to him.

Instead of the gentle caress Carl had been planning he cuffed her tits with the back of his hand. She yelped in pain, her heavy breasts bouncing amusingly. Holding her lead close to her collar he pulled her head down towards the ground, then pushed her so that she fell on her face. With the weight of his foot upon her back the girl started to sweat with fear.

Sheba was excited. It was years since she'd been a working dog, chasing and flooring burglars when they ran helter-skelter through the alleys. This creature didn't smell the same though. She gave an outstretched ankle a slow, experimental lick. Salty, yet somehow sweet as well. She licked again, further up. The calf, then the back of the knee. The creature moaned and wriggled. The men were talking.

"So Tom, where do you want to have her? Shall we take her back to the house and tie her back on her bed… a little more securely this time!" Carl shifted his weight slightly so that she would feel the pressure of his booted foot, "or do you want her out here?"

"Here, Carl. Now. The bitch has given us enough of a run-a-round, I've had my fill of waiting. But I want her trussed like I had her. We need a branch to tie her to, any laying around?"

It didn't take them long to find a suitable branch, six foot long, two inches thick, good strong wood. The whore was whimpering a little. She still lay prone under Bredon's boot, and the dog was licking her thighs, the big hot tongue washing the girl carefully, concentratedly, the way a bitch licks her puppies.

They pulled the girl onto her back. Someone had brought rope, and they tied her to the branch, first her wrists, above her head, then her ankles close to her wrists, pulling her tail up so that her pudenda was displayed and open. It was a position Bredon had always liked. He had a book of Japanese Erotica with an 18th century illustration that showed a genteel lady getting raped by two ruffians, and she was strapped just the same way.

Stuart moved in with the camera, and the other men spread the pussy lips to completely reveal the girl's intact virginity. Someone carefully slipped a single finger into her little hole. They laughed to see her fuck juices trickling in a welcoming stream. Tom got out his cock, ready to force himself upon her whether she wanted him or not, though to judge from her slippery cunt… he slipped a finger in and out of her, relishing the tightness of her hole… she wanted cock pretty badly. He began to kneel down, ready to penetrate her, Stuart close by with the video. But then the boss said, "Wait."

Charlotte lay strapped into complete helplessness, watching the men as they readied her to be fucked. Tom was looking at her as though she were a delicious meal he was about to devour. His cock looked huge to her eyes, eyes that had never seen an erect penis before. It jutted out of his trousers like a stiff, red pole, upon which she knew she would be impaled, whether she wanted him or not. She knew she was presented as an object to be enjoyed, her legs and arms were strapped out of the way because they were irrelevant to what was about to take place, only her sexual parts were of interest, and above all, it was her cunt that was the focus of attention. She was aroused as never before. She felt excitement pulsing through her cunt and clit and ass. But she was terrified to have so entirely lost control, to be so utterly helpless. These men could do anything they wanted to her, they obviously had every intention of taking her by force.

"Wait!" It was the black-haired man they'd called Carl: the boss. He spoke quite quietly, but with real authority. She wondered what was going to happen. Tom looked irritated at the interruption, but she noticed he fell back without a word. She shivered with apprehension as the dark man knelt down in Tom's place, and bent his face to her pussy. She had no idea what he might do. He spread her lips with his two hands so that her flesh was pulled taut, her swollen clit rising up towards his mouth.

And then he began to lick her.

Nothing Charlotte had ever experienced came close to the sweet intensity, the overwhelming exquisite magic, that now poured through her entire pudenda and rippled out in never ending waves so that her whole small body began to throb as though submerged and saturated with heaven. She lost all consciousness of the group of men standing around her, of the dog, of the wood, of where she was and who she was. Her whole self dissolved into a pure liquid stream of sensation, her bound fingers curled as though to stroke or grasp, she looked with awed adoration towards the dark head slowly working between her pale thighs. "Oh…!" she said, or rather breathed, very quietly. And it was an exclamation of amazement, and thankfulness, and even love.

He lifted his head and again those dark, knowing eyes looked into her. A sardonic smile twisted his lips.

"Do you want to be my bitch?" he asked, fingering her clit now with the same expert skill.

"Ohhhh…. yes…ohhh"

There was no hesitation in her reply. He bent his head to tongue her once more, and she was off again, floating in swirls of sensation, carried along on a blissful tide. Again he stopped. She said, "Oh!" again, but now it was with disappointment, frustrated desire.

"Then you'd better understand. If you are my bitch, you do what I say. You'll be mine to fuck whenever I choose, of course. But also mine to share, mine to punish, mine to work."

As he spoke he rubbed her clit in little circles; she writhed with pleasure under his touch. Then he took his hands away from her, and just as her whole body had been in ecstasy before, so now her whole body ached for his touch.

"Please…?"

"No more. Not unless you want to be my bitch."

There could be only one sensible reply to such a ridiculous bargain. The world was full of men who'd be only too happy to give Charlotte cunnilingus for hour upon hour, if she so desired. But Charlotte was drunk with desire, and it was her clitoris, not her mind, that was in charge of her decisions. She was governed by sex, by sexual need.

"I want to be your bitch," she said.

"Call me Master then, you little slut."

"I want to be your bitch, Master."

Carl stood up, grinning broadly at his employees.

"All yours, Tom. Got that on film, haven't you, Stu? Good. Partytime, lads!"

To Charlotte's shock and dismay, Tom now took the place of the man to whom she had just promised herself. His flies were open again, and Charlotte stared open-mouthed at his huge cock, and then, before she had time to protest, this hot, bulbous monster was pushing against her virgin opening. He drove down hard, until, with a sudden, stinging pain she was torn. She was tight, her body resisting him, but he forced his whole length inside her, and started to fuck her roughly, hammering his tool into her again and again and again.

As he fucked her she could hear Carl's voice. He was explaining something to the others, his voice brimming with satisfaction:

"It's because she's a true submissive, you see. A truly submissive girl, when faced by a dominant man, has very little resistance. Very little resistance indeed. Her whole body sings out to be dominated you see. And once I stimulated the slut's clit... a submissive's clitoris is like a control button. It really is, yes, a switch by which you can control her. Turn her on and she's yours, she can't help herself. Really, you can't expect a submissive to be chaste any more than you would expect a bitch in heat to be chaste. That's all she is, a bitch in permanent heat, touch her clit and she'll do anything you want. More of a toy than a whore, really. Look at Tom shaft her! She didn't know that was what she wanted, but look at her face! What a slut!"

Charlotte didn't want to enjoy it. She knew she had consented, but she had been tricked, and she was angry. She had understood that by agreeing to be Carl's bitch she was also agreeing to each and every one of these men enjoying her, but she had assumed her Master would fuck her first. She didn't want to give him the satisfaction of seeing her moan with pleasure under this common man. But somehow, she couldn't help herself. The glorious sensation of being filled spread through her with each hard buck of the man's driving hips. He thrust into her so deeply that with each penetration her exposed clit was deliciously crushed under his weight, he quite literally 'banged' her, his cock reaching to the depths of her cunt in a way that would have been painful if he'd been just a little longer, but as it was, it was enrapturing. Waves of ecstatic sensation built up and up inside her, until she was close to orgasm. At that moment he lifted his hands from her hips and brutally grasped her nipples, pinching and tugging them so that her breasts were pulled into peaks, bolts of fire shooting through her abused flesh. It was this vicious treatment that finally brought her to a thundering orgasm, so that she screamed and moaned, and tried to kiss the man whom she'd been tricked into accepting. He returned a kiss, of sorts. He pressed his mouth very hard against her own, and forced his tongue deep into her, bringing his hands up to her face and hooking his thumbs in the corners of her mouth so that his tongue could penetrate her as deeply as possible. She felt as though he was not kissing her, but instead fucking her mouth, using his tongue as a surrogate cock. Then he was off her, and it was the turn of another man.

Or rather, another two men. The sight of her mouth being force-fucked with tongue was an obvious incitement to stuff it with cock. Someone sat astride her and pressed his oozing penis between her lips. She licked at it, learning for the first time the musky scent of male genitalia, the salt taste of pre-come. She felt another cock pressing at her sore pussy, but she could not see which man wielded it, all she could see was the shaft and belly of the man using her mouth.

He started to thrust into her, each movement taking him a little deeper. She began to gag, but he just paused until she had recovered, then resumed his thrusting. Gradually she was able to take him deeper, her throat accepting the invading organ. Now he held her head still, and used her mouth exactly as he would a cunt, shifting his legs until he was almost lying on top of her, pounding in between her pretty lips. At the same time the man using her cunt hammered into her, even rougher than Tom. She knew all too well that she had consented to being used thus, had told the dark man that she was his. And now she thought she understood what being 'his' was to mean. She was his property, and her wishes were irrelevant.

As if to ram this point home, the man pounding her vagina reached to grasp her breasts, squeezing them hard in his fists, twisting the sensitive flesh so that she tried to yelp. But of course, she could not voice complaint, not with a mouthful of rock-hard cock. However, her attempt at crying out was pleasing to the man enjoying her throat, as she opened a little wider which enabled him to penetrate even more deeply. To her shame, even this brutal treatment pushed her nearer to another climax.

Both men orgasmed at the same time, one shooting his load deep into her belly, the other pulling out as he came, to cover her face with a splattering of come. She lay there limp and shaking whilst they clambered off her, but before she had time to do more than draw breath, the next two were upon her, using her in an identical manner, so that she felt as though it was not two different men at all, but rather the same ordeal or pleasure, stretching on and on. She was already learning that fundamental lesson: how to give pleasure whilst expecting none herself. This thought was so arousing to her, appealed so strongly to her masochistic nature which fed upon humiliation and abuse, that she came again, the rapid contractions of her cunt hastening the orgasm of the man who was plundering it.

They got off her and she lay exhausted. Five big men had enjoyed ravaging and deflowering her slender body, there remained only one who had not yet had his pleasure. Carl was looking at her again, looking at her spunk-streaked lips, and his smile held no warmth.

"Untie her," he commanded, and he leant back against a tree watching her, whilst his lackeys followed orders. When she was free, he took hold of her lead and yanked her to her feet.

CHAPTER THREE

He led her out of the wood, into the dazzling sunlight. She was unsteady on her feet having been tied in such an extreme fashion. When she stumbled he supported her, wrapping his thick, hard fingers around her slim arm.

He led her back towards the house, over the perfect, manicured lawns. The sun was very hot now, and she was desperately thirsty. The German Shepherd bitch must have felt the same, for she trotted ahead of them across the grass to where the fountain water bubbled and gushed. By the time they reached her she was drinking steadily, the sparkling water dripping from her hairy maw.

"You may drink," said Charlotte's Master, "but wash your face, first."

So she washed the sticky come from her face, then dipped her head next to the un-collared dog and drank together with the animal. Quenching her thirst, side by side with the beast, she realised for the first time that they were both bitches, owned by this man, serving him, their Master. She shivered at the knowledge, for she thought she knew which of his female animals he would treat more kindly.

He let her drink her fill, then he told her to wash her snatch. The rim of the fountain was hip height, so she climbed in and squatted in the chilly water, carefully washing the streaks of semen from her thighs. All the time he watched her, holding her lead loosely, so she felt almost free. The other men sat around on the grass, talking amiably and occasionally making some crude reference to Charlotte's body. She flushed to hear them, and did not return their gazes, but kept her eyes averted and concentrated on washing herself.

When she was done he called Tom over to hold her lead. Then bringing her hands together in front of her Carl began to bind them, wrist to wrist. The rope was rough, it prickled slightly and he wound it tight enough to bite firmly into her flesh. She stood meek as a lamb, and made no protest as he coiled the rope again and again around her wrists, then finally knotted it. Then he casually looped it high around the fountain, and pulled the end. Charlotte was tugged forward, her groin pressing up against the cold marble edge, her body bent horizontally forward from the hips so that her face rested on the smooth, wet stone that jutted just clear of the water near the centre of the fountain. Her arms were pulled up above her, against the central pillar. Her full breasts hung down into the icy water.

Either side of her the fountain spouted and gushed in two small waterfalls that filled her ears with sound. She could hear nothing now of the men on the grass, would not have heard her Master had he bothered to speak to her. Nor could she see him, her lips kissed only cold stone.

She felt hands at her ankles, again wrapping rope around, coil after coil, then knotting it tight. Then they were pulling her feet apart and tethering them to the ground, so she stood with her knees very slightly bent, her legs spread enough to allow easy access to her genitals, her thighs pressed against the curving bowl of the fountain. The edge of the bowl was rimmed with delicate flutings. Whether by chance or design, one of these pressed now between her labia, so that her already swollen clitoris rested uncomfortably on the jutting stone. She shifted her weight slightly, from one foot to another, and the stone prodded her clit like a cold, stiff, finger.

Waiting for what seemed an age, her heavy breasts ached from the chill of the water that flowed from deep under the ground and was never warmed by daylight. And yet the heat of the sun was fierce now directly behind her, so that her thighs and buttocks were burning, and sweat pooled in the arched curve of her back. She had never felt so naked or exposed. She could see nothing of her captors, whilst they could see the most intimate parts of her own self.

She caught a flicker of movement out of the corner of her

eye, and the next moment hands brushed over her waist, slipping something around her, looping it round twice then buckling it tight. The buckle dug into her flesh. It felt like a man's leather belt.

Again she waited. How long passed? Maybe ten minutes, maybe more. Then hands again, fiddling with the belt buckle as the leather had gone slimy from its soaking in the cold water. They took the belt away. She wondered why they had wrapped her with it, only to remove it without putting it to any use.

Suddenly a heavy bolt of fire shot through her proffered bottom. Thwack! A hard slap of leather against flesh, so hard it almost felt like a punch. She screamed and bucked in shock, but her ankles were immobile, there was no way to escape. Another blow, this time on her back, and again she screamed. In the pause before the third blow struck she felt cold water trickling down from the line of fire where the belt had landed. It ran down the curve of her buttock, then trickled round to drip from her labia. Suddenly she understood: her assailant had soaked his belt in the fountain water, purposefully to slicken the leather. By the time the sixth blow landed she had given up thinking and was simply twisting this way and that in a vain attempt to avoid the punishment that was evidently her due.

And yet... maybe it was just the pressure of the stone rubbing her clit with every tiny movement of her body... or maybe it was the vibrations that rippled through her pubis from the repeated blows to her buttocks... surely it could not be the beating itself that was making her pussy wet with sexual need? She longed for the beating to stop, not so that the pain would stop, but instead because the pain made her ache to be penetrated again by cock. The memory of the cocks pounding into her tight hole swam in her mind. All she could think about was cock, and how she needed it, how much she needed to be fucked. Her clitoris throbbed painfully, desperately hungry for a man's touch.

He must have known what she was feeling. Thick fingers spreading her pussy lips, slipping over her clit. She knew by the easy feel of the rough male hand that was assessing her that she was dripping with sex juices.

Suddenly a weight upon her back, her little body pressed against the stone and her breasts crushed against the basin of the fountain. He was leaning over her, his mouth close by her ear.

"You love it don't you, slut? You're dripping fuck juices, all you want is cock. You love learning your place. Little Miss High and Mighty. Little Miss Posh Bitch. Little Miss Whore, who lives for cock! It's true, isn't it? You're a pain slut, and all you want is to be fucked. Tell me. Tell me you're my whore bitch and you want my cock inside your cunt."

He seemed to know exactly who she was, what she was thinking. She shivered. Was it in fear, or excitement? She felt intoxicated.

"I'm your whore. Your bitch. All I want is your cock inside me."

"Where do you want it? Tell me, I need to hear you say it: where do you want my cock?"

"In my cunt."

She flushed, and stumbled over the obscene word. He laughed.

"I know you do, whore. But you're not going to get it. I'm going to take your ass." With that he pulled away from her. Another blast of fire as the belt resumed its tanning of her behind. The pain was even worse now as she was already sore, and the blows rained down fast and furious. She screamed and begged, but if he replied she could not hear him through the noise of the water. Tears ran down her cheeks. She knew she wanted it, oh God, she knew he was right and she wanted it. And yet it was terrible.

Just when she thought she could bear it no longer the blows stopped. He must have moved away, she felt the warmth as the sun again fell on her smarting bottom. She must be red raw.

A sudden pressure at her anus. With horror she remembered what she had been told about the size of his penis. Nine inches, those were Tom's words. Surely he must have been exaggerating? But Charlotte somehow knew that he'd meant every word.

But this was just a thick finger investigating her asshole. It pressed repeatedly, but her tight hole resisted entry. A pause. What was he doing? Surely to goodness he wouldn't beat her again? She started to tremble in terror, she was so open, so vulnerable, and they could do anything they wanted to her. At that thought her vagina clenched in a delicious spasm, and her pussy dripped with whorish invitation.

Now a coolness against her ass. Her raw skin stinging… what had he sprayed on her? Then the finger resumed its probing, and immediately she understood. It slipped easily inside her, there was no longer any resistance. He had lubricated her to make the penetration easier, and doubtless more pleasant for him. The finger was fully inside her; moments later and another digit pressed its way in. As he started to pull at her hole she realised that she was impaled not on two fingers, but rather upon his two thumbs. He had hooked them into her, and now his fingers sunk into her buttocks and pulled his thumbs separate, so as to stretch her hole. She squirmed in humiliation at the thought of what he was doing. He worked away at her, stretching, teasing, tugging; then slowly pulled his thumbs out.

Moments later she felt another blast of the cool spray, then the burning hot tip of his cock pressed against her anus. Little by little she could feel her muscles relax under the pressure, little by little the swollen organ forced its way inside her. It hurt, and she cried out. He stroked her reassuringly, then held her hips and resumed the inexorable penetration. He was very patient, but she instinctively knew that he would not be satisfied with anything less that the whole of his shaft up to its hilt inside her. Her ring stung with the stretching.

Suddenly there was a feeling of surrender, the pain lessened, she realised the width of him was inside her body. But could she take the full length of him? What would he do if she couldn't bear it? He kept pressing forward, less patient now. She was strapped in an ideal position to accept him, and after a few moments she felt, with a peculiar mixture of shame and triumph, the scratch of his pubic hair against her buttocks. Her anus burnt with the width of the tool that he wielded. He felt unimaginably huge.

At first he fucked her gently. But after a few moments he must have decided she was ready to be used as he wished to use her, and hammered into her as roughly as the men who had used her cunt. Great waves of sensation were rolling out from her ass, her whole pelvis seemed to throb with arousal. He held her hips and bucked into her like a rutting animal, and as she felt the sudden spasm of his orgasm, she too came, moaning and crying like a creature possessed. When he was finished he leant forward and again lay heavily upon her. She realised he was still fully dressed, as had been all of the men as they had enjoyed her. She had never been more naked.

He pulled out of her, and moved away. The sun resumed its burning of her behind.

The man's spent semen gradually trickled from her body. She waited patiently, humiliatingly conscious of the picture she must present to anyone who was looking. She felt alone now in a separate world, cut off by the noise of the water and her state of subjugation from what was going on around her. Was anyone still looking at her? Had they gone? What would become of her now?

And yet still her pussy throbbed with passion. With a sinking heart Charlotte wondered if there was any humiliation that she would not find arousing. If there was, it was as yet undiscovered. But then, she reflected, her journey from virgin to whore had been so rapid. She knew now that she was a whore. Her Master had told her so, but she hadn't needed telling. She had been fucked by six men, and she'd wanted every one of them.

The men lazed on the grass, replaying Stu's video shots. He'd done a good job. There were some especially nice shots of the slut trussed in the wood, and all the close-ups of her being penetrated were excellent. Carl Bredon's favourite moment was the footage of his own cock, breaking and entering her tight ass. He was proud of his massive tool, and even though he said it himself it looked fantastic, her tight puckered hole (as evidenced by the 'before' shot) stretched nearly three inches wide to take the thick root of his cock. To think that pretty little girl had so easily surrendered to nine inches of meat. And with hardly any tears. Oh, but she'd be crying plenty over the next few days. But not through rough anal usage, he had no intention of damaging her. He was getting quite fond of her, the way you do get fond of pets... the arrogant little madam was already becoming so touchingly meek... but his reason for care was more that he had no intention of reducing her value.

He looked up towards the fountain, where the girl still stood, bound and helpless.

"I think I'll untie her, let her stretch out a bit. We want her good and flexible." The others nodded agreement, and went on discussing the video they were going to make.

He walked over to where the slight figure waited for whatever indignity or pleasure he should choose to inflict, and luxuriated in the knowledge of his total power. Her buttocks were scarlet, the rest of her flesh almost white in the brilliant sunlight. Her hips swelled delectably from the tiny waist, and her nipples in the freezing water were as pinched and hard as bullets. He reached a hand into the water and stroked them, enjoying the rigid flesh, enjoying the responsive tremors that rippled through her. He bent down to inspect her asshole. As he placed his hands on her buttocks to spread them apart he felt her tremble. That was good, it was right that she should be frightened of him. She was the sort of bitch who got slippery at the same pace as she got fearful. He felt her pussy. Sure enough she was dripping wet again. He resumed his examination of her anus. A bit red, but no damage. She might look like peaches and cream, but she was a whore right enough, a natural born slut.

His belt was still lying in the fountain water, coiled like a dark snake ready to strike. Stepping back he casually he wrapped the buckle in his hand and let fly with all his strength, the leather landing on her red bottom with a satisfyingly loud slap. The helpless girl screamed and bucked, trying to pull away as blow after blow found its target; he paused so that he could hear her crying and begging for mercy. Smiling to himself he continued to lash her, letting the leather land now upon her thighs, inching the blows steadily closer to her pinkly swollen lips. Finally he brought a blow directly up, to land with considerable force upon her pussy, and was gratified by her loud shriek of pain. As he rebuckled his belt around his waist he noted with satisfaction that her pussy was oozing fuck juices all down her thighs. There must be a limit to how much pain she could enjoy before it lost its attraction, but apparently he hadn't found it yet.

He unpegged her ankles and unhooked the rope, leading her to the group on the grass with her wrists still bound.

"You can rest for a while. Over there, with the other bitch." He gestured towards the sleeping dog.

Charlotte lay down on her front quite near Sheba, though it was the last place she wanted to be. She wasn't generally afraid of dogs, but then a dog had never taken her neck in its jaws before. She wondered if Sheba would bite if their Master told her to. The thought made sweat prick her armpits. Sheba woke up, sniffed her and padded closer.

44

Lying down by Charlotte's back she started to lick her neck, those same slow, steady licks. Maybe the dog wouldn't hurt her. There was something gentle about her tonguing. Charlotte craved comfort: her buttocks still ached from the brutal beating, and her pussy felt sore and abused. How cruel this man was, to beat a woman at her most sensitive spot!

The sun beat down fierce as ever. She pulled her arms up by her face, to shield herself from the glare. Her face now in a small cave of bare arm, grass underneath, a crack of brilliant blue sky between her bound wrists. The grass smelt wonderfully fresh. It had been cut only yesterday by the gardener. Oh Lord, thought Charlotte. The gardener! Where was he now? The thought of a man she'd ordered around, (somewhat haughtily if truth be known), witnessing her humiliating fall in status brought a flush to her cheeks. She glanced furtively around her, but could see no sign of him.

"Rested?"

She jumped at the sound. Her Master was watching her, that sardonic smile once again twisting his mouth. She swallowed, uncertain what to reply. But the question had been rhetorical.

"On your back."

She reluctantly obeyed. He moved behind her. The other men were a few yards away, still lazing in the sun. Now they watched, rubbing their crotches as their cocks stirred, ready again to sample submissive flesh.

"Peg her down. On her back, legs spread but not so far they are taut, spread and relaxed. Arms above her head. Pegged at wrists and ankles."

In less than thirty seconds they had her splayed as he described. The sun's glare was intense, she shut her eyes but it was still so bright. A hot red glow through her lids.

"Did you bring a hood?"

A pause. Then Tom knelt by her face, holding something black, shapeless. She could smell the sweet stink of leather.

As he tugged it over her head she felt a sudden chill that covered her skin in goose bumps and puckered her nipples. Then she was plunged into her own separate space. Utter darkness. No holes, no light. She twisted her head from side to side, trying to get away, but she could feel straps across her throat, hands buckling them tight. But then a curious feeling of calm swept over her. Perhaps, she thought, this is how a horse feels when it is blinkered.

And then she was lying there, powerless. Naked, spread, completely open. Unable to see what they were doing, no way of guessing whether the next touch would be of hand, or of cock, or of belt. Her sore ass stung as the grass prickled against it.

Something warm, trickling onto her belly and breasts, dripping along her thighs. A sweet smell… what is it? Oranges. Oranges and lavender. It must be oil. Hands start to rub her, gliding over her stomach, down her thighs, across her chest. Yes, oil. Thumbs circle her nipples, bringing them to tight hard buds. Palms press up her thighs, stopping enticingly close to her naked lips. With shame she realises there is more than one man using his hands on her, there are two of them.

No. More than two. Now hands stroke along her arms, from her bound wrists to her armpits, circle her full breasts whilst still her nipples are toyed with. She is moaning with arousal, but doesn't hear herself.

Glistening with oil, the girl's lithe body looked even better. Carl's hands moved nonchalantly over her breasts, perfect hemispheres, firm and luscious. She writhed under his touch, already moaning as though close to orgasm. He liked seeing her hooded; just a body, not really a person anymore, just female flesh for him to explore and enjoy. Her stomach formed a small, planar hollow, her navel an oval shadow against the pale skin. The thighs were long and slender, despite her diminutive stature. Strapped open they trembled, setting those beautifully smooth pussy lips aquiver. Her defenceless crack was exposed for all to see, her hymen obliterated now by the steady pumping to which she'd been subjected, a darkly inviting hole, the dark centre of a dull red rose. The bud of her clit was swollen and fat, jutting stiff and pink, needing attention. He dipped his head and began to lick.

Charlotte felt herself dissolving into a thousand brilliant fragments as the hot tongue lapped and beat upon her throbbing clit. She seemed to be spiralling into a glorious nothingness, as though her whole self were disintegrating into stars of light. Within moments she was swept into a blasting orgasm. If she hadn't been hooded she would have gazed at her new Master with adoring eyes, as it was she opened her eyes only to see nothing but the blank darkness of the hood.

Suddenly she heard voices, but enclosed in the thick, dense darkness of the hood she couldn't make out what they were saying. Two men, arguing maybe? But no, it wasn't heated enough for that, more the sound of two men negotiating, bargaining. Then hands upon her again, and her tethered limbs were being freed.

They pulled her onto all fours and again pegged her into place. Her knees were slightly spread, and of course, she understood by now what that meant, they wanted to use her again. Hands against her throat, unbuckling the hood, and the next instant she was squinting against the brilliant light. But only for a moment: a male figure moved in front of her, his body blocking out the sun.

He was so close she didn't have a chance to see his face before the hard penis was being pushed against her mouth. In one shocked moment she realised both that the man was dirty, for a sour unwashed smell came from the grey nest of pubic hair from which the thick, reddish organ waved, and that he was not one of her previous assailants. But she had no time for further speculation before he pushed impatiently into her, and grasping her head tightly between his two, roughened hands, began to drive into her throat.

As she tried to open wide enough to accept him without gagging, Charlotte felt something smooth and cold pressing against her pussy lips. Whatever it was was far fatter than a cock, and she would have whimpered as it was forced into her, but with her mouth stuffed with an old man's thick meat she could only make tiny squeaks of protest. The smell of his pubes was disgusting to her, acrid and sour, and he was so deep inside her now that her face was beginning to be buried in them with every thrust. The object pushing into her vagina finally overcame her weak defences and suddenly slipped deeply inside her. Her lips were stretching painfully wide to encompass it, and with a sudden wave of heat she felt the utter humiliation of her situation.

A rough voice above her said,

"Look at me, bitch!"

It was sickeningly familiar. The cock using her throat slipped to her lips, so that she had a chance to look up at the leering face of old Mr. Pearson, the gardener. As she flushed in shock and shame he crowed,

"That's my lad Harry, ramming a marrow up your cunt, you stuck up whore! Do you like it?" And then, to Harry, "Ram it in, lad. Really stuff her with it. Ha, you knew marrows was for stuffing, didn't ye, bitch, but I bet you never thought one would be stuffing you!"

He laughed at his own joke and pulled his cock right out of her mouth, rubbing the slippery organ over her face as Charlotte yelped to feel the marrow thrust repeatedly into her so recently virgin hole. She thought she could not be humiliated any further, but at that moment fingers began to play her clit, and she knew that she would soon be orgasming for these horrible men. As the old man's cock rubbed all over her pretty face she saw beyond him, to where her Master reclined comfortably on the grass; as ever his lips were twisted in that cruel smile, evidently enjoying the show. Next to him another man held a video camera.

As she realised what she must look like, recorded for posterity by that unfeeling, impassive, electronic eye... naked on all fours, and with an old man playing with her breasts and rubbing himself against her face, his grandson behind her stretching her so unnaturally wide with such a grotesque implement... her shame deepened unbearably and with it her arousal. She came in perfect time with Mr. Pearson, who deliberately splattered her lips and hair with the thick, grey gobbets of his semen.

"Lick me clean, you dirty whore."

To be called dirty by this filthy old man should have struck Charlotte as ridiculously unfair, but she couldn't help but agree with him. Her deepest fears, that her secret desire to submit would bring her to a state of complete subjugation if ever a man were to touch her intimately, were now being realised. She had been used by a man she could never have found desirable; ugly, old and filthy. She had been frigged as though she was some porn slut. And not only had she been a willing participant in her own degradation, she had even found it sexually exciting.

Fingers were pulling now at her tautly stretched cunt lips, displaying the ridiculously penetrating vegetable so that the camera could take perfect shots of her debasement, and she understood at last how totally she had been tricked. There was nowadays only one sensible way to market hard core pornography: via the world wide web. Men from every part of the globe would be able to log in and stroke their hard cocks as they saw her body so thoroughly and helplessly used. She wasn't just being enjoyed by eight men, she was to be enjoyed by thousands. Anyone willing to pay her Master would be able to see her penetrated, and see her loving it.

She knew just what sort of a site it would be, she'd seen them often enough herself. One of those with a discreet little message at the bottom, reassuring the viewer that her participation was voluntary, despite any appearances to the contrary. And it was true, she had agreed to belong to that cruel man who sat happily watching her shame, and this was the outcome.

Hands moved to her clit again, and the fat marrow was again shoved rhythmically into her vagina like a giant's pounding cock. The camera moved close to her face, capturing the splatters of semen that still stuck in absurd streaks to her cheeks and lips, capturing her whimpers of discomfort as she accepted the monstrous dildo that invaded her, capturing, finally, her wild shrieks and cries as she came again in yet another thundering orgasm.

She slumped, exhausted, onto her face in the soft green grass of what had been simply her family lawn, and was now instead a backdrop for obscene male entertainment. The marrow was being eased from her body, and she knew the camera would linger upon the gaping hole of her cunt, and that thousands of eyes would soon be looking at it, into her, knowing just what she was.

CHAPTER FOUR

They let her rest there for a while, whilst they helped themselves to more drinks from Henry's amply stocked cellar. Daddy had never been much of a drinker, but Henry had very obviously enjoyed worldly pleasures, spending freely on the best vintages and educating her previously naïve palate. Now these common men sat around on Henry's lawns, guzzling his best wine as though it was cheap supermarket plonk and discussing how they'd turned his step-daughter into a whore.

"Aye, it does me a power of good seeing her tied up for shagging like that, she always were such a stuck up little madam, you'd never've believed it. Thought she was a princess she did, reet stuck up bitch. Her mother's alright, she knows her place, I've caught sight of her a fair few times, sucking her new husband's knob in the summer house. The bitch's father wasn't up to much, he let his missus rule the roost, but once she married Henry Withers she soon started learning how to please. She had to, she'd have been out of this 'ere house if he hadn't come along with his money and rescued her, she knew she'd better work at keeping 'im happy."

The men all laughed. Charlotte was pretending to be unconscious or asleep, her head down on the ground, though pegged as she was her arse was still unavoidably high in the air. Her thighs ached. But she had her eyes open a tiny crack, and through the heavily-lashed slits she watched the men as they joked and drank. Her cheeks were now burning with anger at hearing their salacious talk about her mother.

John Pearson, the gardener, turned his red and wrinkly face towards her, glaring malevolently at her from small, shrewish eyes. He was hideous, as ugly as a Rumpelstiltskin, he must've been well into his seventies. Remembering the sour taste of his thick cock in her mouth she felt a wave of disgust and revulsion. His hands had been on her breasts!

His penis had pressed into her throat! The incongruity of her coupling with this foul old man was shocking to her, she could imagine the picture they made, her beautiful young body used so crudely by his collapsed and scrawny frame. She remembered again the all-seeing eye of the video camera, and knew that it was his very ugliness that would make such images so popular: men loved to see gorgeous young girls suffering to be penetrated by those to whom they would never submit were it not that their will had been utterly subjugated. What could be more humiliating?

"I haven't had her yet."

It was the grandson speaking. He looked to be about eighteen, and his voice was quiet, almost shy. She wondered how long he'd been gathering his courage. Carl turned to him with slightly raised eyebrows.

"I seem to remember you wielding a marrow rather effectively."

Laughter all round.

"Aye. But I want my cock in her. I want to fuck her."

Carl smiled.

"Be my guest. Which hole would you like to use? Take your pick."

With that Carl turned away, and resumed his chatting with the older men. No one seemed very interested in what the boy would do. He picked himself up and came and stood over her. Now she could see only his hulking great feet in scruffy trainers and the bottoms of his baggy jeans. He knelt down in front of her, and she kept her eyes almost shut, wondering how he'd take her. He seemed nervous, maybe he wouldn't have the confidence to wake her. She closed her eyes completely as she felt his hot, sweaty hands steal under her to caress her breasts, staying motionless, as though the touch had not reached her. His fingers rubbed her nipples in gentle circles, then again stroked the round heaviness of her tits; still she pretended to sleep. Suddenly impatient, he grasped a tit in each hand and squeezed, brutally hard, asserting his superiority in the manner he had seen his grandfather use. She bolted upright, screaming and straining at her tethers, looking at him in shock with wide beseeching eyes. But it was rather too late to expect kindness, she had insulted him by ignoring him, his irritation was warranted and she would soon regret her arrogance.

He squeezed again, this time letting his nails dig red crescents into the soft flesh, smiling as he saw the tears spring to her eyes.

"Do you want me?" he asked.

She started to speak and faltered, so he pinched her nipples between his thumbs and forefingers, watching her face as he steadily increased the pressure. She felt her pussy flood with fuck juices and began to whimper, in pain and arousal.

"I said, do you want me?"

Despite his cruelty she felt bolder with this young man than she had with the ones old enough to have fathered her.

"Feel my pussy. You'll be able to tell if I want you."

He laughed, and reached a hand round to her tail to feel her sopping cunt.

"You tart. You'd want anyone, wouldn't you? Anything. Animal, vegetable, mineral… you'd want it." He got hold of her clit and nipped it between his fingers so that she screamed, her scream tailing away into a low, aroused moan..

He unzipped his flies and a short but extremely thick cock sprang out, already rigid, and with a pearly drop of pre-come glistening at the tip. He rubbed it against her face, anointing both her eyelids, then rubbing the naked glans down her nose, towards her mouth. She started to lick. He tasted salt; he tasted good.

He moved round behind her. A moment later she felt the hot head of his organ pressing against her still-sore front hole. It hurt, and her muscles clenched in an involuntary attempt to avoid penetration. But wriggle and squirm as she might, there was to be no escaping from the relentless pressure. He gradually forced himself inside her, whilst she whimpered and trembled at the stinging pain. Even when the whole length of him was finally inside it still hurt as he pushed in and out.

He reached a hand under her to stroke her clit for a moment, and she felt herself transfixed, immobile under the duel onslaughts of pain and pleasure. Then he slipped one hand through her collar, wrapped the other in her hair and hung on as though these were her reins, fucking her hard enough to make her whimper again.

The older men hadn't been paying them any attention, but at her increasingly pathetic cries they turned to watch. Through her tears she saw Tom undo his flies, the better to stroke his own swollen shaft.

Carl stood up, and unfastened his belt once more. He settled himself on the grass in font of her, leaning back happily, totally relaxed and nonchalant, watching her face as she wept yet moaned with pleasure. He hooked her mouth open with his thumb and pressed the tip of his still damp belt to her tongue, then fed the leather into her in coiling ripples until her mouth was stuffed full. The belt tasted strong and alien in her mouth. She tried to spit it out, but he put a hand on her head and the other on her chin, clamping her mouth shut, the rest of the belt dangling from her lips like a immensely long, brown tongue. She was salivating all over the leather.

After a few minutes, during which Harry used her cunt steadily, almost gently, Carl pulled the strip of slick and darkened leather from her lips, looking at it in approval, then smiling at her in that evil manner he had.

He walked round out of sight behind her. There was a moment's pause, then she heard, a loud 'Thwack!" as the belt lashed against skin. But not her skin. Accompanying the noise came a sudden jerking thrust from the youth inside her, and a yelp of surprised pain. Another "Thwack!" and another deep thrust so that she cried out herself. Then the blows began to rain down fast and furious upon the buttocks of the boy who was enjoying her, driving him on to ever rougher use of her in the same way that a sledge-dog is whipped to make him pull harder.

Poor Charlotte's cheeks were wet with tears now, her cunt was being plundered far more vigorously than when the older men had used it and she could only be thankful that Harry has chosen to penetrate her vagina not her anus. Just when she thought she could bear it no longer the boy bellowed like an ox as he climaxed, then slumped his full weight onto the unfortunate girl. Tethered as she was she had to choice but to remain in place, her slim thighs trembling.

Tom came forward, his engorged penis ready to have her again.

"No, Tom, I want her back in her bedroom now, where you found her." Carl's arrogant drawl was imperious. He's used to ordering people around, Charlotte thought.

Tom turned away with a nod of assent, but not before she'd seen a flicker of emotion cross his stolid features. Did he resent the way in which Carl had assumed possession of her? It seemed likely, considering that it had been Tom who had found her.

Carl took her back into the house, leaving the other men sprawled with their drinks on the lawn, stripping off their shirts to enjoy the sunshine as though they were on holiday.

It was cool inside the old house. The large rooms seemed very dim and still, they smelt of lavender furniture polish and cut flowers. Carl let her show him the way to her bedroom. He had fastened Sheba's chain lead to her collar again, but he held it quite loosely. She didn't try to pull away, but meekly preceded him up the stairs. As docile as my other bitch, he thought with satisfaction.

Charlotte's bedlinen was still dishevelled, pushed into

ripples and folds that resembled the white petals of a blown rose as it begins to disintegrate. Looking at the bed she found it hard to imagine that only a few hours before she had woken here alone, still safe, still a virgin, still governor of her own destiny.

Carl sat down on the bed, but didn't say she could sit. So she stood there, feeling slightly stupid, waiting for him to speak.

"Show me what you were doing when Tom first saw you this morning."

Charlotte flushed, she'd been expecting this. Hesitantly she moved to the little Faberge box on her dressing table, and pulled out the cord. As she took it to Carl the cold chain lead shifted softly against her shoulder, heavy and oppressive.

"Show me what you do with it."

He watched her and chuckled as she fastened the cord to her nipples, she felt herself colouring under his gaze. She turned back to him, the cord dangling slack between her breasts.

"And then? Show me exactly what you were doing."

Charlotte's blush deepened as she moved to the mirror, hooked the cord above it and slipped the loop over her wrist. She parted her pussy lips with her fingers and her nipples were pulled painfully upwards as the cord tightened and bit into them. Carl was chuckling.

"You really are a natural slut, aren't you? And you like pain… fascinating," he drawled. "But then why were you a virgin? You love cock, you were gagging for it, why've you not had a man before? Do you prefer girls?"

She could tell from his tone of voice that he found that possibility exciting.

"No… it's not that. It's just I knew, I've always known, where it would lead me."

"And where might that be?"

" Out of my own control… to a loss of autonomy. I knew

56

that it'd affect me too deeply, that I'd be intoxicated by it. I'm not the same as other girls."

As she spoke she looked sadly at her reflection in the mirror. Dried trails of semen encrusted her cheek, silvery white now, flaking off. She had been right, she reflected. She felt as though she'd unwittingly embarked upon a path into a dark forest. Where it would lead she didn't know, but there was no way of turning back, no branchings, no possible deviation. Perhaps it was more as though she'd hurtled off down a bleak hillside on a toboggan, with no way to steer, and no brakes.

Carl was standing behind her now. She watched his reflection in the mirror. He was tall, over a whole foot taller than she was. His chest was broad and swarthy, his shoulders muscular. He slipped the loop of cord from her wrist, and over his own, looping it over and over so that when he rested his hands around her tiny waist her nipples were pulled painfully high in an exaggerated version of her own mild torment.

She whimpered in pain, and he chuckled again, and reached his fingers down the smooth curve of her belly to part her silky labia. Now her nipples were pulled so high that the mirror reflected back an absurd image of a girl whose breasts were tugged up into sharp pointed cones. She moaned softly, as he began to stroke her clitoris, each movement of his fingers jerking her breasts, increasing the torment. She tried to stand on tiptoes to lessen the tug, but he just looped the cord once more around his wrist, so that now she had to stay on tiptoes just to keep the pain constant. She strained and trembled and then felt the hot thick wedge of his penis, pressing against her cunt hole. As he entered her she realised that because he was so much taller he had to lift her slightly to settle her onto his cock, so she was able to relax onto him, her poor nipples slightly less stretched than before. His cock felt huge inside her, almost as big as the marrow, far bigger than young Harry's organ.

He started to fuck her. Slowly. Steadily. She felt his hot breath at her ear.

"You're mine now, slut. You... belong... to...me."

He punctuated each word with a thrust of his cock, and then, on the last word, she felt the huge organ convulse and fill her with his load. He pulled swiftly away from her, his ejaculate already dribbling down her slender thighs. Her abused nipples were scarlet, her breasts ached.

He tied her, spread eagled on the bed, his semen and Harry's trickling from her vagina, more evidence of plunder still seeping from her anus. He tied her tightly, so that this time she had no chance whatsoever of loosening her bonds, and then he left, shutting the door behind him. She heard his heavy footfalls trudging down the stairs, fading away as he moved towards the back of the house. Out again to join his brave comrades, she supposed.

Outside her window the birds were still singing.

Charlotte dozed fitfully as she lay there, despite the discomfort of her bonds. It was past midday now, and whenever she woke she was sharply conscious of hunger gnawing at her belly. She could hear the sound of voices down below, and the clink of silverware against china. They must have found something to eat. The smell of roast meat came wafting tantalisingly up towards her, making her salivate. Of course, they'd found the leg of lamb she'd bought for the dinner party. She'd completely forgotten, she had five friends coming round tomorrow night, what on earth would they think when they saw her like this? But maybe the men would have gone by then, maybe she'd be able to tidy the place up, go into town and buy fresh meat, serve up a delicious dinner as though nothing had happened, as though she hadn't spent the preceding day being gangbanged and beaten. Charlotte sighed. She knew she was fooling herself. These men had her in their power now, they had no intention of letting her off lightly. Maybe they had no intention of letting her off at all. It was as though a cold breeze had suddenly gusted through the open window. She felt chilled, despite the burning heat of the day. Carl Bredon and his cronies, what would they do once they had finished with her? She knew the answer to that, she felt sure of it. There was something so practised, so easy, about the way they'd settled down to fuck and abuse her... this situation was novel for her of course, but not, she now realised, for them. And if they made a habit of this, then it stood to reason that there would never come a time when they had 'finished' with her. A time when she was free to go. She remembered one of the words she'd overheard. Merchandise. She shuddered. It seemed more than likely that the future that now lay in store for her was one of permanent debauchery and whoredom, a life spent with her legs repeatedly spread to please numerous anonymous men, who would have little if any concern for her feelings on the matter. Her groin felt suddenly hot, and she wished she could reach a hand to touch herself.

Her sore ass rubbed uncomfortably against the wrinkled linen, and she shuddered again as she thought of the pain of the beating, and how her squeals had apparently aroused her Master. That was what she could expect then, a life of casual penetration and cruel beatings, a dramatic reduction in status from free woman to owned bitch.

Her pussy was getting wet again. But she knew this future was not what she wanted, not really. Not for ever and ever. Suddenly she realised there was one glimmer of hope for her. Carl was evidently a powerful man, a man with money, a man with contacts. But so was Uncle Henry. In a month Uncle Henry would return from holiday with her mother, and she would be rescued. After all, Henry wasn't going to be too happy to have a houseful of the great unwashed, swigging his wine and muddying his parquet. She began to feel a bit better.

But could she survive a month of this subjugation? A

month of having her mouth unceremoniously stuffed with dirty cock, her back and buttocks whipped, her vagina forced to accept whatever instrument it might amuse her captors to wield?

Footfalls just outside her door; she looked up as it opened. Stu came into the room. He was stocky, blonde. She hadn't seen that much of him as he'd spent most of the time filming the other men using her. He didn't say a word now, didn't even look at her face, he just started untying her wrists. Then he sat her up and brought them behind her back and wound smooth cord around them to strap them together, wrist to wrist, elbow to elbow. Like this her shoulders were pulled back, her full breasts jutted forward like so much displayed meat. Finally he untied her tethered ankles. But before she was free he wrapped her chain lead around his wrist several times. She would not be allowed to make any further bids for freedom.

Once he had her trussed to his satisfaction he pulled her off the bed, and marched her on a short leash across the landing to the bathroom, pushing her roughly ahead of him towards the shower. He locked the door behind him, then let her lead fall, and quickly stripped. Charlotte wondered about escaping from him, but with her arms so uselessly trussed it would've been impossible. How could she possibly climb down the apple tree, like this? How could she even undo the bolted door? So she waited meekly whilst he undressed. He picked up her lead again, unbolted the door, and stepped into the shower, dragging her after him, then he forced her to her knees.

Now he turned the faucet on full, and began to wash himself in the torrent of near scalding water. Charlotte could hardly breathe, kneeling helpless on the glossy tiles, water gushing over her in an unbroken flood. Sopping hair covered her eyes and face, clogged her nostrils. With her arms pinioned behind her she couldn't even push it back out of the way. She felt his fingers twist into her hair, pull her head back. Now the full force of the water was on her upturned face.

He was pressing something to her lips. At first she thought it must be cock, but it was perfumed, cool and slick and unyielding, hard. She opened her mouth just a tiny way, and he forced it between her lips. Opening her eyes, trying to peer through the stinging water, she saw what he was holding and pushing into her mouth. A huge, dildo, grotesquely realistic apart from its absurd size, a crude, pink colour. It had a sickly sweet artificial scent, and as her lips parted to accept it, as she knew she must, she realised it was made of soap.

He pushed the soap dildo deeper into her mouth. She was starting to gag, and the taste of the soap made her feel nauseous, but she knew what he wanted, and knew she'd better do her best to please. The dildo pushed into her throat and she strained to keep open, to allow entry. It was massive, but being soap it was also very slick now. As she held her throat open he pushed it into her, and began fucking her face so deeply that the solid soap balls pressed against her chin.

She was frothing at the mouth now, her lips lathered by the invader. There was too much water on her face, and with her mouth so stuffed she struggled to breathe, inhaling hurriedly through her nose whenever his body blocked the spray enough to grant her air. Suddenly she felt terribly claustrophobic. The dildo was just too big, the torrent of water too unremitting; she wanted to escape. But whether sensing her distress, or perhaps just by chance, he chose that moment to slide the surrogate cock from out of her lips. However, before she could be too thankful, he replaced it with his own swollen flesh, pressing hotly, impatient to enjoy her.

"Now, clean me," he said.

Charlotte's mouth was soapy from the dildo, her throat greased to slickness by the suds. The cock slid in with no

61

trouble at all, in one swift movement. He felt burningly hot and almost soft in her mouth after the rigid inflexible length of the dildo. He held her head in his hands and pulled her swiftly back and forwards on his cock, each thrust pressing her face deep in amongst his wet, still musky, pubes, her mouth frothing still, and the alkaline burn of the soap making her throat sting. She could neither fight him nor aid him, kneeling helpless before him, her arms bound into irrelevance, her role in this sexual act was entirely passive. She might as well have been a doll for all the attention he gave her.

The situation must have been to his liking for he orgasmed quickly, pulling just a little way out so that his load filled her mouth, sudden and sour. She knew better than to spit out the choking explosion of thick come, so she meekly swallowed it down, her throat burning again from the soapy mixture.

She had expected him to be finished with her. His spent cock hung limp, quickly shrinking back to softness, but the dildo was still hard of course, and now he turned his attention back to it.

He pulled her to her feet, and turned her to face the wall. He pressed her forwards, so that her full breasts were painfully crushed against the cold tiles. She felt something, slippery, hard, against her puckered anus and then a steady pressure, as he began to force the soap dildo up inside her.

Her sensitive tissue stung, she was still sore from Carl Bredon's penetration, the way his great length had so remorselessly taking her anal virginity. The dildo was even larger, it had been designed as a joke novelty item, never intended for use. But little by little the man pushed it up into her, holding her by her bound arms and pressing hard, relentlessly, so that finally her muscles relaxed and the shaft slid inside.

It hurt, it was too big, her ring stung and burned. She squirmed in pain, but that only made it hurt more. The man held her still, waited for her to relax, then continued to press the monster deeper inside.

Tears streamed down Charlotte's face, indistinguishable from the gushing water, as she forced herself to relax, to accept what was happening to her. She was shivering uncontrollably, and she suddenly couldn't help but piss herself.

Stu had decided the penetration was deep enough. He wanted to fuck her, not damage her, he wasn't fool enough to think she could take the whole length of the huge instrument. Now he began to slide the monster in and out, fucking her in short, gentle thrusts. From nowhere Charlotte felt the steady swell of an orgasm build rapidly inside her. It was immensely deep, and when it reached her it was as though a wave of huge power was engulfing her. Her cunt and anus squeezed in ecstatic ripples of response, but that hurt so much, with the thick wedge of soap still inside her, that she cried as she came.

He slid the dildo from her body, and immediately slipped his newly erect cock in its place, gliding inside in one movement as her hole was still open from his manual thrusting.

As he started to fuck her ass, pressing her against the tiles, again hurting her breasts which were still sore from Bredon's abuse, she became dimly aware of voices in the bathroom. Then Stu pulled her away from the wall, his cock still inside her, and continued his fucking with her up against the clear glass side panel of the shower cubicle.

She could see through the glass, and with shock realised they had an audience. Relaxing comfortably in a chair, only a few feet away, was Carl Bredon himself. Another man squatted next to him, but his face was obscured by the all-seeing eye of the video camera. Her breasts were pressed repeatedly against the glass in a steady rhythm of the fucking. The man inside her held her by her bound arms, and her hair. He knew he was being filmed, and he knew how to put on a good show. Charlotte knew exactly what she must look like, the way her tits would appear ludicrously huge, flattened against the glass, the way she must look totally humiliated and debased, as indeed she felt. Once, years ago, she'd seen a beautiful film, 'Time of the Gypsies'. In it there was` a scene that she knew she was supposed to find upsetting, when the innocent young woman has her first taste of sex, pressed up against a window for all the men to see her casual defloration. But Charlotte hadn't been upset, she been aroused and hungry and ashamed.

Carl was still smiling at her, with that cold cruel smile that rarely seemed to leave his face. She felt a sudden wave of irritation; she'd like to wipe that smile away. When would it be his turn to suffer humiliation? Probably never: she seemed to have entered a world where women were toys to be used and men casually ruled the roost.

Stu suddenly climaxed and immediately withdrew. His semen trickled from her used hole in thick burning drips. He turned off the water, and pushed her out of the cubicle, leaving her to shiver in the middle of the room whilst he wrapped himself warmly in two of Mummy's best Egyptian cotton towels from the heated rail. She stood there, shaking and dripping, her hair trailing in wet snakelets down her ivory shoulders, her sore red nipples hard as bullets in the sudden chill. The camera panned up and down her body, its shiny eye drinking in her taut belly, narrow thighs and naked, dripping lips, before focussing on her displayed breasts. At a word from Carl, Stu turned her around and bent her forward. She felt his hands spreading her buttocks apart, and knew the camera was devouring the image of her abused and reddened anus.

The bathroom was large, as were all the rooms in her family home. The bath itself was grand and opulent, a luxurious modern copy of a Victorian cast iron bath, with curling lion's claw feet, and ostentatious gold plated taps. It stood in the centre of the bathroom, thick cotton mats all around. To one side was a bidet in the same style, and it was upon this that Carl's eyes now alighted.

"Over there. Bend over. No, right over, get your face between the taps! And keep your legs straight, if you want any food this week!"

Charlotte did as he indicated, bending over the bidet so that her lips rested between the taps on the cold white ceramic basin, her legs spread wide so as to bring her face down far enough to accomplish this, her bound arms jerked skywards.

She waited, trembling, hideously uncomfortable. Carl took her chain lead and wound it round and round the taps, then undid her collar, slipped the leather loop of the lead handle over it, and refastened it round her neck, making sure it was good and tight. She was now immobilised, bound in place by her neck. She rested her forehead against the shiny white rim of the bidet.

Again she waited, still wet, growing colder by the minute. Water trickled down her body and dripped from her nipples into the basin. Bredon had evidently sent Stu to get something, for he returned, a little out of breath by the sound of it.

"Will these do the trick?"

"Excellent. Strap them to her legs."

Her Master had evidently not been confident that she would be capable of keeping her legs straight, for now she felt smooth wood being pressed up against her thighs. Peering between her legs she saw Stu was binding two of Daddy's old walking sticks to her, with leather straps that wrapped tightly round her calves and thighs. The curved handles of the sticks dug into her pussy on either side of her labia, pinching her lips between them like a cruel wooden vice. She wriggled and then whimpered, as her movement made the pinching worse.

Carl got up, and stood behind the tethered whore. He

reached between her legs and inspected her crushed lips, noting with pleasure how uncomfortably the wooden sticks pressed into her. He trailed a finger over her pussy, inspecting it. This position afforded an excellent view of her genitals. Her asshole was red and sore in appearance: good. Pain without serious damage, that was his ideal.

She was shaking now, probably from the position as much as from the cold. Her delicious breasts hung temptingly vulnerable beneath her, like rich ripe fruit he could pick and plunder at will. He felt his cock stir in his pants, growing rock hard. This was going to be an exceedingly pleasurable beating. At this point he didn't much care whether or not the pain he inflicted would be within bounds she would willingly suffer, his mind was focussed on the far more important consideration of his own enjoyment. He thought he might use the cane, this time. It would be good to raise some welts upon her perfect white flesh. Or maybe the cat. But first, a few more details...

"Bring me the harness of narrow leather straps."

When Stu returned Carl took the bundle of cords, and dropped them into the bidet. He put in the plug, and turned on the hot tap. The basin filled with steamingly hot water. The fine leather bonds looked like a bundle of seaweed as they soaked, dark strands entwined and twisted. He knew the whore could see what he was doing, and that she didn't understand his purpose, for she was watching carefully. He could also tell she was frightened, for though her trembling thighs could possibly be explained simply by the discomfort of her position he had noted also that her breath was coming in short, hurried pants. Her neck was blotchy from her shallow breathing, mottled with red as though she'd orgasmed, but he'd seen enough frightened women to recognise the cause. Knowing that the beauty was both terrified, and, totally under his power, made his cock as hard as bone. He unbuttoned his flies, and let the lord she must learn to worship rub casually against her belly and breasts, anointing her with a fine trail of pre-come like a dog marking his territory.

Stu had also brought with him the cat o' nine tails. The knotted leather hung limply from Carl's belt as he casually fingered the whore, enjoying her little shivers and barely audible whimpering. He pressed a finger between her squeezed fuck lips, finding his way straight to her clit, noting with satisfaction that it was fatly swollen and slippery with her juices. He rubbed it with the length of his finger and she moaned in appreciation. It was time to punish her.

He felt the soaking leather ties. They hadn't been in the hot water for long enough yet, he needed them soft, stretchy. No matter, he could begin the slut's chastisement without them, all the better if it was a long drawn out punishment. He had plenty of help here, after all. They could whip her for hours if need be, if the whim took him.

He raised the cat and brought it down with full force upon her raised and defenceless buttocks, still nicely pink from his earlier beating. She screamed with gratifying intensity, jerking her head up the tiny distance made possible by her short chain so that the leather collar bit into her neck, leaving a reddish mark on the delicate skin as she subsided. Before her scream had died away he lashed again, at the same spot. And again. And again. Her buttocks were already flaming red, and tears were coursing freely down her cheeks. Was she begging him to stop? He didn't hear, he wasn't listening to her words, she was chattel now, she had agreed to be his and now she would begin to understand what 'being his' would entail. He claimed complete jurisdiction over this slight body: it was his to fuck, or order fucked, his to arouse, and his to degrade and torment. Only his rights mattered: as she had been foolish enough to submit to him, she would obviously have to bear the full brunt of the consequences.

Again he brought the cat down on her smarting buttocks. And again.

"Please, Carl, no!"

Her pathetic plea for mercy would have been irritating enough, but she doubled his fury by having the temerity to use his name, instead of addressing him with proper respect as 'Master'. He lashed her again, this time allowing the knotted leather to land with stinging precision upon her pinched pussy lips. She screamed again, and he paused so that he could fully enjoy the sight of her weeping and confused face. He could see that she was sexually excited.

Bending forward, he hissed in her ear:

"What is my name, whore?" his voice dangerously soft, daring her to err again.

"Carl. Carl Bredon," she managed to sob out.

Grinning with malice he brought the cat down once more upon her genitals.

"WHAT IS MY NAME, WHORE?" he bellowed.

The unfortunate girl was trembling from head to foot in terror. He trailed the cat gently over her swollen labia, back and forth, back and forth.

"Well?" his voice was icily soft again.

She must finally have understood her mistake,

"M-m-m-master," she moaned.

He reached the handle of the cat between her clamped lips and rubbed it slowly back and forth, noticing with satisfaction that it rapidly began to glisten with her copious fuck juices. The slut moaned each time the smooth leather rubbed over her hidden clitoris.

The dye had leeched slightly from the soaking leather straps, turning the basin of water the colour of brandy. He reached to test them, and found them as pliant as he could have wished. The girl could count her blessings, she had some time to recover; he would pause in his punishment in order to strap her as he wanted. The harness had a section like a bra, but with no cups to obscure the displayed flesh, instead it had two circular loops that surrounded the breasts and could be tightened to fit. Reaching down from the centre front of the bra were two more straps that slipped between the labia, then up between the buttocks, buckling to the back of the bra above her waist. He fastened the harness onto her, then adjusted the straps so that her tits were encircled by loops of leather so tight that they dug into the pale flesh, leaving her orbs painfully pinched at their roots. Then he shortened the twin straps that lay between her pussy lips, again buckling them so tightly that they cut into her belly, and, above all, pressed painfully tightly into her groin.

She had stopped screaming, but was moaning gently, obviously in a fair amount of discomfort mingled with a burning sexual need. Good. He wondered if she was intelligent enough to realise what lay in store for her as the leather bonds dried out; somehow he doubted it.

CHAPTER FIVE

Charlotte wriggled and squirmed in her restraints, but the movement only made her more uncomfortable. At least he had stopped beating her. Her bottom was still stinging from the rain of blows, she was sure it must be bright scarlet and her poor pussy throbbed from the lash and the pinching sticks. As if she wasn't already suffering enough now he had bound her in the leather cord that nipped her breasts and pressed into her clitoris. Behind her she was aware of the omnipresent video camera, recording every detail of this barbaric treatment. Perhaps she might be able to steal the cassette. The men weren't bothering to hide their faces. If Uncle Henry saw it she was sure he'd have them all jailed. The thought that Carl Bredon might have that annoying smile wiped off his face, by an avenging angel in the form of Uncle Henry, gave her a little courage. The fact that her body was responding to this cruelty with a throbbing need for penetration made her all the angrier.

The three men left the room, closing the door behind them, leaving her there, bent over in this ridiculous position, arse in the air like a duck looking for food. She blushed to think that anyone who entered the bathroom would be immediately greeted by the sight of her raw and smarting posterior. As the door was behind her, and as the lowly position of her head thus meant that she could see only the legs of anyone entering the room, she realised that someone could enter the bathroom and then enter her, with her having no idea as to his identity.

But no one came. She stood, bent and uncomfortable, waiting for something to happen. The minutes wound on. Every now and then she'd hear voices from downstairs, quite close by, and each time she'd be on tenterhooks, expecting someone to open the door. But no one did.

Gradually she became aware of a growing change in the leather straps that bound her breasts and pulled between her labia. From the start they'd been uncomfortable, too tight, digging into her tender flesh. And as time went by she'd been aware that the discomfort was increasing. However, she'd assumed this was simply the inevitable intolerance that comes with any drawn out ordeal, that it was hurting more because her body had had quite enough of being bound. Now she realised, with horror, that the pain was steadily increasing, and then suddenly she understood why. As the leather dried it was shrinking, losing its elasticity and becoming shorter. Her breasts, hanging almost in her face, were swollen taut and purplish now, the leather cords cutting deeply around them in a manner that was excruciating and getting worse by the minute. But worse still were the two cords that cut between her labia. They had originally been drawn tight, right on top of her clitoris. As they shrank they cut steadily deeper into her most sensitive place, which was already swollen and pinched by the two walking stick handles.

She shifted position, pressing up on her toes to try to lessen the pain. But the cords just moved imperceptibly on her body, bringing fresh waves of agony to her pinched flesh. She jiggled desperately, almost violently, from foot to foot but could find no release, managing only to increase the throbbing desire that seemed to spread from her clitoris to every part of her. Whilst she was doing this the door opened without her noticing it, and again the video eye sat gloatingly recording every wriggle, every moan, every sob, until she realised, with a start, that she was not alone, when Carl's voice said:

"Make sure you have a shot of that pretty face, the tears trickling down. I think it is perhaps time to resume her education."

Only a few seconds' pause after he spoke these words, then the next swipe of the cat landing on her already raw behind. She screamed and didn't have time to catch her breath before a second blow struck, this time on her pinched and swollen pussy lips. A third blow, across the sensitive tops of her thighs. Then a pause, and she felt the cat trailing gently against her dangling breasts, almost stroking her.

"I'm going to move her. Her breasts are too protected like this, I can't get a good swing. And I'm looking forward to seeing how she responds to them being whipped, now they've been so effectively bound."

She could hear the rich amusement in his voice.

His hands were on her collar, unfastening her from the taps. In a few moments she was free to lift her neck. As she straightened she wobbled and would have fallen, but Carl wrapped one of his immensely muscular arms around her slender pinioned ones, and half walked, half dragged her over to the mirror. She didn't want to see herself in this condition and dropped her gaze to their feet. Hers: tiny, naked, with opalescent pearly polish on her toenails; his: large, long, encased in expensive Italian leather shoes.

"Look at yourself, slut!" as he spoke he wrapped his free arm in her long mane of hair and yanked her head back, so that she saw her reflection.

She hardly recognised herself. Her eyes look wild, and far away, more animal now that human. Not the eyes of a pet, no. They reminded her more of the wild desperate eyes of a doe as the dogs set upon it. Her pussy lips were pinched and red, and the cruel cord that pulled between them split them apart so that the red meat of her most sensitive flesh could be seen within. But it was her breasts that caught her attention and held it, so that she stared, almost mesmerised by her own body.

They bulged in front of her like swollen purple fruit, the skin taut, the nipples jutting dark. The leather bonds pinched around their roots. She understood for the first time in her life how beautifully designed for cruelty a woman's body is. How many ways there are of using her lovely femininity to hurt and degrade and yet still arouse her.

As she gazed at her unfamiliar reflection Carl released

her hair, and brought the cat with which he had been beating her up to her face. She saw for the first time the instrument of her abuse, and shivered as he let the knotted cords trail slowly over her cheeks and lips. He moved it down her neck, caressingly light, her skin tantalised by the delicacy of his touch. When he reached her breasts he let the cords trickle softly over her swollen orbs and nipples, bumping each nipple gently with the knots. Even this touch was uncomfortable, so tightly was she bound. She understood what was coming, and as he tightened his grip on her hair and arms so that he held them both with a single arm, she started to mew in frightened anticipation, her pussy burning hotter than ever in wild inexplicable need. He raised his other hand, the hand that held the cat, and her eyes were fixed on it in terror. As though in slow motion she saw it swing down towards her breasts, and then the lash contacted her skin and she screamed in sheer agony. Whatever pain her buttocks had suffered it was nothing compared to this.

He must have been pleased by her reaction, for she felt his cock pressing at her through his trousers. Again she watched as he raised the cat high in the air, and brought it down, even harder than before, stinging her engorged flesh. She hadn't time to recover before he brought it down a third time, and this time the pain was so overwhelming that she lost control, and pissed herself, all over his expensive Italian shoes.

Bredon was furious. He pushed her to the ground so she fell on her back, and lashed repeatedly at her trussed tits and pussy. She yelped and writhed, but she could do little to protect herself with her arms so uselessly strapped behind her, and her legs strapped to sticks so that closing them was agonisingly impossible.

"Clean me up, you dirty whore. Lick my shoes clean!"

He settled himself comfortably in the chair, and she tried to struggle to her knees to obey him, but with the sticks still bound to her legs this was impossible.

"Remove those walking sticks, Stu" her master commanded.

It was quickly done. Now she could bend her stiff legs at last. She managed to kneel in front of him, and bent her head to lick her urine off his glossy shoes, tentatively lapping, her nostrils full of the odours of piss and shoe polish. The blood was rushing back into her fuck lips now they had been unclamped and they tingled painfully. The leather cord shifted and rubbed against her clit which was throbbing and swollen. As she licked she was dimly aware that her sex juices were flowing copiously.

She was shocked to realise that her whore's body found even this degradation exciting. Yesterday now seemed like a mythical lost world. She found it increasingly hard to remember there had ever been a time when she was more than a toy for male pleasure. For that seemed to be what she had become. A sex toy, an aid to pleasure for a gang of heartless men, who would penetrate and beat her as they wished. Her whore's cunt clenched at the knowledge of her utter subservience, and she remembered, ruefully but with a certain amount of satisfaction, that she had consented to being used like this.

She had closed her eyes, and now she felt fingers on her clit, then slipping into her vagina.

"My, my, what a whore you are!" she took pride in the surprise in Carl's voice; he clearly hadn't expected her to still be aroused after all this ill treatment.

"Stu, call Tom would you, I think it's time this little beauty experienced some double penetration, don't you?"

Both men laughed.

"Come, my dear, time for a change of scenery."

He frogmarched Charlotte out of the bathroom and down the wide sweep of the stairs. Tom was just coming out of the dining room, and he leered salaciously at the sight of the trussed girl. Stu must have relayed Carl's message, for Tom's hugely erect cock was already jutting from his open flies. The men took her to the kitchen, where a row of large, black, iron hooks hung from a dark oak beam, brightly arrayed with decorative, shining copper pots and pans. Charlotte thought incongruously of all the times she had helped Mummy in this kitchen, baking buns or shaping gingerbread men. Carl gestured to Tom to remove one of the pans, then swiftly untied her wrists, only to retie them in front of her, then bring her arms above her head towards the iron hook. It was far higher than she could reach, but Carl merely hooked the rope over it, then pulled, so that she was raised first onto tiptoes, then higher, so that finally her feet dangled helplessly a foot off the ground.

Carl wound the other end of the rope around the foot of the Aga stove, and turned to look at his prize. She looked very lovely, hanging there. He reached between her swollen sex lips and pulled the leather cords that were digging into her pussy, spreading them apart so that now, instead of pressing upon her clitoris, they pinned her labia open. Her displayed pink flesh gleamed thickly with fuck juices.

Her Master took the cat from his belt, smiling as she shuddered in fearful anticipation, and again rubbed the handle back and forth against her clit, till she moaned with pleasure in supplication. Then he unzipped his flies, took out his massive organ and penetrated her front fuck hole in one single, violent thrust. She yelped in shock and pleasure, then quivered as another cock pressed to gain entry. Tom was standing behind her, the tip of his rod against her sore anus. He smeared something cold against her burning hole... butter, fresh from the fridge... then pressed again. Now his cock slipped slowly inside her. It was stingingly painful, but gradually she succumbed to the relentless pressure and he drove fully into her.

Charlotte was overcome by the sensation of fullness. The men began to fuck her slowly, swinging her easily back and forth between them, fucking her the way two men might saw a tree with a double-handled saw, pulling it first one way then the other. As Carl was in her to the hilt, Tom slid back so that his penetration was shallow, when Carl pulled back, Tom buried himself up to the hilt. She had become a delightful toy, so easily used and manipulated, and the knowledge thrilled her shamefully.

Now they began to fuck her harder. No longer was she swaying gently between them, instead it was one brutal thrust after another after another. On and on and in and in went the pounding cocks. Tom had been holding her by the hips, but now he reached up and seized her bound and painfully tender breasts, squeezing them roughly, enjoying her cries. Carl's hands kneaded her buttocks that were still raw from the whipping. She felt an unfamiliar orgasm build deep within her, blasting her in waves that radiated from her asshole, shaking her through and through. As she came, her fuck holes spasmed in intense contractions, bringing the two men using her to delightful climaxes. As they slipped out of her Carl said,

"Let's go get a drink," and without even looking at her he walked out of the room, zipping his trousers closed as he went. Tom followed suit.

But she wasn't alone. The other men had all gathered to watch her enjoy two cocks at once, and now they knew it was their turn.

"How about a double vaginal for the video?" asked one of the men. He was smaller than the others, almost dwarf-like, an ugly little fellow. Charlotte realised that she hadn't seen him before, that he had not yet had her. That was soon to be rectified. Someone brought a box for him to stand on, and the foul man pulled out a huge, brownish cock, and without further ado shoved it quickly inside her cunt. Then to her mortification the ancient old gardener, John Pearson, went round behind her and started stuffing his own rod in the same hole.

Charlotte whimpered in impotent fury and shame as the two men, neither of whom she would have even deigned to shake hands with a mere day ago, began to enjoy her so recently virginal pussy. The video camera manoeuvred under her so as to get a good view of the two cocks sliding together in and out of her reddened hole.

Others amongst the men held her ankles and pulled her legs apart, stroking or pinching her thighs as they did so. Someone reached a hand to her pinioned sex lips and nipped them sharply with his nails, before rubbing her clit with relentless intensity. To her humiliation she started to orgasm again, moaning so loudly as she came that the video camera panned to her face, recording every detail of her open-mouthed ecstasy. When the men had finished with her she slumped in her bonds, all resistance gone for the time being, defeated not by the men but by her own whorish body.

"Cut her down, we can't use her mouth with her strung up like that."

And the next thing she knew she was on her knees on the cold stone floor, hands pulling her thighs apart, fingers reaching to probe her cunt and anus. Something icy was pressing against her lips, and as she automatically opened them, having grown used to the demanding manner in which she was to be used; a tubular ice lolly was shoved into her mouth. She sucked, gratefully. She had neither eaten nor drunk all day, and the sweet water lolly tasted heavenly.

Suddenly it was pulled away from her, and a long throbbing penis unceremoniously stuffed in its place. Ah, now she understood. The lolly had, of course, not been for her pleasure at all, but entirely for theirs. Its purpose was to chill her mouth, to enhance the sensation when she fellated them.

Dutifully she sucked upon the cock, licking her tongue repeatedly up the shaft, toying gently with the oozing glans, running her lips again and again over the sensitive juncture of the head and body of the organ. It was a relief to fellate a man, rather than just have him use her throat as though it was another cunt. She closed her eyes as she enjoyed sucking him.

The man quickly reached orgasm, pulling from her mouth to splatter his full load over her lips and cheeks. As he came she realised that others had been masturbating near him, for when she opened her eyes all she could see were cocks, three or even four of them, close to her, hands urgently beating them to climax. Load after load of thick creamy semen spurted onto her pretty face, stinging her eyes, coating her mouth and chin. She flushed with shame to think what she must look like, as globs of come dripped from her eyelashes onto the stone flags. And yet she simultaneously felt a strange fierce pride, as though she'd been blessed by their holy water.

Someone got a spoon from the drawer, and carefully scraped the come off her face, quite gently, not wishing to scratch her. He held the overflowing spoon out to her, but she shook her head, and refused to open up, not wishing to be fed on semen. But they pulled her mouth open, and made her eat it anyway. The slimy muck tasted bitter and she was disgusted, but when some slipped back out of her mouth they scraped it off and fed it back in, until she had swallowed every drop of their precious spunk. Every time they humiliated her she could imagine no worse degradation, and yet moment by moment they contrived to debase her further. And each time the demon whore inside her rose to the occasion so that she found herself enjoying even this shame.

She was glad when they let her suck the lolly again, even though she knew what that meant. It was half-thawed now, and disintegrated into fragments in her mouth. Before she had time to suck or swallow them, another cock was pressing between her lips, and she began again to fellate the man with all the care she could muster. She thought the pleasures her lips and tongue provided would be enough for this man also, but he wanted her throat as well, and after she'd caressed him with her tongue for ten long minutes, her jaws aching from being so wide for so long, he plunged deeply into her throat and held her head to fuck her hard.

She was almost delirious now, from the hunger and the beatings and the fuckings and the orgasms. She barely noticed as someone fingered her wet vagina and then thrust his cock inside her. But then the two men using her began to fuck in rhythm, so that both were deep inside her at the same time, thrusting into the slender body increasingly roughly so that she felt as though she were a barbecued delicacy, skewered meat. With shame she accepted the climax that soon blasted through her.

When they had finished, other men took their place. She had stopped looking at their faces now, she was growing used to being accessible and penetrable by whosoever should wish to have her. Her new role in life was to service cock, and it was upon the unceasing flow of erect phallus that she focussed, licking and sucking and opening and relaxing as necessary.

When finally they were all finished with her, she was a sorry sight to behold. Her hair messy and tangled, in places matted with semen, her cheeks likewise smeared with come and tears, her breasts still swollen and purplish now from the leather cords that bound them so tightly, all her fuck holes, including her mouth, red and bruised from so much brutal usage. Someone pulled her to her feet, and she rose unsteadily. Hands fumbled around her tits, undoing the cruel straps so that the harness fell away from her. Totally naked, apart from Sheba's leather collar and clinking chain, she was led out onto the driveway.

It was early evening now. The walls of the house still radiated heat, the stone mellow gold in the setting sunlight, but a chill breeze ruffled her hair as they led her to where a man was washing the cars. He was lathering the Lamborghini, white suds frothing over the shiny yellow bodywork.

"Mick, we've been driving this one pretty hard, wash her off for us would you?"

Mick turned from his work, and laughed to see the bedraggled slut.

"Tie that beauty on the bonnet of this beauty," he said, and left them to do so, whilst he busied himself washing a Merc that was now parked next to it.

Charlotte was pulled onto the slippery yellow bonnet, splayed like an X, a rope from one wrist looping round behind the car and then coming forward and ensnaring the other, a rope leading from one ankle behind the nearest front wheel, under the car, behind the other front wheel and up to the other ankle. The men went back indoors. Turning her head she could see Mick, carefully lathering the Merc.

She began to shiver. The sunlight was still golden but it no longer held any warmth. The metal underneath her felt chill and hard. Her whole body was sore and aching from the cruel treatment she had received.

Finally Mick finished working on the Merc, and made his way back to the Lamborghini. He dipped his sponge in the sudsy water and began to wash the bonnet again, this time including her naked body, but not paying it particular attention. He just washed her as though she were part of the car, a decorative insignia perhaps, she thought wryly.

The water was hot, the sponge soft. Again and again Mick's hand pressed the sponge over her, washing her ankles and calves and thighs, washing her open pussy as though it was no more significant than the windscreen wiper blades, washing her belly and still aching breasts. When he got to her head he continued in the same casual manner, so that she gasped and spluttered as he covered her nose and mouth with the sopping sponge. Her semen-clogged hair received the same, nonchalant treatment.

When he was satisfied that both car and whore were spotlessly clean, he turned on the hose. It was a power hose that delivered a hard jet of water under extreme pressure, useful for blasting away grime. She heard it splashing hard against the rear of the car. He gradually made his way forward, then aimed it at the bonnet, directing the blast back and forth over the shiny expanse, again regardless of the bound girl.

The water burst over her, freezing cold and drenching. When it hit her breasts it was as though they were being beaten again, or perhaps slapped by rough hands. The man laughed as they bounced around, pummelled by the jetting water. She started to scream, but at that moment got a faceful of icy water, and was gasping for breath when the hose moved on.

Only when the pulsing stream of water reached her red and parted labia did the man adjust his pattern of cleaning to allow for the fact he was cleaning a woman as well as a car. Carefully he spread her swollen lips with one hand, then directed the blast of water straight up into her vagina. She yelped in shock at the cold, but already he was pressing the rubber hose closer to the car to give her asshole the same treatment. This time he actually eased the rubber nozzle into her burning hole, and she shivered as she was thoroughly cleansed.

Finally he turned his attention to her clit. Looking her in the eyes for the first time, smiling lewdly, he brought the full power of the water stream directly onto her swollen nub. The effect was electrifying. Within moments she felt an orgasm rising inside her. When she came, with the hard current of water still pummelling her clitoris, the over-stimulation was more than she could handle, and she tossed and struggled in her tethers like a bound animal. When she finally opened her eyes it was to see him leering at her in a knowing way.

Mick began to rub the car down, using a can of some sort of wax, and polishing the gleaming metal to a deep shine. He used a different sort of polish for the chrome, yet another for the rubbery black trim that surrounded the screen, and finally yet another for Charlotte's lovely pale skin. He switched cloths, and rubbed her all over with a rich spicy oil. She caught the scent of cloves and oranges and cinnamon, massaged carefully into her trembling flesh. Cold trickles of water ran down her neck from her still sopping hair.

Then, without a word, he turned and walked back into the house, leaving her alone, naked and helpless, tied like a trophy to a rich man's car.

The sky began to darken. Round to the west the clouds were stained a lurid, bloody red, but above her the sky was a clear and deepening turquoise. The stars were coming out. She shivered. Under her back the car felt cold and hard and unforgiving. She wondered what the men were doing inside the house. Looking that way she could see the brightly lit windows, and occasionally snatches of talk and laughter drifted out from the open windows round at the back. Though she knew that if they came it would only be to use or beat her, still, she wished they would come. An owl hooted and she shivered again. Would they leave her here all night?

Just then a sudden burst of laughter made her look up. The front door was open and three men were coming out onto the driveway. Carl Bredon, her new master, and with him the ugly dwarf-like man who had shared her with the gardener. The third man was much older, he must have been in his seventies, tall still, with a thick thatch of white hair. He carried a silver cane, though he didn't appear to need it. The three were talking in loud, braying voices, and from that and their expensive suits she recognised them as the aristocracy amongst the band of men who were oppressing her, they had such an unmistakable air of power. Something about that easy knowledge of their own power, of their natural authority, reminded her strongly of someone else… but the memory was elusive and she quickly gave up trying to place it.

The three walked over to the Lamborghini. Carl was talking.

"What do you think, rather a beauty, isn't she?"

"Indeed. What's her top speed?"

"Not pushed her to the max, yet, too many speed cameras around here. Tomorrow I'm heading up to London, I'll put her through her paces then."

With a peculiar sense of chagrin Charlotte realised that they were talking about the car, not her. Was it not enough for them to reduce her to a sex toy… it seemed as though they were intent not only on treating her like an object, but upon emphasizing the fact that she wasn't even a particularly important object.

Suddenly the old man raised his silver cane and used it to prod at her still tender breasts. She yelped in protest, but he didn't show any sign that he'd heard. He slipped the cane to her pussy and prodded again, sliding the rubber tip inside her vagina, and poking her as though assessing the quality of some meat.

"And what about the slut? Looks as though you've also been putting her through her paces."

"Yes, I'm rather pleased with that acquisition, too. She was a virgin only this morning, you know." The men all tittered. "This house was her family home, until we decided to requisition it for her initial training. She's shaping up nicely. I'm thinking of bringing her to your party on Wednesday, I thought that might be quite educational for her, what do you think?"

His voice was plummy with amusement. The older man laughed.

"Certainly, I'm sure you're right. And if you should feel the need for a more formal 'education' than you can provide at home, I'd be delighted to break her in for you. Slaves are my speciality as you know, and a body of this quality is exceptional. But I dare say you have your own plans for her?"

"Indeed, Sir Jonathan, I know you are the undisputed expert. Sinclair Precision Components has an international reputation second to none. Incidentally, I have some entertaining designs I've been working on, I wonder if you might take a look? I know you have extensive workshops for the production of specialist items."

"Delighted to help, Carl. I'm always glad to assist in the disciplining of females, it's such an entirely pleasurable occupation. May I?"

There was a pause. Then a bolt of fire shot through Charlotte's left breast. As she screamed it was the turn of her right breast to feel the cat, which Sir Jonathan had borrowed form Carl Bredon. Finally a blow to her spread pussy completed the triptych of subjugation.

The outstretched slut whimpered and moaned, fresh tears gracing her pretty cheeks. The men turned away, laughing.

Chapter Six

Charlotte thought for a few desolate minutes that the men meant to leave her out all night, strapped to the car like a Greek sacrificial maiden awaiting the dragon that would devour her. But as she began to shiver with renewed intensity the side door of the house opened, and a figure came towards her. At first she could not make out who it was, for the light was behind him, and all she could see was a bulky silhouette, but as he drew near she recognised the amiable features of Rich. He smiled at her, quite kindly, and started to unfasten the ropes that strapped her to the car.

"Time we got you to bed, you'll have another hard day tomorrow."

He spoke with a quiet satisfaction. Again Charlotte got a strong impression that the men had done something similar to this before, that she was not the first girl they'd enslaved. Enslaved. She turned the word over in her mind, testing it, tasting it. Yes, that's what she felt like, a sex slave. She'd been thinking they'd turned her into a whore, revealing her slut's nature, as though her virginity had never been the white of innocence, but rather the white of an undeveloped photographic print, that looks as though it holds no secrets, but once treated appropriately reveals its true self. And that was accurate enough, up to a point. But a whore is in charge of her own destiny; she may be bullied, but she is also paid, and she can choose which cocks she services. A whore can still say 'no'. Charlotte knew she'd been given a choice, and that all that had happened to her had thus been of her own volition, and even now she had no regrets. But it was as though having made that choice it was considered both final and absolute, her permission would never be asked again. And so, she was a slave. She had voluntarily become a slave, but a slave has no rights, no right to choose, no right to say no, no right to protest that she made a mistake.

She had freely chosen to become a woman with no choice.

The thought that she was now entirely at the disposal of whatever cock Carl should permit to use her made her flush with arousal. Why was it so intoxicating to become an object, a sex toy, a mere thing for men to use? She didn't understand it, but somehow the knowledge that she no longer had even the most basic rights over her own body, that she was owned, the way an animal is owned, made her feel very safe and warm and wildly sexualised.

Rich led her into the house by the side door, locking and bolting it behind them. The front door was of course reserved for guests and visitors, whores should use the door that led to the outhouse and utility room.

On the washroom floor there was a large wicker dog basket, and Sheba was curled up in it, fast asleep.

"In there," said Rich, gesturing at the basket. His voice was casual, but she could sense amusement behind it.

Charlotte stared at the animal, and back at the man.

"Go on!"

There was steel in his voice now, and he was reaching for the whip which she now noticed dangling from his belt. She hopped into the basket, and lay down, her chilled naked body pressed against the warm hair of the dog's coat.

He reached in his pocket and brought out two padlocks. One he used to padlock her chain lead to the copper piping that led to the washing machine. The other he clipped onto her collar, to make unfastening it impossible. Then he turned on his heel and walked out of the room, switching off the light and shutting the door behind him. She heard the bolts slide into place, and knew there was no chance now of escape.

Charlotte reached to her collar, and fiddled with the fastening. With the padlock securing the buckle there was no way she could undo it. She got out of the dog bed, and felt her way to where her lead handle was padlocked to the pipes. Could she pull them off the wall? Experimentally she tugged; they didn't budge at all. She pulled again, this time using her full strength: nothing.

She got back into the basket, and snuggled down next to the other bitch. Despite the situation in which she now found herself... her still-sore pussy and breasts and buttocks, the hunger that gnawed at her belly... she fell quickly into a deep and dreamless sleep.

She awoke in the middle of the night, realising she was burningly thirsty. She climbed out of the basket and walked towards the sink, but the chain was too short; she couldn't reach the taps. Her foot caught against something on the floor, and she felt cold water slop over her toes. The dog bowl. She paused for a moment. She had very little choice: she could yell until she woke someone up and they came and gave her a drink... if they gave her a drink: she had the feeling that waking the household would be more likely to merit a beating... or she could wait till morning, and try to sleep with this raging thirst, and hope that they gave her a drink then... or she could sit on the floor and drink water from the dog bowl.

There was no real choice, that was obvious. So she lifted the bowl to her lips and drank the water all down. Then she snuggled back next to Sheba's hot, unstirring body, and fell deeply asleep once more.

"Wake up, you lazy slut!" A booted foot prodded gently at her belly. It took her a little time to wake and remember where she was. The memories crowding into her head seemed so fantastical that she would have thought the whole preceding day had been some dark and disgusting dream. But there was the collar firmly buckled around her neck; she was entirely naked, lying in the dog basket, and being nudged awake by the toe of Rich's boot.

Next to her in the basket was a warm and hairy empty space where the dog had been sleeping. A cold breeze gusted into the room, making her shiver, her nipples tightened to hard buds. The door into the garden was wide open.

The man was pouring fresh water into the dog bowl. Charlotte was still very thirsty, so she climbed out of her basket and lifted the bowl to her lips.

"No, bitch!"

Rich landed a stinging slap across her cheek. In shock she dropped the steel bowl, which fell to the floor with a noisy clatter, cold water spilling all over her breasts and belly.

She looked up at the angry man, confused and trembling.

"Don't use your hands again, or I'll be forced to strap them behind you!"

Something in his voice made Charlotte realise he'd find it very pleasant carrying out his threat.

"Lap, like the bitch you are. You can start by licking up all the water you've spilt!"

He was unfastening the long whip that dangled from his belt, and as she still hesitated he flicked it with stinging accuracy against her delicate pink nipple. She yelped in pain, and bent her head to the stone floor.

The water had made quite a puddle. Charlotte lapped and licked, feeling grateful that Mrs. Pearson, the gardener's wife, did such a thorough job when she came in to clean. When she finally had the floor dry enough to satisfy Rich, he poured more water into the bowl. This time she lapped like an animal, on all fours in front of the dish, lowering her face to the water. It was hard to lap like that, water kept getting up her nose, but finally she finished it. Rich immediately refilled it to the brim. She looked up at him.

"Drink it"

It was a command, not a question, so again she drank. She felt bloated with water now. Sheba came running in from the garden. Charlotte noticed she wore a smart new collar.

Rich was opening a can of dog meat. In horror, Charlotte

suddenly noticed he was spooning it into two bowls. He saw her shocked face and laughed, setting the bowls down in front of the two owned females. Sheba began to guzzle her food. Charlotte stared, aghast.

"Better eat it up, else Sheba will wolf the lot." Rich spoke with a sadistic pleasure in his voice.

"I'm not eating that!"

"It's up to you. But unless someone's kind enough to give you some table scraps you won't get anything else today. Apart from some spunk, most likely," he added reflectively.

Charlotte dipped her head, and sniffed the meat. It smelt horrible. The thought of eating it made her nauseous.

"Then I'll just have to starve," she said defiantly, but with a tremor in her voice. She felt so hungry and so cheated that she was close to tears.

"Please yourself."

Sheba finished her meal, and started to eat Charlotte's.

Charlotte watched her in glum silence. There was a growing pressure in her bladder that she'd been ignoring. She needed to urinate, but was putting off asking, fearful of what response she'd get. But she couldn't wait any longer. She looked up at Rich.

"Please, I need to piss."

He looked at her and didn't reply. But he went to where her chain lead was locked to the pipes and undid the padlock. Then he led her out onto the lawn.

The grass was thick with dew, sparkling like jewels in the bright early morning sunlight. It was cold under her bare feet. As she walked her steps made a pathway of deep emerald over the silvered lawn. She waited.

"Well get on with it!"

He sounded irritated, but at the same time secretly pleased. She realised with another flush of shame that he meant her to piss on the grass like a dog, and that he was enjoying her reluctance to behave like an animal. Still she hesitated, unwilling to suffer this humiliation in front of him. He laughed.

"Get down on your haunches and squat, bitch, piss like an animal, that's all you are to us now."

The pressure in her belly was unbearable. Charlotte squatted down with her legs wide apart and urinated, a gushing steaming stream. She was blushing furiously. The man was laughing in pleasure.

"You certainly did need to go. And I doubt you'll be so high and mighty about it next time, will ye?" He reached a rough hand towards her breasts and casually stroked them.

"My, but you've got a nice pair of tits. Seeing you didn't like that meat you can suck on mine."

And he pushed her onto her knees, unzipped his flies, and stuffed a hot swollen cock into her mouth. She started to fellate him expertly, but he pounded unkindly into her throat, holding her head steady in his large, scratchy hands. He orgasmed in a matter of seconds, pulling back just far enough to fill her mouth with the glutinous mass of come. Charlotte swallowed, though the slimy semen sickened her, trying not to remember his words about all she'd have to eat being spunk.

Rich led her back into the house, chained her back to the pipes and left her alone once more.

The house was quiet, but every now and then she'd hear a sound of water running or a door closing that told her the rest of the men were gradually waking up. After an hour or so the door abruptly opened, and Carl came in. He was wearing a silk robe, and looked well rested. He smiled when he saw her, another of his nasty smiles, as cold as metal.

"So I gather you don't like the food? Excellent, it'll make it all the more amusing when you finally accept your situation and eat it. You will eat it, you know. Oh yes, you'll soon be licking your bitch-bowl clean."

As he spoke he trailed the cat across her naked thighs and buttocks. She was still huddled in the dog bed where she'd been dozing, unsure of how she was supposed to behave. Too late she realised her mistake.

"Well stop lounging around, you idle whore, get out of there! Sir Jonathan was telling me last night that he feeds his whores nothing but semen for their first twenty-four hours, part of the breaking in process he says, really teaches them their place. That's on their knees, pleasing men. I see no reason why you should fare any better."

He was sitting back now on the one chair in the room and parting his dressing gown. His monstrously huge cock sprang out of it. She obediently knelt before him and started to suckle the great head, running her tongue around the shaft, flicking it against the glans, concentrating with all her might on pleasuring this man. He sighed deeply, and leaned back in the hard chair.

She began to deep throat him, diving her head onto his massive tool again and again, trying her best not to gag. He seemed to be enjoying her ministrations, and as she took him fully inside her he began to stroke her hair, gently, almost lovingly. His hands strayed down to her breasts, caressing them, brushing his fingertips over the surface of each nipple in turn, his cool, fine touch making them pucker with arousal.

He came quickly, it was his first orgasm of the day. When his semen spurted into her mouth she swallowed it neatly, thankfully, feeling again as though she'd received a benediction. Her Master opened his eyes and looked at her lazily.

"My, my, Charlotte. You've certainly learnt a lot in a short space of time. You did that as expertly as any whore I've used."

Charlotte flushed, confused. He was paying her a compliment, of sorts, telling her that she was performing her one role, that of whore, exceptionally well. But somehow she felt hurt and disappointed. His touch had been so gentle, she had for a moment felt loved. She was too innocent, not only of sex itself but of the whole game of love and conquest, to understand something that most girls learn very young: that what can seem to a woman a tender caress can sometimes be, to a man, just another part of the sex act and as such have no emotional significance whatsoever. For so it was now: whilst Charlotte had savoured that delicate touch, and assumed it spoke of love, her Master had actually just been enjoying the smooth silk of his whore's skin, the fine texture of his whore's hair. This man was brutal, but that did not mean he didn't appreciate the finer sensual pleasures of life, and the exquisite beauty of the slut's body could certainly be counted amongst those pleasures.

Carl stood up, readjusting his robe. He was looking at something above the washing machine, his eyes very bright. Charlotte followed his gaze: the old drying rack.

"Come here."

She did as he bade, standing in front of him patient, though trembling slightly, as he lowered the rack till it hung just above the washing machine. He seemed to be assessing its possibilities. Looking around the room, his eyes lit upon a bundle of new washing line. That familiar evil grin creased his mouth unpleasantly. He wheeled the machine sideways, out of the way.

"Lie down on your belly on the floor here."

He gestured at the dusty ground where the washing machine had stood. Unquestioningly Charlotte lay down on the cold stone flags, watching a small spider scurrying in alarm through the dust near her cheek, wondering what diabolical game he had in mind this time. She heard creaking as Carl lowered the drying rack to the floor, so that it rested across her naked body. It's cold iron bars weighed upon her flesh, so looking down on her prone body she appeared striped by the black metal. Carl pulled her arms, brought them up above the rack, down behind her back, so that now her wrists were together behind her back at waist level, with the bars of the rack between them and her body. In the same manner he lifted her feet and brought then towards her wrists. Essentially, he was wrapping her in a hogtie around the metal rack.

He bound the cord around her wrists and ankles, fastening her helplessly in place. Then he started to weave the cord tightly in and out of the iron framework, so that her breasts became cruelly trussed and so the cord slid between her labia, pulling deeply into her groin so that she began to moan and struggle ineffectually. He looped cord round her knees and bound it tightly to the frame so that her knees were widely spread, her pussy open and accessible. Then he raised the rack, so that Charlotte hung high in the air before him.

He surveyed the trussed slave with a look of satisfaction.

"One more little detail…" he muttered, as if to himself.

He pulled the washing machine back to its original position, so that now it was directly beneath the suspended girl. Then he wedged a broom so that it stuck up vertically from the side of the washing machine, shifting the machine till it was properly aligned, then lowered the rack, and with it the trussed Charlotte.

He lowered her until the broom handle pressed uncomfortably hard against her already pinched genitals.

"Let's see what happens on spin cycle."

He was already chuckling. He pressed a few buttons on the washing machine then settled back in his chair to enjoy the show.

The machine clicked and hummed, then sprang into life, vibrating softly as it started to spin. Charlotte moaned as the broom handle began to vibrate too. The machine spun faster and faster, overwhelming sensations spreading through her pussy from where the wood pressed against it. Carl came forwards, and delicately parted her pussy lips, then pressed the washing machine very slightly towards her. Charlotte shrieked in wild arousal, the vibrating wood was now hammering upon her swollen clit. Within moments an orgasm engulfed her.

As she came down from the orgasm she squirmed in her bonds. Her clitoris was exquisitely sensitive after her climax, and the still pounding wooden vibrator was unbearable. But there was to be no release, Carl watched and made no move to help her, though she begged to be allowed time to recover. She felt her body inexorably wrenched towards another orgasm. Shuddering and crying at its intensity, she came once more.

To her relief the machine was beginning to slow down. She hung there, dripping with sweat, her breasts aching from the tight cord that her unkind Master had used to bind them.

Carl's penis was rock hard again. It gave him such pleasure to exercise his control over the slave's body. He chuckled to himself, relishing the word, 'slave'. She was his now, to do whatever he liked with. What fun!

The strapped broom had worked better than he could have hoped, but already he could see ways to improve the spectacle. Without a backward glance he left the room, enjoying the knowledge that the unfortunate girl was quite unable to do anything but wait, hanging trussed and ready for whatever humiliation he had in store for her next.

It was over an hour before he returned. He was now fully dressed, and accompanied by most of the men who had enjoyed her on the previous day. Rich, who was very good with his hands, moved the washing machine and started to modify the broom-vibrator. The whore couldn't see what they were doing, and this was perhaps as well, for Rich felt sure she'd baulk at the sight of the huge rubber dildos he was attaching to the broom. Using heavy duty tape he bound the two shafts to one side of the broom, carefully adjusting them so that they projected at different angles, then binding them absolutely tight.

They shifted the washing machine back into place, carefully easing the helpless girl so that her body hung a little more vertically so it would accept the surrogate cocks that now jutted obscenely from the wooden shaft. There were two, a slim one at the perfect angle for penetrating her anus, a fatter one to stuff her cunt. Both were large enough to start with, but what the hapless slut didn't yet know was that they were inflatable. When Rich had driven them deeply inside the moaning girl's slender body he turned to Carl, and smilingly handed him the pump. Bredon turned to Sinclair.

"Sir Jonathan, would you do me the honour of inflating these devices?"

"My pleasure, Carl."

The old man started to squeeze the pump. Within moments the whore was moaning and whimpering. Only yesterday a virgin, and already forced to take dildos as wide as a man's wrist. Sir Jonathan stepped closer, peering at the stuffed fuck holes to ascertain if she was stretched enough.

"That should be enough, for now. Do you happen to have any pegs?"

Someone started the machine.

Charlotte moaned as the huge dildos that filled her fuck holes began to vibrate. The wooden tip of the broom handle still pressed against her clitoris, and the total assault on every part of her pubic area, the intense mixture of pleasurable and painful sensation, flooded her mind so that she lost all sense of self.

Sir Jonathan was standing in front of her, his face close to hers. He was looking her right in the eyes, and she shivered with fear. There was something menacing about this old man. She had some instinct that, more than any of the others, this one really relished cruelty. He reached down, and caressed her bound tits, rubbing his thumbs back and forwards over her nipples so that she groaned in pained arousal. Now he pulled on them steadily, lengthening them, the delicate tissue rigid under his rubbing fingertips. He smiled at her, reached down to the bag he held in his other hand, and brought out a peg. He held it up in front of her scared face, letting the wood touch her lips.

"Have you been pegged before, you little slut? No, of course you haven't. Well, there's a first time for everything."

He pinched the peg open wide, held it to show her, smiled cruelly and lowered his hand. The next moment Charlotte screamed as a bolt of fire shot through her aching breast. Blinking back tears she peered down to see the wooden peg viciously clamped onto her nipple. Sir Jonathan held up a second peg, and, ignoring her pleas, let it, too, snap shut in place. He flicked the pegs gently with his fingers, and she was humiliated to find the sensation was arousing. Desperately uncomfortable, but still, arousing.

But he hadn't finished yet. Again the hand disappeared into the bag, again he showed her the peg, as though to exacerbate the torture by ensuring she had several panicked seconds of anticipation. This time the peg sank shut into the smooth creamy mass of her breasts. It didn't hurt so much, but nor did it arouse, directly. But as he repeatedly dipped his hand, smiled at her, and attached yet another peg, then another, then another... so that when she finally looked down, her eyes wet with tears, she saw tits that bristled absurdly, almost covered with jutting wooden pegs... she felt a deep sense of shame, and of submission, and was aroused by the knowledge of self that he had given her. For what Sir Jonathan was teaching her, what he had taught so many wilful girls to accept, was that ultimately only male pleasure is important, but that ironically enough, through accepting this inalienable fact, a truly submissive woman can be brought to experience the deepest pleasure of which she herself is capable.

Now her bound breasts bristled all over with pegs. He ran his hands lightly over them, flicking the ends, so they tugged and pulled, and she moaned again, though no longer hearing herself. The vibrating dildos were forcing her towards yet another orgasm, and as old Jonathan Sinclair stroked her pegged breasts as though he was smoothing unruly hair, she exploded in a climax so deep that she travelled quite outside herself, almost delirious, rocked by wave upon beating wave of painful ecstasy. She pissed herself, but she was too far adrift to even notice. She gazed at Sir Jonathan with adoring eyes.

They cut her down then, and fucked her without ceremony, taking it in turns to hold her legs spread as they took her, bent over the still vibrating washing machine, or on her belly on the floor, the pegs digging painfully into her tender flesh, or held aloft and on her back by four of them so that a fifth could stand between her legs, pumping into her. By the time their passion was spent she was dripping with semen, it streaked her cheeks and lips, oozed from her anus and pussy, covered her breasts in a sticky slimy lacquer. She had swallowed more loads than she'd been able to count, her mouth rarely empty of thrusting cock.

And she'd also lost count of the orgasms. It was as if by finally submitting totally to the men who now owned her, something within herself had been freed by her enslavement. She felt more beautiful, more desired, and more womanly than ever before in her life.

They left her alone for the rest of the day, chained by the lead to the pipes again. She had an instinct that they just had other business to attend to, and anyway, there was no rush about using and enjoying her; she wasn't going anywhere. She would stay there, awaiting their pleasure, totally available and beautifully submissive.

That evening Rich opened another can of dog meat, and this time she ate it. It tasted disgusting, even worse than she had imagined, but as she ate her pussy grew wet with fuck juices, because she knew that they had succeeded in their goal of turning her into a sex slave. Rich must have known the effect her acceptance would have on her, for as she ate he slipped a hand between her legs and felt her hot and slippery cunt.

"Good little whore," he breathed in her ear, and easily and dextrously brought her to shivering orgasm with a few expert rubs of his fingers.

Her friends came round for the meal to which she had invited them; she heard them ring the doorbell, heard voices in the hall. What was said to them she did not know, but they left without trying to find her. Probably just as well, she thought, for the Charlotte they had known no longer existed.

She slept late the next morning. When she finally awoke the room was hot. Sheba was sniffing around the bowls, clearly thirsty. A few minutes later Rich appeared, refilled the bowls with water, and let them out to piss on the grass.

When they went back in he set bowls of meat down in front of them. Sheba's was dog food again, straight from a tin. But Charlotte's bowl was an odd mixture of meat, fresh and tasty, several kinds of vegetables, and some rich and creamy pudding.

"It's the leftovers from yesterday's dinner," said Rich, answering her unspoken question.

Charlotte almost wept with gratitude, and ate the lot at top speed.

"Why...?" She didn't know how to phrase the question.

"You may be a slave, but you're human. You need human food. The dog meat was just to teach you your place. Once you'd accepted it... and I could certainly tell that you had accepted it," he laughed as he spoke, "then you could be treated a little more kindly. But be warned, if you show the slightest resistance, if you show any signs of forgetting the lesson Sir Jonathan taught you, then it'll be back to dog meat. So behave yourself!"

With that he grinned, and gave her rump a hearty slap.

She had a lovely day, spending most of it lying dozing on

98

the lawn with Sheba. The bitch was allowed to roam freely around the garden, but Charlotte was chained to a metal stake. The chain was long and made of dark steel that hung cold and heavy against her breasts. It was padlocked to her collar, the other end padlocked to a ring welded into the stake. If she had wanted to escape she'd have had to uproot the stake from the ground. But she knew that was impossible, she'd watched young Harry Pearson hammering it deep into the earth with great swings of a stone mallet. There was no chance that she could get away.

Late in the afternoon Rich came to fetch her. The sky was darkening, dark slate clouds that threatened rain threw the lush garden into an ominous, deepening gloom. As he un-padlocked her chain the first drops fell, great fat droplets that burst chillingly over her bare skin. Rich led her indoors.

Carl was waiting for her in the lounge.

"Come and sit here."

He gestured towards his feet. Charlotte dutifully sat down on the thick carpet, very conscious of her nakedness as the long wool fibres brushed against her thighs and naked mons. Carl was leaning back comfortably on the expensive leather sofa.

"I'm invited to a house party that starts tonight, at Sir Jonathan's mansion in the dales. You will accompany me. I've picked out suitable clothes from your wardrobe for you; they're on the bed, in what used to be your room. You will go and bathe, and dress, and make up your face. You can wear your hair up if you like, I'll leave that choice to you. Just make yourself pretty, as you would for any ordinary party. You have two hours. Oh, and you must wear only the clothes I have placed ready on the bed."

Charlotte wondered what he meant, 'any ordinary party'. So this party would not be ordinary. Maybe he just meant that it wasn't every day one was invited to a mansion by a member of the aristocracy, but somehow she had the feeling that something else lay behind his words.

Rich took her to the bathroom, and fastened her chain round the foot of the bath before leaving her to her own devices. She ran the iron tub brimful of very hot water, crumbled in some expensive scented bubble bath, and settled down into the steam.

Her genitals stung slightly in the perfumed water. Not surprising considering how thoroughly they'd been used, she thought ruefully. She lay back, letting the water cover her right up to her nose. A few days ago, relaxing in the bath would have been a pleasure so commonplace she'd have hardly regarded it, but now, it seemed like untold luxury.

Eventually she decided she'd better get out and prepare herself. Wrapping a big towel around her she scrunched mousse into her hair, so the waves curled into pretty ringlets. She peered at her face. Really she had little need for make-up, her skin was flawless and her eyes huge without resort to artifice. But he had told her to make-up her face, and she knew better than to ignore an order.

She skimmed the merest trace of foundation over her fair skin, and pressed powder upon it. The artificial velveting made her look like a young girl dressing up, she thought. She started on her eyes. She had a feeling that she knew what Carl required, and she could only hope her guess was correct. She rimmed them with a dark kohl pencil, smudging the outline so her eyes looked back, sad and beautiful, from the mirror, then brushed dark brown powder onto her lids. She rummaged in her make-up bag for the right sort of lipstick. Nothing seemed quite what she needed, so she made do with a dull pink.

She was dry now, and her face painted, all that remained was to dress and put up her hair. But she couldn't leave the bathroom, she was still chained. She opened the door, and listened. She could hear men's voices downstairs, but she didn't dare call out and disturb them. Never mind, she'd fix her hair and then wriggle quickly into her clothes when they came for her.

Her auburn curls were almost dry. She piled her hair carefully onto her head, letting a few tendrils spill in snaking curls down to her neck. She surveyed the effect in the mirror. She looked very lovely and very sophisticated. But she knew that somehow the lipstick wasn't right.

Footsteps on the stairs. She turned as Rich entered the room. She hadn't bothered to close the door, she was getting used to being naked, to having no privacy. Rich surveyed her and smiled.

"Very nice," he said, "Come and get dressed."

Charlotte flushed when she saw the silk skirt Carl had picked out for her. It was the same flimsy blue skirt that she'd been wearing that day when Henry had begun to ogle her. She'd washed it since, and the slightly stiff pale stain where her fuck juices had moistened it was gone, but the memory was still fresh in her mind.

She looked around for underwear, wondering what he'd have chosen. There was none there. The only other item of clothing on the bed was a tight knitted-silk vest top, very low cut, incredibly clingy. The back was a delicate beaded spider's web of glittery threads, sexy and chic, one of her favourite garments.

But she couldn't wear it without a bra! The vest fitted like a second skin, without a bra she'd look little better than naked, her nipples would be embarrassingly obvious. She scanned the bed again, frantically. The only other thing on it was a pair of ridiculously high heeled black stilettos.

"What are you looking for?"

It was Rich, she'd almost forgotten he was there, holding her chain loosely in his large red hand. He sounded amused.

"I… there isn't any underwear," She knew as she spoke her words sounded ludicrous, the dismay in her voice absurd. She'd spent the last two days being fucked and sodomised by about a dozen strangers, what need did she have of underwear? But he told me to dress up, she thought to herself, he said make myself pretty, he said we were going to a party. The reality was sinking in, and she felt dismayed, even though she knew she had been foolish to expect anything else.

"He doesn't want you wearing underwear, you silly slut. You're going to this party as a whore, what did you expect?"

He was smiling at her, and the smile was very like Carl's. A cruel smile; he was enjoying seeing her disappointment and shame.

Without another word she turned to the skimpy clothes. Her hands were trembling as she pulled them on. Then she fumbled with the buckles on the strappy stilettos. When she had them on Rich took held of her arms, pulling them behind her back, steering her over in front of the mirror. She looked at her image and blushed.

It was extraordinary how much difference the absence of underwear and the presence of the dark eye make-up made to her appearance. The girl who gazed back at her certainly looked chic, but also wanton, available. The tight top skimmed over her full breasts, hiding nothing. Her erect nipples poked through the fine fabric, their puckered shape clearly visible, their darkness showing through the pale silk. The heels could only be worn by a whore. Someone chuckled.

She turned to see Carl, surveying her appreciatively. His eyes trailed lasciviously over her body, lingering on her breasts as they strained against the tight top, and her honey-coloured thighs disappearing under the skimpy silk. He frowned.

"Wait a minute."

She could hear him, rummaging in her mother's room. She felt furious and resentful, all over again. What right had this man to invade her house, use her body as though she was some cheap whore and go through Mummy's things?

Carl returned, smiling. Evidently he had found what he

was looking for. He held out a lipstick.

"Wipe that off your mouth, use this one instead," he commanded.

Charlotte took a tissue and carefully wiped the pink lipstick away. She took the slim gold tube that Carl held out to her, pulled off the lid, twisted up the shaft. The lipstick had barely been used, one of those impulse purchases that linger in drawers, inappropriate and best forgotten. It was bright glossy pillar box red. Charlotte held up a compact mirror and carefully applied the lipstick. She imagined it looked absurdly, crudely bright on her pale face, ridiculous in fact. She looked at Carl, waiting to hear him tell her the other was better. But he was smiling, as though he'd got exactly what he'd wanted. This time it was he who pinned her arms behind her, and held her in front of the mirror.

"There, girl, what do you see now?"

Charlotte looked. Gazing back at her was one of those women she'd occasionally seen in London, hovering round the hallway salons of expensive hotels. The girl in the mirror was inarguably a high-class prostitute, a whore, a slut. Or, in this case she thought bitterly, a sexual slave.

CHAPTER SEVEN

As Carl dressed for dinner he thought back to his last conversation with Sir Jonathan.

"A slave must be continually reminded of her place," the old man had said. "At my party tomorrow night there will be two kinds of female: Sinclair slaves in training, being groomed in the art of pleasuring, soon to be ready for sale; and the women my guests bring along... all sluts of course." Both men laughed. "The thing about a girl like Charlotte is that she has an innately arrogant nature. It's unavoidable when a female grows up in an atmosphere of wealth and privilege. She's never been taught her rightful place... on her knees with her mouth full of cock..." Again they laughed. "...and as she hasn't grown up knowing that women were put on God's great earth for male pleasure I'm afraid you can never assume she's finally learnt that she's just here to serve you. And so you must remind her. Again and again and again." As he spoke he waved his wrinkled hand through the air, punctuating each word with a delicate slap on his open palm. "And never stop reminding her. The best way is to humiliate her. Let her see other women receiving your attention whilst she is treated with no more concern than your car or even your chair. Humiliate her, and keep on humiliating her. Let her taste the lash every day, without fail. And if you should sell her on... and such a pretty whore will bring you a nice profit, even though amateurishly trained... then make sure that her future master knows she must be continually reminded of her one role in life. My favourite term nowadays for such a girl is 'cock-holster', it so effectively delineates her purpose. That's all she'll be when she's completely broken in: a collection of holes to receive cock."

Carl smiled as he fastened his gold cufflinks. He hadn't been offended by that 'amateurishly trained' remark. Everyone knew that the long-established Sinclair family slave trading business produced the best quality sluts in the world. All exquisitely lovely, all trained to perfect submissive obedience.

He had intimated to Sir Jonathan that he would bring Charlotte with him for the house party, and the old chap had waxed lyrical about the various ways they could bring the 'uppity bitch' to heel, once she was helplessly inside the old Tudor mansion that was his family home; a daunting place, where over the centuries many innocent young girls had been degraded into whoredom. Carl's smile took on a sadistic gleam. The old man really was rather cruel, and he did seem particularly taken with Charlotte, she was very much his preferred type. Perhaps the slave trader would take her under his personal wing for part of the visit. Somehow Carl got the feeling that Charlotte would not soon forget such an encounter.

The car was spacious, the back seat easily wide enough for Charlotte, flanked by Carl and another man she didn't recognise, evidently a friend of his. The chauffeur in front of them was impassive, paid not to see the misbehaviour of his affluent clientele. Carl and 'Steven', as she gathered the friend's name to be, talked over her, casually stroking her thighs as they discussed share prices and real estate. The car purred smoothly through the lush countryside. Summer was at its height and the trees seemed almost over-laden with foliage now, it hung over the road, dark green and dense, so that often it seemed as though they were driving through green underwater tunnels. After an hour or so they reached a major road and sped along, towards the city.

Soon they were sitting in dense rush hour traffic. Charlotte's thighs were naked and slightly spread, as Carl had pulled her skirt up to expose them, and each man had nonchalantly pulled her legs apart to better expose her soft flesh. The fine wool of the men's suits rubbed against her naked knees and softly prickled her thighs. When Charlotte looked out of the window she saw that the passenger in the neighbouring car was leering crudely at her, sticking his tongue in and out suggestively. She looked away, blushing with shame, and the car moved on, but after that, each time she braved another glance it was to find she was being observed by one lustful drooling man after another. She was glad when the traffic eased and they once more sped invisibly past the respectable homes of the good women of middle England.

The journey took hours. After a while Steven's hands began to roam more intently over her flesh, pulling her skirt right up to her waist to reveal her naked sex lips, already glistening with moisture. The car was stationary again, this time queuing at traffic lights. Charlotte again felt eyes upon her and she could not help but look up. A motorcyclist was next to them, peering intently in at her. He was staring her right in the face, not eying her body with lubricious pleasure as all the other observers had. The expression on his face was close to a frown, and she could not guess what he was thinking.

She had a feeling that Carl and Steven had also noticed him, for at that moment Steven slipped a thick finger into her crack, and brought it, shiny wetly, to her lips. She sucked as he obviously wanted, tasting the sweet salt of her own body.

"Carl, would you mind…? I think there's room in here for her to kneel down. Actually I'd like to bone her ass but that can wait for later."

"Be my guest, I never tire of seeing a slut with her mouth full of cock, one of life's simple pleasures."

Charlotte was pushed to her knees. Steven already had his penis out. Looking at the bulbous monster as it jutted at her face she remembered her image in the mirror. She was a whore now, she'd better get to work. She glanced up at the motorbike rider. He was still watching her, that same odd expression on his face. Again she flushed with shame, then bent her head to her task. She started to fellate Steven, carefully caressing his cock with her tongue and lips, her cheeks burning with the knowledge that the unknown man outside the window was watching her prostitution. Then the car set off again, juddering and vibrating under her. The men were still talking business, in fact Steven seemed no more interested in what she was doing than if she'd been massaging his feet. When he came it was in the same, nonchalant fashion. He merely gripped her head tightly before ejaculating a small load into her waiting mouth. She swallowed quickly, she didn't want any of the semen to stain her party clothes.

Watching her fellate Steven must have aroused Carl, for now he pulled his cock out of his trousers. Charlotte shuffled over on her knees and took him into her mouth. Again she worked hard as the men chatted. Sucking away as the car purred steadily towards their destination, feeling it turn corners, accelerate, brake, accelerate again, felt deliciously degrading. When Carl climaxed she swallowed neatly, savouring his sour load.

"Nearly there."

From her position on the floor Charlotte couldn't see much out of the side windows, but through the back windscreen she could make out tall trees towering either side of them in the gathering dusk. She heard gravel crunching under the wheels as they pulled to a halt. Carl opened the door.

"Out."

Meekly she followed him.

They were standing in front of a gaunt, stone mansion. The door was open, and light and laughter spilled down the steps towards them. The evening was still warm, but Charlotte felt her nipples harden at the sound of so many male voices.

Carl took her by the hand, and the three of them ascended the steps. It felt strangely intimate, to be holding hands with her Master. He led her into the house. A butler was standing by, he ushered them into a large room, humming with conversation.

The room was very grand, ornate mirrors graced the walls, grandiose chandeliers hung from the ceiling. The walls themselves were covered in dark red velvety paper. The whole effect was of luxurious, almost ostentatious wealth. A country house, but not the sort of country house that is open to the public at weekends, humming with the hoi polloi craning their necks to see how the other half lives. No, this was very much a private house, the property of a very rich man. But she didn't take in much detail of the beautiful room, her attention was drawn to the other guests, and most especially, to the other women.

The men were dressed as one might expect for a society party. She had been to plenty herself, though never one quite this showy. But the women...

Many of the girls were dressed similarly to herself. Pretty clothes, but revealing, sluttishly disarrayed. Skimpy, low-necked, halter tops, which gave the viewer occasional glimpses of naked nipple, acres of bare back, skirts so short that when a girl sat down her shaved pussy lips were clearly visible. The girls were dressed so wantonly that they could have resembled back street whores, but they were all far too beautiful to be ordinary call girls. They looked healthy and fit. She thought again of her reflection in the mirror, and decided that 'high class whore' fitted not just herself, but these other girls.

But there were other women, and Charlotte couldn't take her eyes off them. Around the edges of the room sat naked girls, as though forming a sort of frieze. They were all in exactly the same position: Sitting on a very low metal bench, their legs very widely spread, their arms strapped behind them. Each girl wore a collar, some of iron, a few of black leather. And each girl's feet were bound at the ankle to the girls' on either side.

In a few places the frieze was broken, a gap, presumably waiting to be filled by another bound girl. Charlotte looked at the empty section of bench. Something projected upwards from the surface at a sloped angle, something dark, as though made in one piece with the metal of the bench, something long and thick and phallic.

Carl was talking to two of the other men. Again it was the same dull conversation, the state of the market, what were good investments… she didn't bother to pay attention. As Carl talked he casually petted her, the way a man might with his girlfriend at any party. But whereas in such a situation normally the man's hands would only stroke the girl's waist, and perhaps give her bottom a little pat, Carls hands were roaming much more freely over her. He stroked her breasts repeatedly, making the nipples hard and erect, so they jutted ever more obviously through the thin fabric. And sometimes his hand strayed down to her pussy, stroking the silk against her lips. Steven, too, occasionally fingered her with that same nonchalant air, taking her permission so much for granted it was clear it could never have crossed his mind to do otherwise.

A noise behind her made her turn her head. Someone was whimpering. It was a girl, dressed very much like herself in short skirt and skimpy vest, her dark nipples clearly visible through the clinging cream silk. Two men were pulling at her clothes. First her top was pulled off, revealing heavy, golden brown breasts. Whilst it was being pulled over her head, her face covered with the fabric, the other man pulled down on her skirt, exposing her hairless pussy. Charlotte drew in her breath in a little gasp: the girl's labia were pierced by a two thick metal rings, buckled together with a small padlock. She felt simultaneously a wave of pity and her vagina clench with sympathetic arousal.

Soon the girl was entirely naked. She must have been told to lift her hair out of the way, for, still whimpering, she did so as a third man buckled a wide leather collar tightly around her neck. One of the men pulled her arms behind her back, and Charlotte saw them strapped there, strapped at the wrist, then on the forearm, then just above the elbow. The straps dug into her honey coloured flesh, Charlotte could see it bulging slightly either side of each bond. The girl's breasts jutted out provocatively now her arms were so trussed. She was moaning and wriggling as though she wanted to escape but her struggles lacked conviction.

The man who had stripped her top stood in front of her, idly twiddling her nipples, which were now stiffly erect. The girl let out a sharp yelp of pain and surprise as he suddenly twisted them viciously. He slipped a finger between the rings that fastened her fuck lips, and pulled it out, glistening wet with her sex juices. The small crowd of onlookers tittered appreciatively.

A manservant approached, bearing a small silver tray, lined with dark red velvet. Lying upon the velvet were objects of metal, some shiny, some dark and matt. Charlotte wondered what they were for. As if in answer the man whom Charlotte guessed to be the girl's master, the one who had cruelly twisted her nipples and made her cry, reached to the tray, carefully selecting from the choice of implements displayed. He smiled grimly and picked one of the dull metal objects. It looked to Charlotte rather like those bull clips that are used in offices to fasten sheaths of papers together. Without a word the cruel man let the clip snap shut onto the unfortunate girl's nipple. As she cried in pain, the other nipple received the same brutal treatment.

Charlotte watched spellbound, remembering the pain as the clothes pegs had snapped onto her own delicate tissue, sweating slightly as she imagined how much more painful these metal clips might be. The master turned his attention back to the tray. Again he made his selection, then fiddled with the clip on the girl's right breast. Charlotte watched in horrified fascination as the man began to add weights to the whimpering girl's clipped nipples. More and more weights he hung from them, until the previously perky breasts hung down, the nipples stretched by the excessive weight, now almost an inch long.

The poor girl was whimpering steadily by now. The master said something to the watchers nearest him... Charlotte couldn't quite catch his words, but as he spoke he gestured at the girl's pussy. Charlotte looked, and was shocked to see the girl's sex juices were now flowing so freely that her labia were glistening wet, and a pearly drop of moisture hung suspended from her crack. What a slut! Charlotte thought to herself, she's actually enjoying this!

The crying slut was now led towards a gap in the decorative frieze of bound whores. Charlotte peered again at the low metal bench. With another involuntary gasp she realised what the projecting phallic like objects were: huge iron dildos, double dildos. She had assumed each girl was just resting her bottom upon the bench, reasonably comfortable except for her bound arms, but no, each whore was impaled upon two surrogate cocks. Charlotte began to tremble. Was it with fear, or excitement? She couldn't tell.

The men began to press the slut onto the cold iron. They were tugging at her buttocks, to ease the anal dildo inside. She was moaning still, but Charlotte had little sympathy for her now she knew that this brutal treatment aroused her.

Finally the girl was completely impaled, so that her buttocks rested on the bench. The men tugged her ankles apart, and Charlotte saw that they'd removed the padlock and opened the girl's sex lips. Between them, the monstrous black iron dildo disappeared up inside the slender girl. She was wriggling and moaning still, but Charlotte could see how wet the dildo was.

Jonathan Sinclair nodded his head towards a nearby footman, who went to the end of the bench and flicked a switch. A low, almost inaudible humming filled the room. Suddenly one of the impaled sluts gave a wild shriek of arousal, closely followed by moans from the other girls.

They were wriggling and twisting, some panting, others giving voice at steadily increasing pitch. As their shrieks and moans increased in fervour Charlotte realised with shock that they were orgasming; the iron dildos inside them were vibrating. These girls' sexual response was controlled by the men who owned them.

As the girls came they started to groan, their sensitised pussies wanting escape from the remorseless vibrations. But their owners had no pity. Charlotte watched open-mouthed, guessing correctly, that the vibrations would continue until even the most unresponsive slut reached climax. In this way the more sensitive girls were forced to come again and again.

"Ahem."

A small cough, close by her ear, brought her attention abruptly back to her master and the men to whom he had been conversing. They were staring at her, their eyes travelling up and down over her body. She followed their gaze, saw her jutting nipples, then saw with shame that the silk skirt that Carl had been stroking against her labia was stuck there. A patch of silk was dark and wet, and clinging to her pussy, outlining every detail of her parted sex lips. A sudden flash of memory: Uncle Henry leering at her in the car. Had Carl chosen this skirt on purpose? But no, he couldn't possibly have known.

"You certainly enjoyed watching that little show, didn't you, slut?" Carl's voice was knowing, mocking.

One of the staring men reached forward and roughly poked his index finger right into her crack, forcing the silk skirt actually inside her body. Charlotte was so shocked she stepped back, right into the waiting arms of Carl. He wrapped her arms tightly behind her, so that the other man could resume his investigation of her body unimpeded by her struggling.

The man began to frig her with his finger, stabbing it again and again into her hole. Charlotte looked down and saw the silk pulled tight over her lips, the thick finger thrusting crudely into her. Carl reached round with one arm and began to fondle her breasts, then he started to slip the narrow vest straps down off her shoulders.

She squirmed and wriggled, trying to escape from this far too public humiliation. For a large crowd of men had gathered around to watch her being handled, and, they probably hoped, manhandled.

With a final tug the vest slipped down, revealing her jutting breasts. An appreciative murmur rose from the onlookers.

"Excellent tits," brayed a pompous sounding voice. "Nice package all round," came another.

As the finger plunged in and out of her tight hole, the silk rubbed repeatedly against her clit. With horror she realised she was going to orgasm. Carl chose the same moment to begin pinching and twisting her nipples. She knew he was deliberately mimicking the action the other man had used on the slut they'd watched impaled, and the knowledge that he had observed her arousal and was learning how to play her body, to control her, brought her thundering to a moaning climax.

"Oh good show!" came that braying voice again. She saw its owner now, a florid, shiny-faced, extremely plump man, with thick fingers like raw sausages. He was at the front of the group of men who were enjoying seeing her played with, and now he moved forward.

"May I?"

Charlotte pulled away in alarm as his garlicky breath wafted hot and sour over her face. Carl sensed her dislike, and dug his fingers deeper into her slender arms.

"Be my guest," she heard him reply, "do whatever you wish with her."

"Oh I say, that's really very generous," puffed the fat man, getting hold of Charlotte's naked breasts and squeezing them hard.

Charlotte struggled, she didn't want him touching her.

The disgusting sausage fingers fondled and pinched her, roaming all over her breasts and slapping them repeatedly as though he had every right to do this. And of course, he has, thought Charlotte, ruefully. I agreed to belong to Carl, and so everything that's happening is my own choice. The sausage fingers began to lift her sticky skirt. But I don't have to like it, she reminded herself, and resumed struggling.

It was absolutely no use resisting. Any one of the men could easily have overpowered her, and there were dozens of them standing around enjoying the entertainment. As she continued in her futile struggle the fat man pulled her skirt right down, leaving her naked except for her high heeled sandals, and as the crowd again murmured their appreciation of her naked and glistening fuck lips, and her sweet round bottom, so ripe and ready for penetration, she realised from the excitement in their voices that her struggles were actually enjoyable for them. They liked the fat man fingering her… slipping three bunched fingers into her vagina now, and telling everyone what a tight front fuck hole the whore had… because they liked seeing her having to endure the touch of a man she didn't want. She considered just going limp, that'd annoy them, they wouldn't find that such a turn-on. But it was no good, she really didn't want this man and the crowd didn't really matter, what mattered was getting his hideous podgy fingers off her body. She struggled some more.

The fat man looked up from her pussy. He'd been trying to stuff more of his sausage fingers inside her, without success. He glared at her, clearly angry to meet with so much resistance.

"She'd not very thoroughly broken in, is she?" he drawled at Carl, the irritation obvious in his voice.

"No indeed, she was a virgin two days ago. Mind you, she's taken a lot of cock since then."

Carl laughed, and the onlookers laughed too.

"My my, a virgin, what? No wonder she's a little resistant. Perhaps she could do with a good thrashing, what d'you say?"

"Be my guest. I enjoy seeing her fucked, and I especially enjoy seeing her whipped. So really, consider her yours, whatever discipline you'd care to administer will be quite delightful to watch, I'm sure of that."

Hanging from the ceiling in various places, suspended from chains that disappeared into dark holes amongst the fine white plaster mouldings, were large, black iron hooks. The fat man called a manservant over.

"Dangling from her wrists from here, please, my good fellow. Toes a foot off the ground."

Taking her from Carl, the servant strapped Charlotte's wrists together in front of her with a few quick and expert movements. It was clear he'd done this many times before. With equal skill he looped the straps over the hook, then went to a lever at the side of the room. With a slight clanking of chains, the hook rose into the air, Charlotte dangling helplessly from her bound wrists.

The fat man approached her and she kicked out, trying to ward him off. The crowd of men… it now appeared as though all the men in the room were watching her… laughed and slapped each others' backs in appreciation. They obviously found her struggles highly amusing, thought Charlotte, crossly.

"Hmm. A pair of spreading bars, I think."

Someone reached two iron bars down from one of the racks that lined the walls. With similar efficiency the servant buckled the straps of the first bar around her ankles, ignoring Charlotte's attempts to kick. Now she was spread and helpless, her limbs forming an inverted Y shape. But the fat man hadn't finished with her yet. He nodded towards the second bar, and this shorter one was strapped to her thighs, forcing her legs into a properly spread, ready-for-fucking-position. Her labia were thus pulled open, and the men peered at her wet pussy, laughing and making crude comments to each other about how the whore was gagging for it.

The fat man surveyed her for a moment. She was his, now, and both he and she knew it. He looked her right in the eye, smiling with triumph: she could no longer resist, he could penetrate her whenever he chose.

"A gag, I think. One that can be inflated."

He wasn't taking any chances. These sluts could deliver a nasty bite.

The servant gagged her. The rubber gag was soft and flaccid on her tongue, until Carl reached forward and began to pump it. Soon, a huge phallic-like mass stuffed Charlotte's mouth. She moaned in discomfort.

"Adjust the bars. A little wider." It was the fat man speaking. The servant looked at him in surprise; the whore was already fully spread. But he knew better than to argue with one of the houseguests. He cranked the bars wider open. Charlotte began to whimper through her gag.

"Excellent."

For a moment the fat man just stood there, watching her. Charlotte's eyes pricked with tears, she was so spread and so stuffed. She had a shameful feeling that her pussy was wetter than ever.

Then he moved forward, and began to touch her.

Now she could no longer resist, in any way at all, the thick, fat fingers went where they liked, stroking her breasts, caressing her belly, patting her gently on the buttocks. But he didn't just touch her sexual parts... the hot, soft hands went all over her, trailing along her tense thighs, inspecting her calves, fingering her bound arms. Always his touch was gentle. She knew why he wanted to touch every part of her: it was to remind her that she was owned, that total jurisdiction over her slight body now lay with the men to whom she belonged.

When he had touched every inch of her skin his fingers began to probe inside her body. First he forced a thick digit in next to the inflated gag, slipping it round so as to feel her gums and teeth and tongue. Then he resumed his investigation of her vagina, even squatting down to look at her hole as he pressed his finger inside her, then removing it only to stuff her with two fingers, then three, and finally four.

Frigging her quite gently with his four fingers he then bent his head to her swollen clitoris, and began to lick.

Charlotte trembled, entirely unable to prevent the ugly man from stimulating her, entirely unable to prevent the inexorable rise in arousal. Soon she felt her body mounting, step by step, the helter-skelter staircase that precedes orgasm. Muffled moans escaped past the stuffing gag as she grew nearer and nearer to climax. But abruptly he stopped, slipping his fingers back out of her dripping pussy, leaving her hovering on the brink of orgasm. She mewed with disappointment, a small, soft sound escaping from the gag. The men around her laughed.

The fat man was surveying the whip stands that lined the hall, perusing the various devices, all beautifully crafted to assist in disciplining recalcitrant whores. He made his selection and walked back over to the group around Charlotte, the sea of men parting to let him back through to his quarry.

It was a long, black whip. It looked very old, and was in fact an heirloom, having been used by the Sinclairs for chastising sluts for over one hundred and fifty years. Before that it had briefly been a horse whip.

A sudden crack. The first blow struck her stingingly on her belly, quite low, a little above her pubic mound. She yelped, but to the amusement of the onlookers only a little squeak escaped past the gag. Although resistance was useless she was unable to accept her punishment meekly, as she knew she ought. She tried to wriggle this way and that, but all she achieved was a slight swaying on her chain.

The next two blows landed in quick succession, right on her nipples. She tried to scream, but again the gag swallowed her protests. The men all laughed and someone called out,

"Oh good show, George, your aim is really superb."

He began to whip her breasts in earnest, ringing them with stinging blows, so she yelped and struggled and swayed a little more on the hook. The lashing, coming so soon after his exquisite cunnilingus, made her helplessly aroused. To her amazement she felt the stimulation building back to overwhelming power inside her. As the man turned his attention to her behind and the whip fell again and again onto her back, buttocks and thighs she climaxed in a tumultuous, raining orgasm.

She hung limp, totally exhausted and depleted. The climax had sprung from very deep inside her. She had known for years that pain aroused her, but she had not realised she was one of those rare, and, on reflection, perhaps rather unlucky women, who can reach satisfaction from pain alone. She looked at the fat man with a new respect.

During her beating she'd become unaware of the men around her. As she settled back down to earth, her eyes still upon the man who had wrenched such a violent orgasm from her shaking body, she realised they had stopped laughing and were now gathered closer, their faces intent and slightly animal-like. She knew by now what that expression presaged: they were going to fuck her. Of course, the fat man would have her first. She no longer wished to resist him, and as he slipped his thick organ out from his trousers and swiftly into her vagina she accepted his penetration meekly. Not that she had any choice to do otherwise, hanging trussed and bound as she was, totally helpless and subject to the every whim of the men who controlled her.

Moments after the fat man began to fuck her she felt the familiar hot pressure of a penis against her asshole, then fingers tugging at her buttocks to aid the anal penetration, and that painful, but oh so pleasurable, sensation of a cock pushing deeply into her. Now she was impaled on two cocks, and sandwiched between the hot, sweaty bodies of the men who were enjoying her. The man behind her held her breasts, pinching and tugging the nipples in a way that brought tears to her eyes. She looked down at the heavily ringed fingers, marauders intent on possessing her flesh, and she did not recognise them. Whoever was using her it was a man who had not previously taken her.

The man in her anus climaxed first, pumping his hot semen inside her with rhythmic thrusts that made her moan and crave more. But no sooner had he slipped out of her than another gentleman forced his way into her tight hole, and as soon as the fat man had come, pulling away as he did so to splatter his seed all over her belly, where it dripped in thick gobbets down to her mons, another of the manor guests stuffed his hot cock inside her cunt.

The gangbang continued in this frenzied manner, so that hardly had one man left her than another took his place. Only when the gong sounded for dinner did the men leave off fucking her. She watched them leave through the far door, joking and laughing with an exclusive male camaraderie, and hunger gnawed at her belly.

Charlotte hung helplessly waiting, the spent semen trickling warmly down her thighs, right down to her ankles, so many men had filled her. A small puddle formed on the ground under her spread thighs. She wriggled in discomfort as a gaggle of servants of both sexes arrived to tidy the room, picking up glasses, cleaning ashtrays; her bonds seemed more uncomfortable now that she wasn't distracted by the thrusting of cock or the sting of the whip.

She looked around the room again, noticing details now. At the far end, above a great stone fireplace, was a huge oil painting. It looked old, most likely Victorian but possibly older, she thought. But the subject matter was so obscene she wondered if it could be a modern painting, deliberately painted in such a manner and with such techniques as to appear antique. It showed a pair of girls, quite naked apart from harnesses and bridles, pulling a little trap on which two gentlemen sat comfortably ensconced in fur coats and mufflers. There was snow on the ground, and yet the girls' bare flanks and chests were shiny with sweat. Their plump buttocks were crimson, as though they had already received many lashes from the whip the driver held in his right hand. She could just make out the inscription below the painting: "Drive them hard, Sir!" and a date, 1821.

The girls' breasts poked through the harness straps, looking very vulnerable and pale against the dark leather. She could see how their skin was reddening from straining against the harnesses; it was clearly hard work pulling the trap. Their faces looked piteous, their eyes wide with effort and fear. She glanced again at the men in the trap. She fancied that the older gentleman, the driver, was the father of the younger man. So perhaps the inscription referred to the son urging his father to push the pony girls to their limit. Charlotte shivered. Poor girls, what a life! For she suddenly knew, with total certainty, that this painting was as old as it purported to be, and that the two harnessed girls were very real, and the painting quite true to their lives of slavery. She looked at their pussies. As naked and hairless as her own, and like her own, their swollen clits glinted like red jewels half hidden by the silken labia. She realised then that there was nothing new about enslaving women to use them as toys for sexual pleasure, in fact, quite the reverse.

She turned her attention to the bound girls whose trussed bodies formed the frieze around the room. They were all very beautiful, and all very young, early twenties every one. Other than that they were of no particular physical type, with delicate Japanese girls bound next to tall athletic blacks, tanned blondes next to dark-eyed Indians... but all were slim and beautifully proportioned, some with large breasts, some small, but all quite delectable specimens of the fair sex. A meat market, with only the best quality female flesh for sale.

Two of the female servants approached her and looked her up and down, their eyes narrowing. One was about fifty perhaps, the other older, maybe seventy. Both had thin lips, pinched from endless disappointments and jealousies. If she had expected sympathy from these women on the grounds of their shared gender she was to be disappointed.

"What we supposed to be doing with this whore they've got strung up here?"

It was the elder woman who spoke, as she did so she prodded Charlotte's belly disparagingly with the handle of the broom she held.

"Take her down, add her to the line of bench sluts," called a smartly-dressed footman who appeared to be supervising.

"In this state?" the old crone went on, her expression disgusted as her eyes took in the trails of semen all over Charlotte's legs.

"Yes, just as she is, please Mary. I've had very specific instructions about that one. Would you believe…" he was walking over to join the two women in front of her now, "… that just a few days ago she was a virgin? But apparently she was caught pleasuring herself, in full view of the window cleaner I heard, put on quite a show for him, no shame at all, the little hussy."

Charlotte flushed at this distortion of events, but she could not protest for her mouth was still securely gagged.

Attached to the man's belt was a whip, and now he unfastened it, and like Mary, prodded her with the handle.

"I don't think they've whipped her quite enough, looking at her backside. It's not really red at all yet, and you can still make out the individual lash marks. Leave her up for a while and I'll finish the job. You two can watch her face for me, tell me if you think I'm over-doing it."

His voice was rich with repressed excitement.

Crack! Charlotte yelped as the whip tongued her sore behind, but all that escaped from behind the gag was a pathetic squeak. Crack! Again she yelped and wriggled as hard as she could, though she knew that to attempt escape was hopeless. Crack! Tears were already pricking her eyes, each lash of the whip cut through her like fire. Crack! She looked beseechingly at the women servants, for she had heard what the footman had said, and knew that the two matrons had the power to end her torment with a word. Crack! Now the tears tracked down her face. The women in front of her were smiling grimly, the narrow lines of their mouths curled up at the corners, like paper curling in the fire.

"Enough yet?" asked the footman from behind her. His voice sounded hopeful, hopeful that it would not be enough yet, hopeful that he would be permitted to continue abusing the lovely girl for a few more strokes…

"Not nearly enough, I wouldn't say, would you Mary? I'd give her at least twice that, maybe more."

"Thrice," came stout Mary's response, "She looks a bit sad, like, but you can tell she's not in any real pain. And if she chooses to behave in such a whorish manner she's in dire need of a bit of disciplining."

"Right then."

The young footman couldn't hide the pleasure in his voice. Again and again his whip landed on Charlotte's bottom, each blow more painful than the last. As he began the final set of three lashings he seemed to swing his arm with even more force. CRACK! The lash bit against already tender flesh and Charlotte screamed and jerked. But trussed and gagged as she was she simply squeaked and swung. CRACK! Her cheeks were sopping wet with tears by now of course. She began to turn her head this way and that, like a tormented animal. CRACK! CRACK! CRACK! As the last blow fell her head lolled forward; she was exhausted and even crying out was now more than she could accomplish.

"There, that looks far more appropriate."

The footman's voice was juicy now with satisfaction. He

came round the front of her and lifted her chin, surveying her tear sodden face and beaming conspiratorially at his two accomplices for all three knew full well what game they'd been playing, nor did any one of them waste a moment feeling guilt about their abuse of power. It had been a thoroughly enjoyable interlude. After all, it wasn't much fun for an ugly woman being a servant at the Sinclair's, seeing the beautiful slaves and knowing your own body was quite incapable of arousing passion. Seeing them suffer made the jealousy so much more endurable.

They lowered Charlotte to the ground and un-strapped her ankles, thighs and wrists, but immediately they rolled her onto her front and strapped her wrists together again behind her, and strapped her above the elbows too, so that her arms were brought together behind her back, forcing her full breasts forwards.

The footman pulled her upright, but she was so weakened by the restraints and the beating that she could not stand and would have fallen, so he had the two crones support her on either side and half drag, half walk her to the iron bench that ran the perimeter of the room.

The black iron dildos jutted up at her, threateningly. Now she was close she could see how obscene they were, shaped so as to replicate an erect cock, but one of them, the front one, far larger than an ordinary man's cock. The women started to push her down onto them. She struggled as much as she could, but the fat old hags were too strong for her. Besides, they were enjoying themselves, had their hearts in their work, whereas she had far too submissive an outlook to protest with much genuine resistance. She seemed to know that it was her own overblown and rapacious sexual nature that had brought her to this pass, and so her struggles were almost more symbolic protests against her loss of freedom, than real attempts to escape. Either way, escape was certainly impossible, and as Charlotte felt her anus burn as the two women pushed her onto the rear artificial shaft and her vagina was simultaneously stuffed with the mammoth frontal dildo she knew that she had no choice but to accept what was happening to her.

Once they had her impaled to their satisfaction, the foreman commenting on how the still oozing spunk made her easy to penetrate, they bound her ankles to the girls pinioned to either side of her, then left her alone as they finished their tidying of the room. Finally the servants left, leaving her with her sister sluts: mere decoration, as about as important as a Christmas bauble.

CHAPTER EIGHT

Charlotte looked at the girls to whom she was tethered. On her left was a very delicate oriental girl, with such slender limbs and tiny breasts that she would be easy for any man to dominate. Charlotte couldn't help but peer to see the root of the black dildo where it disappeared into her pink flesh. She wondered how such a petite girl could take the monstrous invader, but one glance at the girl's face told her that the poor thing was finding it very uncomfortable.

To her right was a dark-haired, pale skinned beauty, whose raven curls spilled luxuriously down her back, right to her waist. She was of similar build to Charlotte, but her breasts were somewhat larger, the kind of breasts that some men enjoy but women almost always wish were smaller. Charlotte suddenly noticed, with a thrill of shock, that there were fine red incision lines under each breast. So their huge size was not natural; the girl had presumably been recently modified to better please her master. How humiliating, how arousing, to know your body had been changed to make you a more pleasure-giving sex object. Charlotte looked at her almost enviously.

Both of her neighbours were gagged, and both had necks encircled with dark metal collars. She noticed for the first time that chains hung from the collars to hooks on the wall behind them, over which the leather handles were looped. She realised then that Sheba's collar was again fastened around her neck, and the cold chain hung against her jutting breasts, disappearing behind her shoulder. She could not recall at which point of the evening the collar had been buckled around her neck, perhaps it had been whilst she was being taken by the fat man and the others. At any rate, it was there now, a reminder, should she need one, of her lack of status.

Her stretched asshole stung and burnt, as did her poor thrashed bottom. And yet her clit was so swollen and ready for sex that being unable to touch herself was almost intolerable. She wriggled fretfully, the twin dildos making their presence felt so emphatically that she moaned. She wished the shafts would vibrate again, but without the gentlemen to see the show there was no point in that, of course. Perhaps she could bring herself to orgasm just by wriggling on the rods... but as she started to shift her weight from buttock to buttock she heard voices. The door through which the men had all departed was open again, and light and laughter spilled back through to the great hallway. Somehow she knew instinctively that any attempt to seek her own pleasure would be a punishable offence, and she was finding life as a sex slave quite painful enough without any additional punishment.

The men filed back into the room. They looked happy and well fed, several of them were rubbing their round stomachs appreciatively. This was a house of pleasure, and the Sinclairs obviously didn't neglect satisfying any of their guests needs.

One of the gentlemen walked up to the Japanese girl next to her, undid her gag and unceremoniously stuffed his erect cock into her mouth. Charlotte watched, fascinated, as the girl attempted to fellate the man but soon realised he wanted her deepthroating him. Within moments the man, a rough looking fellow with big hands and a big penis, was thrusting fully into the girl, so that her exquisite face was pressed right into his pubic hair with each stab of his cock. He held her head between his rough hands and simply slid it back and forth along his swollen organ, as though, thought Charlotte, the girl was just some sort of sex toy.

All round the room girls' gags were being unbuckled, cocks shoved disrespectfully into their pretty mouths. Charlotte felt her fuck juices begin to flow. Back in the days when she was free she occasionally used to look at porn on the web. Her favourite thing to watch was a beautiful and preferably rather fragile girl taking a man to the hilt in her mouth. She preferred the girl to look as much as possible like herself, liked to imagine herself into the situation. If the girl was bound, or otherwise held immobile, that was even better. And now, all around her, she could see the same thing happening to more than a dozen girls, and very much in the flesh. Her pussy clenched with arousal. When would it be her turn, she wondered. Just when she was beginning to think that every slut in the room was going to be face-fucked except for her, a man approached her. She waited for him to undo her gag, but he didn't. He simply took out his penis and with a few, quick and expert rubs brought himself off, splattering semen all over Charlotte's face.

He walked away without saying a word, or even appearing to look at her. The warm spunk dribbled from her forehead, down into her eyes. Slowly it cooled and congealed. She felt ridiculous sitting there with spunk all over her face, quite unable to wipe it away. Another man approached and again her heart leapt. This time he would use her mouth, just like all the other girls had been used. But no: like the gentleman before him he simply took out his erect rod and beat himself off, again deliberately ejaculating over her face.

Charlotte opened her eyes in time to see him walk away, but shut them quickly as spunk trickled into them and made them sting.

She sat there with her eyes shut. Around her the noise of conversation and laughter rose and fell in disorientating waves. She heard footsteps approach, and slitting her eyes open the tiniest amount she saw a naked cock, inches from her face, a hand sliding up and down it, and then another hot sticky load squirted all over her cheeks and lips and chin.

She perched helpless on the dildos, flushing with shame. Around her the other girls all looked beautiful. Prostituted, certainly, their mouths pleasuring cock after cock. But still, their lips were gleaming red with glossy lipstick. And, she now noticed, a serving maid was going from girl to girl, wiping stray come from each girl's lips and re-doing her make-up, so that she became once more a lovely, perfect, immaculate sex slave.

Whereas poor Charlotte now peered out through a growing mask of drying ejaculate. Men continued to approach her in ones or twos, once even three at once. But they never spoke to her, nor even to each other, as they hurriedly massaged their cocks, covered her face with their semen, and walked nonchalantly off.

It was a long evening for her. As the night wore on, the other slaves decorating the hall were led off, one by one, still in their chains, to eat or sleep or pleasure their masters. Eventually she was left quite alone in the vast room. She had watched Carl leave some time earlier, each of his arms around the waist of a tart, joking and laughing and evidently about to enjoy the attentions of both girls. She had burnt with jealousy watching them, her face almost hidden behind the stiff veil of semen. Now she was finally alone, and the penetrating dildos felt huge and uncomfortable.

After a while the servants appeared and began to clean the room. They totally ignored Charlotte, sweeping and tidying and polishing until the great hall again shone fresh and bright, no trace left of the evening's debauchery. No trace except for Charlotte. Finally, when every whip handle had been polished with beeswax, every iron dildo oiled and every inch of the floor was spotless once more, they went off to their beds, leaving only the footman who had so enjoyed beating her. He walked over and stood in front of her; she didn't look up at him. For one thing, she was too ashamed. She hated to think what she must look like, her face covered with dried come, her pussy red around the thick iron shaft. For another, it was hard to see, her eyelashes were sticking to her skin. It was easier to keep her gaze upon his feet. Only two days ago she'd have ignored a man like him without giving the matter a second thought, she'd considered herself above the common people, and far above those who served for a living. Now she herself was learning to serve, and her status was the lowliest that could be imagined.

The man chuckled, softly. Still she didn't look up.

"Well, look at you. You dirty slut!"

Charlotte stayed silent, but tears pricked her eyes.

He reached to her breasts and supported one with each hand, as though appraising their weight, as though she were meat.

"Nice tits. Very nice. How many men have had you, whore? Do you even know?"

He laughed again, a cold laugh.

"Come on, slut. Let's get you cleaned up."

He unfastened her ankles and removed the gag, eased her up off the dildos and clipped a bar to her collar in place of the chain. This way he was able to make her walk along in front of him, directing her where he wanted, like a marionette manipulated by means of a stick. He walked her ahead of him, out through the door of the hall, through a narrow oaken door she hadn't noticed before, thence down a spiral staircase of reddish stone, the treads so old that they were worn into bowls by the passage of so many feet over so many years. Finally he pushed her ahead of him out into a stone-flagged courtyard.

It was deepest night, but still quite warm. A soft breeze blew across her face, lifting her hair. It carried with it the scent of roses from some out of sight garden. She stumbled slightly, for in her high heels it was hard to keep her balance on the uneven ground with her arms so tightly strapped behind her.

He walked her forwards towards a deep trough of water, brimming with moonlight. Looking up, she saw the fat gibbous moon, hanging overhead like a faded red paper lantern. Swift and sudden he brought the bar by which he manipulated her down, down into the water, so that she was dunked under the surface, thrust deep into such cold water that she would have cried out. He held her there for moments that seemed an age, then brought her up, spluttering and gasping for air. Icy rivulets ran down her breasts, her nipples instantly clenching into hard buds. She started to shiver violently with cold, and with shock, but before she could recover he again brought the bar down and ducked her head under the water. Up she came again, and again she was gasping like a fish, shaking her head like a dog in her panic to rid herself of the water. But then as soon as she had drawn breath he forced her down for a third time. This time she opened her eyes under the surface he held her there so long. But she could see nothing, only her own hair swirling like dark weed, fogging the water.

When at last he did allow her up, he hooked the bar to a tall post close by the trough, then pulled off her shoes and fastened her ankles a yard apart to iron rings set into the stone, so she stood there tethered, dripping with water and shaking with cold. She watched him as he fetched something from the wall, turning a lever… suddenly she was blasted by a hard jet of cold water. He began to hose her down, playing the water over her so that it roughly buffeted her breasts and belly, gushed in her ears, slapped against her thighs. When he was satisfied that her skin was washed clean he moved close to her. She trembled as he parted her labia with one hand, then pushed the hose inside her vagina, douching her with the chilling water. As he reached round to part her buttocks she knew what was coming; the rubber tip was eased into her anus, the icy water jetted inside, washing her clean.

She was soaked now, and freezing cold. She stood watching him as he tidied the hose away, her teeth chattering, her body atremble. The wet stone under her bare feet was slimy smooth and still a little warm from the heat of the day. She wished she could crouch down, lie upon it, or even sink into it, out of sight, out of personhood.

He came back over to her.

"You'll be spending the night with a pair of our ponies. Come to think of it, you'd make a good one yourself, I'll talk to the master about it."

He laughed, and led her off to the stables.

Inside it was warm, a sweet rich scent of hay enveloped her. She could hear the breathing of the sleeping animals in their stall. A small flame flickered, then an oil lamp glowed steady, yellow light filling the stable. Charlotte looked around her, and understood with sudden shock what the man had meant. Lying asleep on the straw, their necks tethered to the wall by iron collars and heavy chains, were two naked girls. That these were pony girls she understood at once, for they were still partially harnessed. The harnesses were exactly like those she'd seen in the old painting.

In a matter of moments the footman had tethered Charlotte next to them. Then he left, shutting the door behind him. She listened to his footsteps as they died away. She heard the bang of another door, some way off. Then she was alone with the sleepers. She settled down to try to rest, but it was a long time before sleep came, for her arms ached, still bound behind her, and the gag still stuffed her mouth. When finally she drifted off it was to inhabit strange swirling dreams, dreams where she was being raped by giants and ogres, and she was orgasming, always orgasming, and she could not escape.

She woke at dawn to find someone standing over her. A huge man, so big in fact that at first she drew back in fear, thinking that her nightmares had become flesh and blood reality . He squatted down next to her, and began to run his great blackened hands over her slender body, smiling in pleasure.

"My, but you're a pretty one. It's a pity we ain't got you here for longer, I'd rather like to be the one who breaks ye in meself. Still, it's three days your master is visiting for. Plenty of time for me to give you a taste of me whip. And

131

me cock for that matter."

He chuckled happily, turned her over onto her belly as easily as if she were a cushion, and without any preamble at all began to force his penis into her asshole.

Charlotte moaned and whimpered. Pressed onto her face in the straw she could not see the cock that was attempting to invade her, but it felt massive. Little by little he drove his way in, until finally he was inside her, sunk to the hilt in her perfect flesh.

He fucked her, slowly, casually, and orgasmed without a murmur. Charlotte cried steadily. He was so huge and it hurt. She tried to ignore the hungry burning in her pussy. As he was finishing she heard voices behind him.

"What you got there, a new holster?"

"Yes, but not one of ours. She's a tart belonging to one of the guests, he wants her taking down a peg or two, she's an uppity little whore they say. So we have free rein to fuck her and beat her whilst he's here, that's for the next three days. Sir Jonathan is going to be treating her to some of his special training techniques later," much laughter at this, "…but anything you'd like to do to her this morning just go ahead. As long as you don't damage her… apart from welts and bruises o' course…Enjoy yourselves, I'm off to feed the other ponies and take the bay and palamino whores out for a good long trot. Mind you don't treat her too soft, now!"

She heard him leave the stable. His last words had been chilling, she knew her ordeal was about to get worse.

She was still lying face down in the straw. Someone got hold of the back of her collar, and dragged her upright, turning her round.

She was looking into the face of a man not much older than herself. He was strongly built and deeply tanned, she guessed, correctly, that he spent his days working outside, his skin already had that leathery weather-beaten appearance that comes from long days labouring in the sun. His hair was a tawny gold, and he'd have been very handsome, if it wasn't for the crude leer that marred his face.

"Nice titties, whore!"

As he spoke he squeezed and twisted her breasts, pressing her firm flesh in his hard sinewy fingers so it bulged softly between them, very white against his tanned skin. She whimpered.

"Let's be having that gag out of your mouth, I rather like to hear a slut scream when she's whipped, don't you Matt?"

Charlotte looked across to the other man who stood in front of the window, silhouetted against the light. He moved forwards, and she saw him clearly for the first time. He was leaner than the man who was manhandling her, his hair and eyes darker. But he seemed very much of the same mould, so that she wondered if perhaps the two were brothers.

Matt reached a grimy hand forward and stroked her belly. She flinched away from his touch, but that only brought her closer to the other man, her buttocks touching the rough denim of his jeans.

"Yeah. You know I likes to hear 'em suffering."

The brothers chuckled.

"What you reckon? Dangling from her feet?"

"Aye, let's do it that way, Todd. With her legs so spread she's begging for mercy before we even start to whip her."

Charlotte struggled as they started to propel her towards the far end of the barn. She could see four stout wooden posts, with various metal rings and chains set into them. That appeared to be where they were taking her, and she didn't want to go. But she was slender and small and female and bound, and they were solidly built, tall men; her wriggles were futile, and served only to further excite her captors.

Her arms were still trussed firmly behind her back, and they had no reason to free them. Todd pushed her over on the hay, flat on her back, clipped heavy iron restraints round each of her delicate ankles and stepped back, watching her.

133

Charlotte started to struggle up, but as she did so she realised the ankle cuffs were attached to chains, and the chains were shortening as Matt turned a winch. First her legs were pulled open and then they began to be lifted off the floor of the stable. She lay helplessly wriggling, her back still flat on the floor, her legs and now her buttocks pulled up in the air. The chains wound steadily into their sockets. Now she was being pulled completely off the ground... just her shoulders still touching... now just her head... until finally she dangled upside down, her legs wide apart.

But still the chains cranked ever shorter. Her ankles were being pulled towards diagonally opposite poles, stretching her further and further open. Soon she was so spread that it started to hurt, and she whimpered and moaned.

Todd ran his hands over her thighs, assessing the tension in the muscles.

"A little tighter, Matt, but not too much now."

The chains again cranked shorter. Charlotte's legs were wide apart now, her pussy pulled open and vulnerable, at the height of the men's waists. Matt fixed the lever so that the tension would be maintained. The blood was rushing to her head and she felt dizzy and confused. She was also frightened, for the men had her totally in their power and could do whatever they wanted to her. She remembered again the words of the groom as he left, and shivered.

"How about a hood?"

Moments later a black leather hood was being pulled over her face and buckled tightly around her neck. There was that same sudden feeling of chill, that made her nipples pucker hard. Then she was alone in the darkness, the soft leather rubbing against her cheek.

For a while nothing happened. She didn't know where the men were. Were they standing close to her, peering into her spread sex lips? Or were they standing some way off, at this very moment raising whips to lash her? She had no way of telling, and she began to tremble with the tension of not knowing what would happen to her.

Something cold touches her clitoris. Cold, and very very smooth, it slips back and forth over her nub. Polished metal? Marble? Her sex juices start to flow.

The thing begins to press against her fuck hole. She realises now that whatever it is, is very thick. Thick and smooth as glass and so cold it numbs her lips as it stretches them wide. Wider. It is beginning to enter her.

She doesn't hear her own whimpers, which have slightly shifted nuance. Before she was moaning in pure pain, now she moans with mingled pain and arousal. She cannot tell where one ends, and the other begins.

The thing presses deeper into her. One of the men must be pushing it down, hard. It's so big that her cunt doesn't want to accept it. But the pressure is huge, steady, inexorable. She starts to groan as it enters her. Then suddenly the battle is over and she has lost; the cold thing has slipped inside her. She feels totally filled. She wouldn't have imagined it possible to be so overwhelmingly filled. It hurts to be forced so open, but she is now so aroused that she knows a few rubs on her clit would bring her hurtling to orgasm. The thought is frightening, for how it would hurt to climax with such a massive shaft inside her!

A pressure now at her anus. No, this is too much, she cannot be filled there at the same time as this monster penetrates her cunt. She starts to moan, no, no, no, no... not because it hurts, but because it is beyond her, she is losing connection with self, she feels lost. But again that cold pressure, that smooth chill pressing so firmly against her asshole that it has to part, it has to give way, it has to allow penetration. And then the cold thing plunges inside her. Her ring burns, it has never been so stretched before.

A cold metal finger prods at her clit. Within seconds she is bucking wildly, helpless under the onslaught of an orgasm. But before the rush of pleasure has even begun to ebb sudden fire shoots through her and she screams in shock and pain, bucking even more vigorously in a futile attempt to escape her punishment. Her fuck honey flows like water. Pain, pleasure... where does one end and the other begin?

Carl settled back comfortably on a bale of straw and watched the two stable hands torment the hapless Charlotte. His cock was instantly rock hard to see her strung up like that, dangling head down, her naked and open cunt conveniently presented at waist height. And watching them force the huge stone dildos inside her had been most entertaining. The dildos were rather special, actually. The surviving remnants of giant priapic statues, that legend had it were used for the ceremonial defloration of maidens, these smooth black marble phalluses were thought to be over two thousand years old.

But the best was yet to come. Sir Jonathan had shown him the cattle prods the previous evening. They had been modified so as to impart only a miniscule shock, no bigger than the shock of static one might receive from stroking a cat, but delivered to the most sensitive flesh of a bound slut the effect was literally electrifying. The tawny haired young man had poked the girl's clit with the prod, trying to get good contact before pressing the switch; all three of the men chuckled to see her explode into orgasm just from the touch. Oh, how delightfully cruel to follow her climax so immediately with a sharp shock of electricity! And before she could recover another, then another. The poor creature bucked like a mad animal, but there was nothing she could do, they had unlimited access to her delicious flesh. Besides, it didn't really hurt that much, it was simply the effects of the bondage and stuffing, magnifying every tiny burst of electricity, Carl didn't feel even the smallest pang of guilt. He watched, stroking his cock as the lads played the prods all over her genitals, encircling her clit with fiery blasts of pain before landing her an especially intense shock right

136

on her pulsing nub. Then whilst one man continued to abuse her pussy the other brought his prod down to her erect nipples, treating each of them to thrilling bolts of electricity.

Poor Charlotte… Carl almost felt sorry for her when she pissed herself, the urine trickling down over her trussed body, running over her breasts and face and finally wetting her long mane of hair. He lifted his hand to silently call a halt to the proceedings.

He wondered how much she was enjoying this. Sexually enjoying it. She certainly wasn't enjoying it on any other level, she'd been screaming her head off. But was this pain more than she could take, were they simply torturing her? That wasn't what he wanted, however entertaining a spectacle she made as she swung around so helplessly. She had been screaming, but apart from when the anal phallus had been pressed into her she hadn't once said, 'no'. And even then, her 'no's had been more like moans of pleasure than pleas that they should stop. Was she now so submissive that she was actually aroused by their cruelty? He sincerely hoped so, because he was really rather enjoying this little show, and he certainly didn't want to bring it to a premature end. He wanted to find out, to know for sure, and it was a simple matter to do so…

There was a rack on the wall behind him, with the usual array of Sinclair tools, including a large rubbery vibrator. He turned it on, and it hummed gently, vibrating warmly against his palm.

He moved over to where the girl's exposed pudenda was spread so conveniently for his attentions, and slowly brought the vibrator down on her clitoris. It took less than three seconds of the softest vibrations to bring her to another moaning, shaking climax. Carl smiled at the stable lads and gestured they should resume their shocking treatment. It was impossible for a girl to come that quickly if she wasn't already highly aroused. So pretty little Charlotte really was a pain slut, even this level of abuse turned her on. What a whore! He inspected the rack behind him once more, selected a long, fine cane, and motioned for the other men to prod her from the front, to leave her naked buttocks accessible.

He walked round behind her. Her bottom was still red from last night's beating, that was good, it would mean this one would hurt far more than it would on unmarked skin. He raised the cane high, and brought it whooshing down with full force, landing neatly on her arse just as she received another shock to her clitoris. The bound girl screamed, piteously. Carl brought the cane down again and again, flushed with the effort, first raising bright crimson weals on her sweet ass, then turning his attentions to her spread legs, caning the sensitive skin of her inner thighs with frenetic intensity. She screamed and moaned and bucked, but was unable to avoid his torment.

Her muscles were gradually pushing the marble dildos out of her fuck holes. He lowered the cane, and pressed hard to drive them back in to her. They were warm now, heated by the whore's flesh. She moaned, not with pain this time, and whilst Matt continued to chastise her with shocks to her nipples and clitoris, Todd strapped a wide metal chastity belt onto her, to force them completely inside. It was artfully designed with a hole for the clit, and so did not impede the cattle prods.

When Carl's arm tired he changed places with Todd. As he held the cattle prod against her pink flesh he felt an exhilarating surge of power. He pressed the button, and was immediately rewarded by a scream, her legs going tense so that she swung slightly from her chained ankles. Again he blasted her on the nub, then again.

He brought the prod down her belly, shocking her on the fleshiest part of her mons, then on her pretty navel, then steadily down until it was aimed between her breasts. He circled each breast in turn, delivering tight spirals of pain, finally blasting her directly on the nipple. Before she could recover her blasted her again on her clitoris.

Her helpless body was soaked with sweat. A low, rank odour came from her as her drying piss turned sour. He needed to orgasm, but he remembered very well what the old man had told him, that utter humiliation was the route to utter obedience. He indicated to Todd that he should remove her hood, then beat off, jetting his spunk at Charlotte's belly so that it trickled down in thick dribbles to her tits. He gestured to the stable hands to follow suit, then strode out into the courtyard. Several workmen were about, some repairing a wall, others just in from the fields for their lunch, and also the grooms who looked after the four-legged horses. He called them all in to the stable and urged them to scent-mark the slut with their come. They stood around the dangling girl, encircling her enthusiastically and rubbing their cocks until hot sticky ejaculate spurted over her from every side. When finally every man had christened her, so that her pussy, thighs, belly, arse, tits and face were dripping with spunk, Carl sauntered off back to the mansion to dine with the other gentlemen. The workmen got back to their tasks, leaving the despoiled girl hanging alone in the stable.

CHAPTER NINE

Charlotte hung there all afternoon. Her ankles hurt, her genitals hurt, her poor abused breasts ached intolerably. But worst of all was the stench of herself, the musty scent of semen blended disgustingly with the acrid stink of piss.

The departing men had left the stable door open, and through it she could see out into the courtyard. There was the great stone trough into which she'd been dunked the previous night. She looked longingly at it now, remembering the feeling of her face being washed clean. And there was the post to which she'd been tethered whilst the footman hosed her off. Oh, how she wanted to be washed, how she wanted to be cleansed! She felt filthy. She was filthy.

A rattling of wheels, a click clacking of heels, and a bright trap swung into view. As she saw what was pulling it her vagina clenched sharply with arousal, which made the overlarge dildos hurt even more. She moaned, softly.

Harnessed to the trap were two young girls, both around her own age. Their arms were bound like hers behind them and they were naked, apart from leather harnesses that pulled between their breasts, tight straps going down between their pussy lips and digging into the soft flesh there. Every movement must make the straps rub and press their clits, thought Charlotte, feeling both fascinated and repelled. The memory of being trussed with cord in her own kitchen came flooding back to her. But these poor girls had to pull a trap like that! Around the grounds, presumably, where any of the staff or guests could see them. How humiliating.

Four men had come out of the house, Charlotte recognised them from the night before; they'd been amongst the guests in the great hallway. Each of them had ejaculated onto her face. She shuddered at the memory of their smelly spunk all over her lips. Now the pony girls were being detached from the trap. They obediently bent over, and the gentlemen proceeded to use them, two taking their arses, two their mouths. As they were fucked the men squeezed their breasts very roughly. One man held his slut's tits as though they were handles, pulling and tugging them with no regard at all for the poor girl's feelings.

Someone shut the door. Without the distraction of the slaves to watch, Charlotte's bonds began to feel quite unbearable. She shifted her weight to ease the pressure on her ankles, but it didn't help. The stone phalluses seemed to bore right into her. She knew she had agreed to all this when she first consented to belong to Carl, but now, for the first time since her willing enslavement began, she really did want it to stop. But she was alone. No one around to plead with. And if someone had been there, would they take any notice if she begged them to release her, she wondered? Most probably not. The thought that she really was a slave, that she really didn't have any choice and that these men really would use her exactly as they wanted, was both terrifying and thrilling. She felt her fuck juices begin to flow once move, and then a thick wave of disgust washed over her.

What kind of female was she that she enjoyed being so humiliated and hurt, used as though she existed only for male pleasure? She remembered Carl's words. A true submissive, that's what he'd said. A true submissive can't say no. For the first time she understood that he was right. She'd not said no to these men, not once, not said no and meant it. She'd behaved like a whore. She was a whore. By enslaving her it was as though Carl had held up a mirror to her naked self, and shown her what she was. At the realisation of how cheap and sluttish she really was under the pretty veneer of niceness, her cheeks burnt with shame. She was dangling upside down from her ankles, arms tied behind her, vagina and anus both stretched wide by huge dildos and her body sore all over from a beating, because she wanted to be. All she'd got was what she'd wanted. She truly was a slut.

It was much later when they came to let her down. They lowered her to the straw and unfastened her ankle cuffs, and then her arms. They unbuckled the chastity belt and let her squat on the dusty floor, the marble dildos slipping slowly from her body.

She was so stiff she couldn't even stand, let alone walk, so they dragged her out to the courtyard, where the light was so bright after the dim stable that her eyes were dazzled. They didn't bother to tether her; they knew, and she knew, that she wasn't going anywhere. They dumped her in the middle of the cobbled yard, and moments later five jets of water began to pummel her.

The water was freezing, and soon she was gasping and shaking.

"Stand up!" bellowed a voice, and without questioning she struggled to her feet, swaying slightly.

The jets of water pushed against her and she almost fell.

"Look at her tits!" called a voice, and she flushed with shame as they made a game of jiggling her breasts around with their powerful hoses.

"Open your legs, slut!"

She stood with her legs wide apart and straight. The water gushed at her sore pussy, and she was glad of the chill of it.

"Not like that, legs bent!"

Charlotte squatted slightly, her feet wide apart, in the position a woman only assumes unbidden if she is flat on her back about to be fucked. The men came closer, the hoses were directed up towards the heart of her. Two of them were slipped into her, the streams of cold water cleansing her, then they were pulled back out.

"Stay like that, bitch!"

Hands reached round from behind her, and clamped a hinged metal cuff around her neck, above her collar. A chain led from it to the post to which she'd been tethered the previous night. The men were moving away again across the yard, fastening the hoses back to the wall of the stables.

The sun beat down on her head, warming her drying skin as the cold water rivered off it, pooling between her legs. Little cold trickles meandered down her hot back from her sopping hair.

It was hard to stand still. She felt a little dizzy, and couldn't stop herself swaying. Standing with her legs spread she felt more animal than human, she felt as though she was a farm animal waiting for the farmer to assess it. She was holding her hands behind her back, not that she'd been told to, but having been strapped like that for so long her arms seemed to naturally go there, as though the message of her submission had reached even her unconscious.

Now that she was dry she began to feel the true power of the sun. She was standing in the full brightness of it, sweating, her chest and back gleaming with moisture. She heard the sound of a door behind her, then footsteps. Several men coming, from the house.

" I see what you mean, father. And he definitely won't sell?"

A tall, dark man, in his late thirties, stepped into view. He looked very like Sir Jonathan. His voice was accentless and cultured, you could tell immediately he had had a particularly privileged education, the sort of schooling that can only be afforded by the most prosperous families.

"No, he won't sell. Pity, I'm sure once she was properly broken in she'd make a crown grade cock-holster. Can't blame him for wanting to keep her, though I gather he has a prior arrangement."

Charlotte recognised Sir Jonathan's voice. A moment later he, too, came into view and stood next to his son, his eyes on her body. The men continued to talk, standing comfortably together in the shade, looking at her all the while, but Charlotte felt strangely invisible. They weren't looking at her as a person, they were just looking at her flesh, just at the meat of her. They talked in front of her as freely as they'd talk in front of one of their horses. Even when they looked her in the face, even when they looked at her eyes, there was no contact, no connection.

She had stopped listening to their words for a moment, and now she couldn't follow what they were talking about.

"Of course, nowadays it can all be done with hormone shots. To look at her I'd guess she'd be highly productive. I hope he'll bring her back for a demonstration, it should be rather amusing."

"I'll ask him to do that, I'm sure he'll oblige. He's asked me to pay her some personal attention this afternoon, he knows of my reputation and thinks she'll benefit from the experience."

At this, both men laughed. The sound was chilling to Charlotte, their voices sounded so cold, so predatory. She shivered despite the heat.

Just then the big groom who had fucked her on her face in the straw that morning came into the yard.

"Ah, Joe. Could you have this whore sent to my rooms in an hour? Leave her standing as she is now, till then. No food, but give her water."

"Certainly sir, how would you like her?"

"Hmmm, let me see. Black rubber slutsuit I think. Cutaways. A corset over the top. Heels. It's about time we saw her dressed like a prostitute, seeing that's what she is. An owned prostitute, of course. A slave whore. A cock-holster. Just a collection of fuck holes, receptacles for cock."

Charlotte's face flushed. She guessed these words were aimed at her, that the old man wanted her to listen and know what he thought of her. As the gentlemen moved away they continued the conversation in loud voices.

"I do so enjoy seeing a new slut's face when you remind her that her cunt is owned, and that henceforth she'll have no say as to who or what penetrates it. And that being penetrated is her sole role in life. Quite delicious to enslave a girl so recently virgin. It would have been pleasant to see this one deflowered, but Carl tells me he has it all on video.

144

Apparently she was quite willing."

The men laughed again, even more heartily than before, as though Sir Jonathan had just told a most hilarious joke.

By the time Joe came to dress her for her visit to Sir Jonathan, Charlotte's legs were trembling from standing so unnaturally for so long. She was dizzy from the sun, her head so hot she thought she might soon faint. It was a blessed release to be led back into the cool dark of the stables.

A small pile of clothing lay ready on one of the straw bales. Joe held up something black and shiny. At first sight Charlotte thought it was a bag for trash, but then she realised it was the rubber slutsuit to which Sir Jonathan had referred. Joe sprayed her body with a fine oily substance that made her skin as slippery as graphite, then eased the suit onto her legs. She felt like a joint of meat, being prepared ready for the oven.

When she was finally dressed in the rubber catsuit she understood what the old man had meant by 'cutaways'. She was encased from neck to ankle in thin, skintight black rubber, but her breasts were naked, as was her pussy. Large holes in the suit exposed these most private parts. It was a reversal of norms, for clothing usually covers the sexual parts first, as they are the most private. This garment covered every bit of her apart from her sexual parts, because to these men those were the only parts of her that mattered.

She felt hideously exposed, more like a prostitute than she could have imagined feeling. At the same time she felt exquisitely sexualised, as though the whole of her sense of self was concentrated in the naked, exposed sections of her flesh. She felt as though she was, indeed, nothing more than her fuck holes and tits.

Joe was holding a black leather garment from which dangled laces. He fastened her wrists in cuffs, then hooked them to the roof of the stable, so that she dangled a foot off the ground. Then he wrapped the corset around her and began to lace it.

Dangling a slut like that stretched her out, made her as slim as possible. Not that this one carried any extra blubber, the only fat on this bitch's sleek frame was that which comprised her tits, plenty there. He stopped work for a moment to fondle them. Very heavy, very firm. She trembled under his touch: very sensitive. He rather suspected the old man would have some especially cruel punishments it store for these lovely titties. Poor girl, who'd choose to be a submissive? They just never could say no, and it got them into situations like this, where they really didn't have any control over what happened to them. His cock was hard, and he wanted to fuck her just as she was, but that would never do, you always sent a whore to the gentleman in a nice clean state, ready for them to despoil. But later, he'd have a bit of fun…

He turned his attention back to the corset and began to pull the laces tighter. It was a long job, and couldn't be hurried. He worked over the laces repeatedly, bringing her slim waist down from twenty-three inches to a tiny eighteen. He wondered if he could get it down a little further… yes… nice. She was now so tiny around the waist that he could actually encircle her with both his big hands. It usually took a few months to get a slut corset-trained enough for that, but this one had a figure made for it.

He undid her wrist cuffs and made her stand facing him whilst he inspected her. Shoes, next. They were black stilettos of course, with five-inch heels. So high that she could only teeter on them with tiny mincing steps. Almost finished. He left her tethered and went to fetch one of the housemaids to paint Charlotte's face.

Holster make-up was always the same, no fashions or wit, it had a very simple purpose. The little maid deftly painted the whore's eyes, rimming them heavily with black kohl, dusting the lids with dark powder and then carefully sticking long false eyelashes in place. The slut now had eyes like some scared little bambi, ever so cute and ever so fuckable.

The only other make-up needed was for the mouth. A bright slut scarlet lipstick, so glossy it always looked wet. It looked particularly good on young Charlotte's sweet, plump lips.

Then Joe told the girl to brush Charlotte's hair. Lovely long wavy tresses, and such a pretty colour. He wished again that she was under his control for longer; he would dearly like to subject such a pretty creature to the full Sinclair slave training. This one would look superb pulling a trap.

The housemaid scurried thankfully away when her work was finished. All the women who worked at the manor were scared that one day it'd be their turn to get whipped and fucked. For the most part this fear was unfounded; the Sinclairs never forced girls into slavery; there was no need, the world was so full of submissives that they always had plenty of stock. And, happily, for some reason it was usually the very prettiest girls who secretly craved to learn obedience. But once in a while a servant at the manor had shown signs of being a submissive. It was impossible to hide your true nature in such a sexualised environment. In that case, the unfortunate girl quickly found her maid's uniform replaced by an iron collar, and her job of changing the bed linen replaced by the job of lying on the bed having her little body stuffed with cock. So an atmosphere of charged fear reverberated through the manor whenever a female submissive was on the staff, for everyone knew that it was only a matter of time before she showed her desires, and tasted the lash for the first time.

Joe strapped Charlotte's arms behind her back, tight straps binding her wrists, then more straps above the elbow. He buckled the black leather very tight. Painfully tight, for she whimpered and shivered in his grasp. He let his hands roam freely over her breasts once more, feeling the weight of them, enjoying the redness of the erect nipples that had still not recovered from the electric shocks. Reaching between her legs he felt her wetness: little slut, she was gagging for sex. He gave her clitoris a playful tweak and chuckled to himself as she jerked in his arms. It always amused him how most laymen seemed to think the phrase 'nipped in the bud' came from horticulture, when really, of course, it was a slave-trading term, meaning the well-used technique of denying an aroused cock-holster her orgasm by pinching the clit hard enough to stem any excitement.

At the far end of the stable was a mirror, and now he marched her off towards it, holding her by her bound arms. She teetered pathetically on the heels.

"There you are Charlotte, what do you see?"

His words seemed harmless enough, but he said her name mockingly, as though there was some joke to which she was not party. Charlotte looked in the mirror, and did not recognise herself.

The girl in the mirror was a whore. The skin tight rubber showed her beautifully-fleshed body to perfection, the full and naked breasts accentuated by the corset-narrowed waist. Because of the cutaway section of rubber that exposed the genitals, one's eye was drawn immediately to the hairless sex lips. She saw with the familiar wash of shame that they were already glistening with her fuck juices. Her pink and swollen clit glinted between them, temptingly visible, still throbbing from the trainer's cruel pinch.

If her clothing had not been enough to mark her as a prostitute her face alone would have done so. Even dressed demurely she would have looked like a slut with a face like this. The eyes, so huge and vulnerable, with the dark lashes that resembled those of a doll, and the scarlet mouth. What are mouths for? Breathing and eating, of course, and also talking, and kissing. This mouth was for sucking cock. Of course, she could still use it to eat, and even talk if anyone should have any wish for her to do so, though that would certainly be a rare event. But the main function of this mouth was clear: the pleasuring of male members by means of lips and tongue and throat.

But the girl in the mirror was less than a whore. A free whore's eyes have that surly bold look, she may be a woman in extremis, but she is a woman who still owns her own flesh, her own cunt. She can say 'no'. Charlotte's cruelly bound arms, which made her breasts jut so invitingly forward, and the leather collar around her neck, which had previously been worn by the German Shepherd bitch... these things marked her out as property, owned flesh. Charlotte wasn't Charlotte any more, and that was why Joe had said her name so ironically. Charlotte was now, quite literally, a sex object, a possession for satisfying sexual needs. Not a person, a thing, a sexual amusement.

Joe watched her face in amusement. He had expected the sight of herself to ram home the truth and he had been right. And now the poor little creature had an appointment to keep with Sir Jonathan. Joe chuckled to himself, his cock rigid in his trousers as he marched the holster back out of the stable, across the yard, and into the house.

He took her up the same spiral stairs that she'd been forced down the previous night. Less than twenty-four hours ago. It seemed like an age. Charlotte felt as though her long-ago promise to belong to Carl had been the first step onto a spinning disc, that now whirled ever faster, and that she was not just being spun around, confused and disorientated, but sucked down, towards some unknown heart of darkness. Had she now reached the bottom, the lowest point? She was being fucked and beaten by unknown men as the whim took them, she could hardly sink any lower.

He led her up a further flight of stairs, along a corridor lavishly carpeted and into a small room, where he handed her lead to a manservant, who took it, fastened it to a ring in the wall and then left, as did Joe. She was all alone, with nothing to do but wait.

Charlotte felt suddenly exhausted. She tried to sit, but the chain that tethered her was far too short, so she had no choice but to stand, swaying unsteadily on the high heels.

The room was unfurnished, but the walls were hung with many paintings. Charlotte's eyes widened as she saw images of women, naked and bound, some being whipped, some being fucked, others, like the hapless pair in the painting downstairs, harnessed to traps.

She was looking at an old painting of a girl on her knees, her wrists bound behind her, fellating an Arabic man who reclined comfortably on a couch. Next to the man lay his wife; dressed in rich fabrics, she held a chain attached to the young whore's neck. The owners were dark, their skin Moorish, their hair black. The young girl at work on her knees had milky-fair skin and dark auburn hair. It struck Charlotte that this girl looked very like herself. She shivered. She had no doubt that the picture depicted a real girl, perhaps one who had stood where she stood now, many long years ago, and who had then been sold to the Eastern couple, doubtless making a healthy profit for Sir Jonathan's cruel ancestors.

"Yes... she does look very like you."

Charlotte jumped at the voice, she hadn't heard the old man enter the room.

"And probably racially prejudiced, like you... I doubt it would have been easy for her to submit to a man with such dark skin. Of course, she wouldn't have been given any choice, and quite right too, racism is an anathema," he glared into her with those beady bright eyes. How had he known she was prejudiced? She tried very hard not to be, she knew it was wrong, but all the same, she couldn't help being rather scared of black men at least when it came to sex. She was too naïve to know whether the folklore pertaining to their size was myth or reality.

"We've got the complete records for every slave trained here," he went on. "They date back hundreds of years. She is number two thousand and twenty five. Her name was Elizabeth, though after training they renamed her Pet. Poor girl, she came from a very wealthy family, but her father was a drunkard and a fool: he gambled away all his money, he was so deeply in debt he'd have had to sell his house. So instead, he sold his daughter, sweet young innocent Elizabeth, who had never so much as been kissed. As you can see, she soon learnt how to suck cock, and all the other ways of pleasing a man. But her father went right on gambling, and lost again of course, and so he sold his wife, and his other two daughters, Elizabeth's younger sisters. One was barely of age, I have her birth certificate and the bill of sale: she reached marriageable age just one day before he sold her. He died, destitute, not long after that. But his wife and daughters all lived long lives of service, every one of them a holster. His wife had the hardest time of it, I believe, being too old when she was sold to please a rich man. She was bought by a captain to keep his crew happy on long voyages, I doubt she ever had less than five men in a night. A little detail of history that is now generally forgotten: everyone knows about ship's cats, not so many people know that each ship also carried a whore. It's all in the records, my dear Charlotte, it makes fascinating reading. Of course, we're less barbaric now. I have no doubt that young Elizabeth was forced into slavery, no doubt that she was forcibly ravished. Whereas you, silly girl, you're here by choice, aren't you?" He smirked at her, his expression knowing. "I don't think I'll ever understand modern young women. Why did you agree to belong to Carl, little Charlotte, didn't you know where it would lead?"

Charlotte's mouth was dry. She had grown so used to being treated like a sex toy that it came as a complete surprise, the old man talking to her. She licked her lips nervously, and swallowed.

"I... I... I don't know. It was just that when he touched me..." she flushed, remembering it was the touch of his tongue that had won her to him, "... I felt so... I just wanted to be his," she finished, lamely.

Old Sir Jonathan was watching her intently, his eyes beady bright.

"As I thought: you don't understand it yourself. You're a natural submissive and they are rarely the brightest of creatures. Pity, I'd rather like to enslave a truly intelligent woman, but all I ever get are stupid little sluts who agree to be cock-holsters in return for five minutes of cunnilingus."

Charlotte's flush deepened. So he knew how Carl had entranced her. She bridled at his insult, though in retrospect it did seem a rather stupid decision.

"Well, little Charlotte. Suppose I gave you the choice again. Would you still choose to be here, about to suffer under my practised hands? Or not?"

Charlotte didn't know what to reply, because she didn't know what she really felt. But her clit was throbbing with need, so aroused was she by the dominance of this man. He must be in his seventies, fifty years older than she was, but his dominance was so intoxicating to her that she knew she wanted to spread for him. But the pain, did she want that too? She opened her mouth to reply at last, but Sir Jonathan interrupted her.

"I'll let you into a little secret, pretty young Charlotte. I don't care," he smiled at her, one of those cold cruel smiles to which she was becoming very accustomed. "I don't give a fig whether you want to be here or not. You could be as unwilling a partner as sweet Elizabeth was when they deflowered her by force, and I'd still enjoy taking you. I don't really care much for these modern niceties. You're female, you exist for male pleasure. That's the mantra I was brought up by, that's the one by which I live. And now, holster, I'll start teaching the lesson to you."

152

As he spoke the last words he unhooked a long whip from his belt, and brought it licking up, hard, between Charlotte's legs. Caught unawares by his sudden change of mood she didn't move in time, so the blow met her flesh with full force, right on her clitoris, so that she staggered backwards with a cry. Sir Jonathan chuckled to himself. Of course, he was lying. It was a point of honour with him that all the girls he whipped and tormented were consenting, in fact he made certain that his own slaves-in-training signed papers to that effect. Nevertheless, it was highly amusing to let the sluts think that there were no limits to his domination.

He laughed at the whimpering girl. "Come on bitch, enough of these pleasantries, welcome to my chambers." And he took hold of her lead and led her through the door to his private rooms.

CHAPTER TEN

Whatever else Charlotte had expected, she had not expected an audience. Somehow she had assumed that the old man wanted her to himself for a few hours. She had imagined that he wanted to fuck her, cruelly no doubt, but that his main intention was to enjoy her body. Looking around the room she wondered now if that assumption was perhaps mistaken, perhaps the main reason for bringing her to his rooms was to provide more entertainment for his guests.

The chamber was luxurious, with plush velvet furnishings and damask curtains. In the centre was a strange object, rather like a vaulting bar, that appeared the be made of textured black rubber. Dangling from the ceiling were various chains and manacles. On the walls were racks, brimful of various whips and other devices for punishing slave girls. Two computer screens stood incongruously to one side.

Seated in comfortable armchairs were around a dozen men, most of whom seemed familiar from the night before. Carl was there, as was the middle-aged man she had taken for Sir Jonathan's son. Two other men bore the same family resemblance: the hawkish nose, the amiable expression, the cruel eyes. Perhaps these two were also his sons.

The other men all looked extremely rich. Gold rings flashed on dark fingers, and the air was perfumed with the scents of fine cigars and cologne. Charlotte noticed with a little shiver that the men were of various races. A heavily built Japanese man, elegantly dressed in a white silk shirt and black suit, two men who looked like they must be visitors from the Far East, and a huge man of Afro-Caribbean descent. She found herself staring at his crotch, again wondering if it was true, what they said about black men. She thought about the websites she had visited in shameful secret, where white girls got relentlessly gangbanged by big black guys. The men all had huge cocks in those videos, but then so did most of the white men in porn.

"She wants you already."

Charlotte flushed. They'd seen where she was looking and were laughing about it. Sir Jonathan held her by her bound arms and displayed her to the seated gentleman, rather like a conjurer displaying the equipment before he performs some magic trick, she thought. The men's hands reached to feel her exposed breasts. Tanned skin against white, ochre skin against white, black skin against white. The black man's hands were enormous, but not large enough to totally cover her pale skin when he gripped her two naked breasts, weighing them in that manner that was becoming so familiar to her and which always made her feel like a farm animal at market. As he held them he looked deep into her eyes, and she suddenly knew he could read the prejudice there. She shivered then, not with rejection of him, but with fear, for she saw her racism had ignited a small spark of anger in him, and that would be bound to make him cruel. As if to confirm this thought he reached between her fuck lips and nipped her swollen clitoris, hard, chuckling when she yelped in pain.

"That's right, Peter, you teach her a little respect. Marcus, could you fetch two of the iron tit-cuffs?"

One of the men that resembled Sir Jonathan went to the wall rack and returned with two circular metal bands, about four inches in diameter and a half inch deep. The old man nonchalantly pulled them over her breasts. They fitted snugly, but not too tight, not uncomfortable. A small circular cog-like knob protruded from each cuff. Sir Jonathan began to turn these knobs, first a few twists on one, then a few twists on the other. In alarm Charlotte realised the circles were shrinking, the iron spiralling against itself: not circlets, but coils. The metal began to dig into her silky flesh as the rings grew ever smaller.

Still he tightened then. Soon she began to whimper in pain, but he took no notice. Blinking back tears she looked

155

from her bound breasts to the gentlemen watching, and saw that several of them had taken out their cocks and were stroking them, leisurely. The black man's was even huger than she had imagined and she couldn't take her eyes off it.

Still Sir Jonathan turned the knobs.

"Owww, ooooh, owww…" she started to moan.

Sir Jonathan clicked his fingers and Marcus brought him a long black object with straps. Without comment the old man stuffed the dildo gag between her lips and buckled it tightly behind her head.

He turned the knobs a little tighter. Now she could only offer tiny squeaks of protest. The audience evidently found this amusing for there was much laughter.

"More?" said Sir Jonathan, chuckling.

"Oh yes," replied Peter, the black man with the huge cock, "definitely more."

Again the knobs were tightened. Tears were running down Charlotte's face. Her breasts hurt and yet her pussy was wet. She felt so ashamed of herself.

"Marcus, could you fetch that hood?"

Marcus went to the racks again, and returned with a black leather object, covered in straps and buckles. Sir Jonathan slipped it over Charlotte's head, and for a brief moment, seeing the men's eyes upon her, she felt again as though he were a conjurer. She, perhaps, was the rabbit, that goes inside the magic box never to be seen again. Then the hood was pulled down over her eyes, that familiar chill as she entered the fragrant dark, and she felt the straps being buckled tight.

Straps around her neck, straps around her mouth, straps around her eyes. The soft leather is pulled tight against her face. She feels panicky, but she can still breathe without problems, there must be holes in the leather by her nostrils even if she can't see them.

Her bound hands are being freed. But only for a moment.

Now they are being brought above her head. Someone leads her mincingly forward and she feels the long rubber bar between her legs. She's straddling it, and it's so high that it rubs against her juicy pussy, pressing her lips open, tantalising her clit. At the same moment her wrists are clipped into manacles high above her head.

A fiery bolt of pain jets through her nipple as some sort of clamp bites shut onto the engorged flesh. Then it is the turn of the second nipple. She would scream, but the thick rubber phallus stuffing her mouth blocks all but the most pathetic of squeaks.

Now something is pulling down on the clamps. She tries to sink lower to lessen the excruciating pain in her burning nipples, but the rubber bar between her legs is changing shape. Before it was gently rounded, now it feels pointed, like an upturned V. It pokes at her clit so she stretches up to get higher, but that pulls on her abused nipples, so she sinks lower again, jabbing her now bruised clitoris. It is impossible to get comfortable, so she wriggles like some helpless trapped animal. The men are laughing but she can barely hear them, trapped in her own world of pain. And yet her clit is swollen and slippery.

Peter watched the whore dance around on the beam. It was good to see her suffer. Little racist bitch, he'd seen that arrogant look in her eyes. She jiggled around, unable to stay still for a moment, chained by her nipples to the floor so there was no way she could escape the jabs of the bar. 'Riding the pony', he thought they called it, but old Sir Jon had an imaginative twist on everything. He couldn't wait to see what would happen to the girl when he set the machine running.

Sir Jon had shown them the rubber bar before he'd led the slut in. Apparently solid, the miniscule ripples in it betrayed the fact it was really made of thousands of fine vertical metal rods, each rod covered with rubber, each rod able to move independently. So the shape of the surface of the bar was entirely controllable. The default shape was gently rounded, like the wooden rail of a staircase, for example. That was the setting it had been on when the girl was first made to straddle it, in cross-section a sort of inverted U. But now Sir Jonathan had turned a lever to lower some of the rods, so the U had grown more pointy, more like V. He had also raised the bar. Peter smiled to himself as the whore continued to jig helplessly about. He knew what was coming next.

Sir Jonathan switched the machine on. It was controlled by a computer and pre-programmed with expertise and wit. The bar was an exquisite piece of engineering. The rods rose or fell as prescribed by the program, making the point of the V travel from side to side, rather as though a wasp had its tail in the air and was swaying its swing about. The girl was still straining to keep her pussy as high as possible. Now the moving V began to shift so that the point was first at one side, then at the other. This had the effect of flicking the slut's clitoris from side to side in hard brutal jerks. Gradually it gathered speed, the girl moaning softly behind her gag as her clitoris was battered to orgasm. She came in a great reverberating wave that didn't seem to stop, but instead rolled on, and on, orgasmic peak following orgasmic peak, all shown by the computer monitor that was rigged up to electrodes in the bar.

The bar relaxed into smoothness as Sir Jonathan turned the machine off, and made some adjustments. Peter winced sympathetically as the older man let a clamp bite onto the poor girl's swollen clitoris. Her little body gave a jerk of shock, followed by a sharp squeak as her nipples were tugged. Like the nipple clamps the clitoris clamp was attached to a chain set into the stone floor. Sir Jonathan adjusted the settings, and turned the machine back on. The rods under her clitoris were still, now. This time it was the rods under her vagina that were active. A broad wedge of them gradually rose, impaling Charlotte on a hugely-thick dildo. It rose up inside her. The second computer screen conveniently displayed a computer simulation of what the rods were doing. Glancing at the screen Peter could see that the ones near her vagina had now formed themselves into an eight-inch long dildo upon which she was impaled. Yet still the dildo kept growing. Soon it was ten inches long, and now it was longer than the slut could comfortably take. She was straining to stand as tall as possible to minimise the penetration, but that made the clamps on her clitoris and nipples tug down even harder, so then she lowered herself, only to find the penetrating dildo insufferable. In this manner, between a rock and a hard place, she was forced to ride the dildo, up and down, up and down, never still, driven by pain. Pitiful little squeaks emerged from under the leather hood.

When he judged the moment was right, the old slave trainer halted the machine. It was obvious that the whore was extremely uncomfortable. Her clamped nipples were dark purple, indeed the whole of her breasts were purpling and shiny swollen from the constrictive tit cuffs. Her clitoris could just be seen in the jaw of the other clamp. She couldn't stop squeaking and she couldn't stay still.

"Her anus is empty."

Sir Jon looked at Peter as he spoke, smiling invitingly. Peter needed no second bidding, he grinned back and stepped up to the wriggling slut. When he rubbed his fingers over her puckering flesh she quivered like a frightened animal. He put the tip of his cock against her hole and began to push into her.

As Peter rammed his way into the bound girl's asshole Sir Jonathan handed out the adapted cattle prods to the other guests. Her flesh was apparently ultra-sensitive from the bondage, for the tiniest of shocks to her stretched nipples and clitoris made her buck uncontrollably. But inflicting pain alone was not what had made Sir Jonathan Sinclair the world's greatest living slave trainer. The trick was to inflict ecstasy at the same moment as agony. As Peter humped her asshole, and his sons and guests sent shocks rippling through her tormented breasts, Sir Jonathan turned on a sleek, noiseless vibrator and held it against the stretched clitoris. Like a violin string when the musician moves his bow, the flesh caught the vibration and within moments Charlotte was blasted into an agonising and heavenly orgasm.

It took most of the next day for Charlotte to recover from her ordeal at the hands of Sir Jonathan and his guests. By the time they unstrapped her she had been barely conscious, overcome by the pain and pleasure which the gentlemen so delighted to inflict. But of course, that hadn't been the end of it. What followed had been a degenerate and violent orgy, with cock after cock forced into her cunt and anus, and after a while her hood had been removed, so they could fuck her mouth and splatter her face with semen. One beautiful girl, dressed for fucking, and ten sexually rapacious dominant men: she didn't stand a chance. By the time they had finished with her, poor Charlotte was a sorry sight: her breasts and pussy marked by criss-crossing red welts where whips had burnt her flesh, her clitoris and nipples dark red and bruised from the cruel clamps, and semen everywhere. They had soaked her with come, marked her as owned. She had come on her face, her eyelids, her cheeks and lips, come in her ears and matting her hair, her breasts were sticky with semen and thick trails of milky spunk trickled from both her lower fuck holes down her thighs.

The final act of degradation came when they stretched her oral lips to see how wide her mouth would go, then proceeded to force both Peter and Carl's huge cocks into it at once. Charlotte struggled to resist them, but there were far too many men, and she was only a delicate slightly-built girl. There was nothing she could do to stop them using her exactly as they wished. And so it was that she ended the day squatting on all fours, some anonymous man under her, filling her cunt, another man… again, she had no idea who… ramming himself into her asshole, and Carl and Peter thrusting together into her throat.

It was a very subdued Charlotte who was hosed down in the yard that evening. And as night fell and she lay tethered on the straw she couldn't sleep. For remembering the day's events her clitoris longed to be stroked, and both her hands were strapped uselessly behind her.

"Wake up, you're due at work in an hour."

Charlotte stirred sleepily. She was lying naked on what used to be her bed, and had now been requisitioned by Carl, her metal neck-cuff chained to the foot of the bed by a heavy iron chain. It was rare that she was allowed to sleep on a bed nowadays, and she had slept very deeply. They had been home from the evil Sinclair manor for over a week, and she was still sleeping like a log every chance she got. Opening her eyes she saw the sun was already quite high in the sky.

What had he said about work? Charlotte didn't understand. Carl was looking at her, his dark eyes twinkling. A sure sign of trouble, thought Charlotte.

"It's Monday. Back to work, remember? You've had your two weeks' holiday."

As he said the word 'holiday' he smirked at her. Seeing she had spent the last fortnight being repeatedly whipped, humiliated and gangbanged it was hardly an appropriate word. But he was right that her two weeks leave from Palmersons was over. Was he really going to allow her to return to work? Her heart leapt. She sat up, staring intently at his face, wondering if he meant it.

"Get your clothes on!"

He had set out clothes for her. Charlotte let out her breath in a silent sigh of relief. Normal working clothes, just as she would have chosen herself, a cream silk blouse and a smart narrow skirt suit. He really was letting her go back. She felt stunned, she could hardly believe it. So it was over, he was letting her go? She felt the strangest mix of emotions.

"No underwear, of course."

So he wasn't letting her go entirely, he was just letting her go back to work. She felt almost relieved. Carl unbuckled her neck-cuff and quickly she busied herself getting dressed and tidying her hair. Her full breasts strained against the silk, obviously naked, her nipples very visible, but she put the jacket on and buttoned it up. She looked perfectly normal, no one would ever know.

"A bit of make-up I think. You know the style." He was looking at her, that unpleasant smile curling his lips. He was holding out a make-up bag: dark kohl, dark shadow for her eyes, scarlet glossy lipstick.

"But… it won't look appropriate for work…" she said, hesitantly.

"Don't argue with me, Charlotte, just do it."

With trembling fingers Charlotte painted her face, then looked again at her reflection in the full length mirror. Her cheeks coloured. Again that whore's face gazed back at her, wide-eyed.

"Come on, we've got to go."

She followed him down the stairs, mincing a little in the heels he had handed to her. They weren't as ridiculously high as the ones she'd worn at the Sinclair manor, but they were still a good four inches, far higher than she would choose for herself. She wondered what Mr. Palmerson was going to think of her, dressed like this. It would be so embarrassing, to see his eyes flit over her body as she was sure they would. But still, it was better to be going to work looking like a call-girl than not going to work at all.

Carl handed her a drink of juice and a roll. It felt strange to be totally unfettered, to be able to eat and drink using her hands.

"Oh, mustn't forget your injection."

She dutifully bent over, her skirt falling around her face, her naked bottom ready for the needle. Carl jabbed it unceremoniously into her buttock. Charlotte wondered again what the injections were for; she'd been receiving them since the second day at the Sinclairs. Was it medicine? But she didn't feel ill, apart from the tiredness from spending so many nights being used, she felt rather gloriously well.

The journey felt strange, too. Carl drove, and she sat next to him in the passenger seat. She felt almost like a free woman again.

At the door to Palmersons he said simply,

"See you soon," and left her.

Charlotte took a deep breath and walked up the stairs to the office.

Chapter Eleven

She wasn't late, but everybody else seemed to be there already, the secretaries bustling about with files and tea as always, a hum of before-work chatter as everyone shared their stories of what they'd got up to at the weekend. Mrs. Hodges, the oldest of the secretaries and a secret power in the firm, turned, about to greet her. Her eyes took in the heels and the lipstick; and her mouth pursed into pinched disapproval.

"Miss. Summerfield. Did you have a good holiday?"

Her voice was not friendly.

"Yes, thank you," Charlotte replied, trying not to meet her eyes.

She looked at her desk and then peered closer. None of her things were on it any more. Her photo of Mummy and Daddy was gone, in its place was a photo of Kylie, bent slightly over showing her bum to best advantage. Someone was sitting in her chair but she couldn't see his face as he was bending down, busy opening a low drawer.

"What's going on, where are my things?"

The head bobbed up.

It was Alistair.

Of all the people she didn't much like at Palmersons, Alistair was the one Charlotte disliked the most. He was her direct subordinate, but he seemed to have a problem taking orders from a woman. He was forever ignoring her suggestions, and going his own way, even when she'd carefully explained to him that she had already tested out the alternative strategies. And the week before her 'holiday' she had found out that he had been going behind her back to the managing director. Even worse, he had presented her own good ideas as his own.

"Alistair. What are you doing at my desk?"

She could hear the rising note of hysteria in her voice, but was unable to control it.

Alistair just smirked.

"I think you'll find it's my desk now. Besides, the MD wants to see you in his office. Straightaway. Pronto."

He smirked again, then deliberately looked her up and down, his eyes lingering on her heels and sluttily made-up face, before coming to hover at the height of her chest.

"Aren't you a bit warm with that jacket on?"

He knows, thought Charlotte furiously, he knows I'm not wearing a bra. She was indeed far too hot, but she had no intention of taking that jacket off. How does he know? she asked herself. Unless Carl…

"Miss. Summerfield. My office please. Now."

It was Mr. Palmerson himself.

"Told you so," muttered Alistair under his breath, grinning even more nastily and then bobbing back down behind his desk. My desk! thought Charlotte, thoroughly confused and upset. She walked past Alistair with as much dignity as she could muster and in through the open door of Mr. Palmerson's office.

"Ah, Miss. Summerfield. Kindly come in. You may close the door behind you."

He was sitting behind his desk in his comfortable leather armchair. A heavily built man in his early sixties, with thick grey-black hair and rather sallow skin, flaccid jowls drooping at either side of his mouth so he resembled a bloodhound. Next to him, a few feet away, sitting on the chair which was normally on this side of the desk, was Carl. Charlotte gaped at him.

"Shut your mouth, dear, it looks ridiculous like that. You're not a fish. And take off that jacket," said Mr. Palmerson.

Charlotte looked from Carl to the MD, then back again to Carl.

"But… what…?"

"My dear," Palmerson's voice was beginning to sound exasperated. "Kindly do as you are told!"

Slowly Charlotte unbuttoned the jacket, then paused, uncertain. Her employer jerked his head in a gesture of impatience, and she slipped out of it. She tried not to look down, tried not to see what she knew he could see perfectly well, her dusky nipples, erect again though God knows why, pushing hard against the pale silk. She saw him swallow.

"Now pull up your skirt."

Charlotte just gazed at him. She understood now what was going on. Carl had betrayed her, he had told her she was going back to work, but he had obviously told her employers at least some of what had been happening. Mr. Palmerson knew full well that she was naked under the skirt. She might have known that Carl wasn't about to let her go back to her normal life.

"Pull up your skirt!"

The barking voice was coloured now with anger, transporting Charlotte straight back to her role of obedient slut. She took hold of the hem and pulled folds of fabric up, revealing her naked thighs, then her hairless silken labia. Mr. Palmerson's eyes bulged. She had always had the feeling that Carl had enslaved and abused other girls before her, now she felt sure that Mr. Palmerson, on the other hand, had never been in this position of abusive power before.

He stared at her pussy, as though he hadn't quite believed what he'd evidently been told.

"Spread your fuck lips for him, holster." Carl's voice this time.

Still looking at the older man, Charlotte parted her labia, revealing her swollen clitoris and cunt already shining wet with fuck juices.

Mr. Palmerson swallowed again.

"I would never have believed it. She always seemed such a nice young lady."

"Just an act, Sir. As you can see, she's a whore, now. She'll do anything you want, anything at all. She's perfectly willing and already rather skilled."

"Strip!" It was Palmerson speaking, but his voice had changed. All remaining politeness and tentativeness had evaporated. It was as though now he was convinced that Carl's words were correct he felt free to follow his most base desires.

"I said, STRIP!"

With trembling fingers Charlotte unbuttoned her blouse, and let it fall to the floor.

Palmerson looked at the half naked girl in front of him. Her naked tits were superb, he would never have guessed quite how good they were until today, for she had always dressed rather demurely, except for those short silky skirts. They were pert and full, rather large in fact, the hard nipples a dark, dusky pink. Suddenly he could almost imagine how they'd feel against his cock…

"Your skirt!"

She began to unzip it, and it slipped down, revealing that gorgeous hairless pussy. His cock was rock hard. He hadn't wanted to fuck a girl so much for years. There was something intoxicating about a female who'd let you bully her into doing just what you wanted. For he knew he was bullying her. Carl had said she was willing, and presumably she must be, for she was obeying his commands without resistance, but he could see her flushed and embarrassed face, she wasn't smiling confidently like one of those London strippers he occasionally watched, she looked humiliated. No, somehow she'd been coerced into this situation. It was that look of bullied innocence that made his cock so hard. He wasn't interested in tarts, but this one was a wholly different creature. And his to fuck! He could hardly believe his luck. He unbuttoned his flies and his cock sprang out, ready for action. It hadn't tasted fresh flesh for years, until today Mr. Palmerson had been a faithful husband, but he instantly decided all that was going to change. He pushed his chair back from the desk.

"Come here. Kneel."

She was evidently used to pleasing men, because no sooner was she kneeling at his feet than she began to fellate him, licking his penis with exquisite tongue-touching that soon had him leaning back, gasping. She began to dive her head over his organ, taking him deeper into her throat with each dip of her head, until finally her lips were right up against his testicles every time she took him inside her. Back and forth worked her pretty little head, Harold Palmerson lay back moaning softly; it was the first time he had ever been deep-throated and he was loving it.

Too soon he came, jetting his load deep inside her in a long orgasm that shook him right down to his shoes. The slut sat back, licking her glossy red lips like a cat that's been eating cream.

"Did she do a good job?" Carl's voice. "When she fails to please, it's a good idea to punish her. Though of course, you may wish to punish her anyway, just for fun."

Just for fun. The words hung in the air between the two men. Harold understood what the younger man was telling him: he could do what he wanted with this girl, no holds barred. He didn't need an excuse, he could whip her just because he wanted to. His spent cock twitched in his lap.

"She did quite well, but it could have been better," he lied, smiling, his voice almost asking permission for what he wanted to do. Carl smiled back at him, knowing full well the whore had done a superlatively good job.

"How would you like her arranged for the beating then?" he said, instantly validating the older man's desire to see the girl suffer. "Bent over your chair perhaps? That'd be a good position should you wish to use one of her holes afterwards."

One of her holes. Harold began to sweat. His wife had always turned down his early requests for anal intercourse, and after a while he'd given up asking. Now he had a beautiful girl who seemed quite willing to do whatever he wanted. Or at any rate, if she wasn't willing she had the good sense not to say so. But first, he was going to whip her. Oh yes. He stood up and perched on the desk to watch the younger man strap the girl into place, bent almost double over the back of his plump leather chair, her wrists bound towards the front feet, her ankles, still perched on their high heels, to the back. Her breasts hung down, exposed and vulnerable, like swaying melons. On sudden impulse he reached under her and squeezed them hard, making the poor girl whimper. At that he felt a moment's hesitation but the combination of a reassuring smile from Carl, and the girl's complete lack of resistance or protest, gave him the confidence he needed. He took her two sweet nipples and pinched them as hard as he could between his thumbs and forefingers. She cried out in pain, and he realised his cock was already growing hard again.

"Look at this," said Carl, gesturing towards the girl's pussy.

Harold walked round behind her and looked. The whore was so wet with fuck juices that they were beginning to ooze down onto her soft thighs. At the realisation that this slut was actually aroused by pain, a sort of dam burst inside Harold Palmerson. He reached beneath the beautiful fragile body and began again to manhandle the lovely breasts, pinching the nipples again and again and again, heedless of her cries, for now he saw that her cunt grew wet with fuck honey faster than her cheeks grew wet with tears.

Carl dipped into his briefcase and offered Harold a choice of implements for administering discipline. Harold mused over the cats and whips, feeling the hard leather, wondering what sound it would make as it contacted firm flesh. And what sound the girl would make…

"Or you could use your belt," said Carl, "that's one of my favourite ways to beat a whore, it's so personal, somehow."

Harold's cock stiffened further in his underpants. He knew

exactly what Carl meant. He unbuckled his belt, and lifted it high, paused for a second, then brought it down on the sweet round buttocks so meekly presented to him. Slap! The girl yelped.

"Would you like to gag her?"

"No. I told my staff what you'd told me about her, they'll all understand what's happening. Do some of the more uppity females good to hear this one getting taken down a few pegs."

He brought the belt down again, harder than before. Slap! And again. Slap! The girl was wriggling around, trying to evade the blows and it was quite amusing to watch her, for strapped like that she couldn't shift more than an inch. That didn't stop her trying. The now red buttocks were jiggling as she tried desperately to escape her punishment. Slap! Her yelps were louder now, and he was sure Mrs. Hodges could hear every cry. Good. That old bitch was far too big for her boots. Let her think it might be her turn next. SLAP! He brought down the belt as hard as he could, and the girl's head jerked as she screamed. Suddenly he realised he wanted to see her tears.

" Could you take over?"

"Certainly, Sir, my pleasure."

He watched from behind as Carl continued where he had left off, noticing how expertly the man landed the belt in a circle of blows that spiralled ever closer to the whore's genitals. He had strapped her legs far enough apart for her pussy lips to be quite visible, and now he brought the belt up hard on her labia. SLAP! Her head jerked up again, and her scream was even louder than before. Harold moved round to the side of her.

The girl's long hair hung over her face. He bunched it in one hand and peered at her. Her cheeks were wet with floods of tears and she had evidently bitten her lip; a large drop of scarlet blood was gathering, about to drip. He bent his head to hers, and licked it away, savouring the metallic taste of her. Then he sat back, still holding her hair away from face, and watched the way the pain clenched her pretty features each time the belt struck. He reached underneath her again, to fondle those sweet firm breasts, noticing with pleasure how quickly the nipples grew hard under his touch. He stroked very gently, deliberately arousing her, circling each nipple with a sure touch until she began to moan softly, in between her yelps of pain. Then he watched Carl carefully, so that he knew exactly when the next blow would land, and as the belt lashed flesh yet again he pinched and pulled the sweet nipples down so hard that the girl would have screamed even without the cruel belt. His cock felt like rock in his trousers. He had to have her, now.

Carl seemed perfectly attuned to his needs, for as soon as he raised a hand the younger man stopped the beating and moved aside.

"Do you want me to lubricate her anus?"

Harold nodded heavily, impatient to be thrusting into the perfect body that was so completely at his disposal. Carl sprayed a mist of cool fluid over the tight hole, and stepped aside. Harold pressed his burning cock against the puckered flesh and, with pleasure so intense it dissolved into pure joy, he felt his glans slide steadily into the tender young meat.

She was moaning now, and he could tell he was hurting her and arousing her at the same time. Good. That was just what he wanted. She was very tight, not surprising considering she had so recently been a virgin in both holes, but he kept up a relentless pressure and as she whimpered and gasped the full length of his penis slipped inside her. He looked down, triumphant, when his greying pubes rubbed up against her silken buttocks, and then he began to fuck her.

At first he was quite gentle. He understood she was valuable merchandise and he didn't want to risk damaging her. But, like a man test driving an expensive motor, his

171

confidence grew steadily, so that by the time he came, two minutes later, he was pounding into her as vigorously as if he had been using her cunt.

After Carl had had her too, Charlotte was untied, and ordered to the bathroom adjoining the office to clean herself up. When she returned Mr.Palmerson handed her a small pile of clothes.

"Get dressed. This is your new uniform. As I expect you saw, Alistair has taken over your former responsibilities, but don't worry my dear, we still have a place for you in the firm."

He was leering at her expectantly.

Charlotte looked at the garments, her eyes widening in disbelief. A miniscule black skirt, a frilly white apron with a bib, a black satin suspender belt and fishnet stockings. And a little white maid's cap.

"That's right," Mr. Palmerson was smiling broadly now in evident pleasure, "You're going to be our new tea girl."

As she hesitated he snapped impatiently, "Well get them on! Hurry yourself, slut!"

He's enjoying using that word, thought Charlotte mutinously. But she did as she was told. First she fastened the slinky suspender belt around her slim hips, then pulled on the fishnets. Both men were watching her closely, and she couldn't help herself, she moved with care, trying to be as erotic as possible in this reverse striptease. Next, the short skirt. So short in fact that even standing up it barely covered her sex lips, and as soon as she sat down, or bent over, her pussy was revealed. Then came the apron. The bib was tiny; it covered the central area of her chest, but her large breasts poked out either side. A less discreet garment it was hard to imagine. Finally the maid's cap. She swept her hair up onto her head and pinned it and the cap in place.

"And you can put your shoes back on," said Mr. Palmerson.

She slipped the black stilettos back on her feet. They looked far more appropriate with this outfit than with her own clothes.

She stood facing the two men when she had finished, waiting whilst they surveyed her, seeing their eyes linger on her breasts and thighs. She felt dirty just from the touch of their eyes.

"Very good," said Mr. Palmerson, "Yes, very nice indeed. You certainly won't be needing these any more." And he threw her blouse and skirt to Carl, who chucked them into the bin.

"Right, off you go. Go round the office, see who wants tea, make them some nice warming cuppas."

Charlotte looked at him in horror. She opened her mouth to speak, but no words came out; she couldn't think of anything to say. So she turned on her heel, and walked carefully out of the room. As she shut the door behind her she could hear the two men laughing.

The first desk was May's. May was a pretty young woman with two small children, she came in part time, working a job share with Sandra who did the afternoon shift. As Charlotte approached her desk she pretended to be busy with work.

"Would you like a cup of tea?" Charlotte asked, her voice a barely audible whisper.

"Er, no thanks," May replied brightly, not looking up.

The next desk was her own. Now occupied by the hateful Alistair. As she moved towards it she could feel eyes upon her. She was sure that behind her back every one in the office was gawping at her, including respectable May. But Alistair was doing as May had done, busying himself with his work, not looking up.

"Would you like a cup of tea?" she asked, and again her voice came out tiny and thin and far away.

"Pardon?" he looked up at her, grinning broadly at the

sight of her ridiculous clothing and her naked displayed breasts.

"Would you like a cup of tea?" she managed to speak a little louder.

"I think what you mean to ask is, 'Would you like a cup of tea, Sir?' isn't it?"

His voice had a nasty edge to it that Charlotte didn't like. Blushing she repeated the question.

"Would you like a cup of tea, Sir?"

"Yes please, whore. And show me your cunt whilst you're about it."

Bright red with shame, Charlotte lifted her skirt to reveal her hairless fuck lips.

"No, whore, not just your twat. Show me your cunt. Spread yourself so that I can see your front fuck hole."

Charlotte just stood there, numb and shaking.

"GO ON!" he barked at her, so loud that she jumped. She reached down, and spread herself, not looking down, not looking at his face, looking up at the fluorescent light, seeing the dust that had gathered above the casing, seeing the fly that had somehow got caught inside and was even now beating its tiny wings in a futile attempt to escape.

Something prodded at her clitoris. Now she did look down, to see Alistair grinning as he prodded her flesh with a plastic ruler, batting her clit from side to side.

"What a big swollen clitoris. My my, you are having fun. Is your cunt big too, or are you still nice and tight? Oh, nice and tight I see." He had thrust two fingers into her and wiggled them around, then abruptly pulled them out and wiped them on her leg. "Now, get me that tea." And with that he went back to work.

Charlotte went round the rest of the office. The women largely ignored her, like May, they didn't even want to see her. The men, on the other hand, were clearly enjoying her new role. Each one touched her pussy or breasts, or remarked on the size of her tits. They took so naturally to

174

their new positions of superiority and abusive power that she couldn't help wondering if they had been thinking of her in these crude terms all the time she'd been working there, but just hadn't had the confidence to articulate it before.

She made the tea and took it round, again subject to invasive fondles, pokes and pinches. When she had put the cup on Alistair's desk he reached up with his left hand and grabbed her right breast, continuing to write and not looking at her, just squeezing her tit hard, as though it was an udder. Charlotte bit her lip to keep the tears from falling. When he stopped she retreated, bruised and humiliated. But where was she to go? She no longer had a desk.

Plucking up all her courage she knocked on the MD's door. Mr. Palmerson's voice called out, "Enter!" and she opened the door and peered in nervously. He was sitting at his desk, evidently in deep conversation with Carl. His face was pink, and she could tell he was still sexually excited.

"Well?"

"Please, Sir... where do I go? I mean, I've made everyone tea that wanted it, and I haven't got a desk anymore." Angry with herself as emotion clouded her voice she bit her lip again, "So where do you want me to sit?"

"Sit? I don't think I want you to sit anywhere. But yes, between duties you obviously need a place to wait till you're next required. Hmm, I'll give the matter some thought. As you are now so decorative I obviously want you on display... but where would be best... well, for now, that desk will do."

He gestured towards a surveyor's desk to the side of the room. It was tilted to make drawing large plans more convenient and comfortable. Charlotte looked at it dumbly.

"Well get on it then! Carl, could you arrange her please?"

"On your back, knees apart, ankles together. You can hold the sides with your hands if you need to. Yes, I know there isn't room for your head, that doesn't matter, it's your tits

175

and cunt we like to look at."

Charlotte clung to the sides of the desk. Her legs were fully spread, her knees wide apart, but her feet were together, resting on the ledge that spanned the bottom edge of the desk. The top edge of the desk was at her shoulder height, so there was nothing to support her head. It lolled down, out of sight of the two men. All she could see was the cream featureless wall.

"Excellent. We won't strap you like that, because that is the position you are to assume without being ordered to, whenever your services are not required. Is that understood?"

"Yes, Sir."

The men resumed their conversation.

"So you've been filming her?"

"Yes. It's one of the best ways to make money from a submissive. After all, you don't have to pay them anything," at this both men chuckled, "and there are no problems with the legalities because they'll let you do anything you want. We've got hours of footage of her being fucked and whipped already, some really nice close ups of her being penetrated. And she's very young and healthy. She's got years of work ahead of her, poor little thing."

They laughed again.

"And you say she's been having the injections everyday for the last week? How soon will they take effect?"

"Only a couple more days."

"Good. It really will be rather amusing. Save us a bit on the provisions bill as well!"

The men laughed even more heartily than before. What were they talking about? She couldn't begin to guess.

CHAPTER TWELVE

Two days later Charlotte woke at dawn to find that her breasts were swollen and hard. They felt like two painful rocks. She was only tethered by her collar, so she moved carefully past the snoring Carl and over to the mirror. She couldn't believe what she saw. Her breasts were huge, the skin taut. She looked as though she'd had them stuffed with silicone. Had they somehow operated on her in the night? She knew it was impossible, but she searched her skin for scars, anyway. But there were no marks.

Her newly massive tits were exquisitely painful to the touch. Even stroking them hurt. Charlotte shivered: what if Carl or Harold decided to peg them when they were in this condition. Her eyes pricked with tears just at the thought of it.

There was a noise behind her, and she turned to see Carl sitting up in bed, his hair ruffled from sleep. He was smiling at her, or rather, at her breasts.

"Ah, I see your milk has come in."

"My what...?" She was nonplussed.

"Your milk, little Charlotte. That's what the injections have been for. I didn't tell you because I wanted it to be a surprise. You know how much we enjoy humiliating you. Those injections, they're hormones. A careful balance of artificial oestrogens and plenty of progesterone. Your tits are hard because they're full of milk. It was Sir Jonathan's idea, actually. 'Carl,' he said to me, 'there's nothing humiliates a slut as much as turning her into a milk slave.' And you are Harold's tea girl, after all," he added, with a nasty snigger.

"But... but... they hurt." Stupidly, it was all Charlotte could think to say.

"So what? We enjoy hurting you. Anyway, they'll get softer in a few days. Come here."

Reluctantly she walked back over to the bed. He started

to stroke her huge tits, quite gently, rubbing his fingers over her nipples which were now darker and larger than usual. Suddenly she felt an intense tingling sensation in both breasts. It hurt, yet it felt pleasant at the same time.

"Oh," she said, surprised. He looked up at her smiling, and began to pull on her breast, as though squeezing it down towards her nipple. Tiny globules of white liquid formed on the tip, and then grew to a steady trickle. Carl dipped his head to her breast and drank. The feeling of his strong lips milking her breast was deeply arousing but also humiliating beyond anything Charlotte had previously experienced. She felt like a used animal. He lifted his head, creamy white milk dotted on his chin.

"Delicious. You must be a Jersey cow to produce such fine quality milk. I'll have to see about getting a milking machine for you." He laughed at his own joke.

He made her dress in her new work clothes and drove her through town. Charlotte stared straight in front of her, trying not to see the leering faces and rudely pointing hands. It was hot again, and Carl wound down her window. They were stopped at traffic lights, when to Charlotte's shocked embarrassment the man in the van next to them actually reached down to squeeze her exposed left tit. She squealed in pain; they were so tender.

"Looks more like a cow than a girl, don't she mate? Nice udders on her!" he called out over her head to Carl.

"You're not wrong. If you want to fuck her, just give me a call; it can be arranged." And as Charlotte blushed furiously he reached over her to hand his card to the ogling driver.

"Thanks mate. Do you charge a lot for her?"

"If you have a good sized cock and you don't mind being filmed, you can fuck her for free."

"Fuck that for free? Can't say fairer than that. I'll be round pronto, I'll bang her witless with ten inches of meat, I'm your man."

When they reached the office Carl left her to go in alone. She tried to slip past the desks without Alistair noticing her, but no chance.

"Woo hoo, what have we here, look at the tits on it!"

Charlotte stood, waiting whilst he stood up and inspected her body. His eyes were bulging in excitement, like some adolescent looking at Playboy. When he squeezed her breasts she yelped in pain. Dots of milk appeared again on her nipples.

"Go make me a cup of tea, udder slut!"

Charlotte scurried off and made the tea. She looked in the fridge for the milk, but there wasn't any there. She wondered what to do. Was she allowed out to buy some? And if she was allowed out, she could hardly go out on the streets like this. She shivered at the prospect.

She took Alistair his tea as it was.

"I'm sorry, there's no milk in the fridge."

He stared at her, a slight smile hovering around his mouth, his eyes knowing.

"Address me as 'Sir', slut!"

Charlotte swallowed.

"I'm sorry, Sir, there's no milk in the fridge."

"I know. We don't need it now we've got a milk slave do we? You really must be stupid, Charlotte, no wonder they thought this job of making tea more suitable for you. Bend over my desk."

Charlotte did as she was told, her arms folded flat under her, resting her aching bosoms upon them.

"Not like that, you stupid slut, I need to get at your udders!"

Suddenly understanding what he had in mind Charlotte froze in horror. Alistair just tugged her into position. She had no will left with which to resist.

She was standing now bent at the hips, her full breasts hanging about six inches from the table. Alistair slid his mug of tea under her right tit. She could feel the heat of the steam rising from it, condensing wetly on her breast. He started to pull on her tit, slipping his hand over the flesh as though kneading it towards her nipple. At the same moment she felt that familiar slightly painful tingling as her milk let down, and then a steady, regular squirting sound. Looking between her breasts she saw the jet of milk spurt into his cup as he continued to paw her udders.

Poor Charlotte was hot with shame. One of the other office juniors was passing, and stopped to watch the show. The way Charlotte was standing meant her skirt was lifted at the back, and as it was so miniscule her fuck lips were exposed. As he watched Alistair milking the humiliated girl the other young man, Charlie, reached between her labia to stroke her clitoris.

"He he he... dirty little whore! She's gagging for it Al, she's sopping wet."

"I'll stuff her then, nothing like a shag to get the day off to a good start."

The men changed places. Seconds later Charlotte felt the hot tip of Alistair's cock pressing against her vagina. He entered her swiftly and began to fuck her with long, slow thrusts. He had enough milk in his tea, so Charlie moved the cup out of the way and replaced it with a plastic memo tray that reached under both her breasts. The man inside her shifted his grip from her hips to her tits and held on tightly, squeezing her tender breasts in time with his thrusts. He was far rougher now, and each time he ground his cock hard against her cervix he yanked on her udders, so that each thrust was accompanied by the noise of milk spurting into the tray.

Charlotte could no longer find words adequate to express the shame and humiliation she now felt. When she realised her treacherous body was becoming aroused and would soon climax she felt quite lost. She was disgusted with herself. There was clearly no degrading or abhorrent practice these men could inflict on her without her enjoying it. She had been gangbanged, beaten, whipped and tormented, her anus used as though it was a vagina, her mouth and face used as though they were nothing more than receptacles for semen, and now her breasts were being used like udders whilst a man she hated casually penetrated her vagina. To undergo such treatment and still be aroused must mean they were right, she really was a slut, a whore, quite unworthy of the respect of normal women. At the thought that she had become nothing more than a toy to gratify her owner's every depraved sexual whim Charlotte came, in a huge blasting orgasm that made her scream with passion. Inside her body, Alistair felt his penis squeezed in delicious intense ripples by her well-toned cunt muscles. The slut was a delightful fuck. He'd been wanting to enjoy her since her first day at work and it was wonderful to turn the tables on her so completely; she'd been such a stuck-up bossy bitch. He climaxed, squirting a big load of sperm deep inside her; he hadn't had a woman for several days. It was good to think she'd spend the rest of the working day with his come trickling down her thighs.

Charlie eagerly took his place.

There was a big meeting due that afternoon in Palmerson's boardroom. Of course, when it came to break time it was up to Charlotte to supply the tea. She had received her instructions from the MD, and as she walked round the chatting business men, enduring no end of fondlings and pinchings of her breasts and buttocks, as she proffered refreshments she had to ask:

"Would Sir like milk in that? Would Sir like cow milk or whore milk?"

Some of the men chose cow milk, but most chose whore milk. Not, thought Charlotte, because they really want to drink my milk, but because they want to see me milked like an animal. Alistair was already a dab hand at milking her, so when the men's pawing hands failed to produce results he would come bounding over and do it for them. He had a permanent grin on his face, and, Charlotte noticed, a permanent bulge in his trousers.

Of course, after the break the men were too aroused to settle down to work again with no release, so Charlotte was ordered to crawl around under the table, sucking off all the bulging cocks. There were so many men, that by the time the meeting drew to a close she was sticky with spunk, her throat sore from so much shafting, her lips bruised from the repeated stretchings and her nostrils full of the sour taste of ejaculate. When Harold Palmerson announced the meeting closed she breathed a sigh of relief, that was the end of it, then. But of course, she was wrong. They pulled her out and began to fuck her, as eager as if they hadn't had a woman for years. They were so impatient to enjoy her that she ended up crouched on the table, one man lying beneath her using her cunt, another plundering her asshole, whilst a third drove deep into her throat. Two other men reached their heads under her and clamped their mouths tightly over her nipples, squeezing her tender breasts and suckling her ferociously to enjoy her milk. In this manner she pleased five or even six men at one time, an impressive use of human resources, as the Personnel Manager remarked as he splattered semen on her pretty face.

It was a bedraggled Charlotte that Tom took home that evening. Carl had delegated the task of fetching her to Tom, for in her filthy, sex-stained state he had no intention of letting her in his car. So she spent the journey home trussed on the floor of Tom's windowing cleaning and decorating van, bumped around between cans of paint and bucketfuls of wallpaper paste. When they finally reached home, Tom hosed her down in the yard, in the same fashion as when she visited the Sinclair Manor. Charlotte knew she was, now, every bit as much of a cock holster as the girls Sir Jonathan trained.

In the days that followed, day upon day of mockery from Alistair, day upon day of servicing every cock in the office, and every cock of Carl's cronies, day upon day of having her breasts milked by whoever happened to be around, there was one tiny ray of hope that Charlotte clung to. In a few days' time her mother and Henry would return from their holiday. How Henry would react to finding Carl and his friends staying in his house and gangbanging his wife's daughter, Charlotte couldn't imagine, but she was certain he would rescue her. But although intellectually she knew for sure that help was on the way, and that her reduction in status from free woman to abused sex toy could not last much longer, still, she could not emotionally feel this to be true. The change in her life had been so overwhelming and total that her previous existence now seemed like a dream, quite unreal, and the prospect of returning to the life she used to enjoy felt almost fantastical. The person she had been, the woman she had been, no longer existed, and it seemed as unlikely that she could change back into her former self as it would be for a flower to retreat into a bud.

Tom watched Carl with growing resentment as he gave the men their instructions for the day. The slut was going to make Carl a packet, that much was obvious. But it was he, Tom, who had found her. Without his phone call to Carl, when he'd had her bound helpless and naked on her bed, Carl wouldn't have had a taste of the money or a taste of the slut's cunt. And now Carl had completely taken over. Tom hadn't even fucked her for the last couple of days, he'd been too busy running errands for Carl. And when the money from the new website, with its downloadable videos of young Charlotte getting fucked in all her holes and whipped till her arse was red raw, came pouring in, as it surely would, who was going to get the lion's share of it? Carl, that's who. Tom was starting to wish he'd never made that phone call. What it was about Carl that made the stupid bitches so enamoured that they would actually consent to becoming a sex slave he had no idea. He couldn't fathom it at all. And whatever it was, it was a skill he certainly didn't share. But fuck it, he could just have raped her, because another thing he didn't share was Carl's insistence that all the sluts they filmed should be willing. He could have called up some of his other mates and gang raped her and filmed it and sold it on the web, then it would have been him making loads of lolly, instead of that arrogant bastard Carl. Suddenly Tom was struck by a thought of such brilliance that it illuminated the whole of his small, dim brain. He could still do it. Of course, she wasn't a virgin any more, but that hardly mattered. He could steal Charlotte away and use her to make his own movies. With him, Tom, as the big-dicked star, covering her in reams of spunk. Hooded of course, he didn't want any trouble. He doubted that Charlotte would be willing, but who cared? He'd steal her away, get a gang of his mates round, and make their own video. He could dump her back here when they'd finished with her, leave it to that tosser Carl to mop up her tears. Tom rubbed his sweaty hands in anticipation. Cunt and cash, his two main wants in life, and he was going to be getting both of them.

Tom bided his time over the next few days, waiting until the moment was right. Finally his patience paid off. Rich was away, and so Tom got the job of feeding Sheba. As the bitch ate up the drugged meat Tom could barely suppress his excitement. He'd already put in a few phone calls to some mates who he knew could be trusted. Poor girl, he thought with a nasty grin, she didn't know what was in store for her, but she wouldn't be forgetting it in a hurry. Now he just needed tonight to be one of the nights when Charlotte slept in the utility room in the bitch's basket. If Carl took her to bed, he'd have to call it off and wait for another opportunity.

He was in luck. Carl had had a long day, and had already fucked his pliant slave several times. Now he just wanted

184

to sleep. Tom settled the slut in the basket, delighting the stupid creature by giving her some chocolate to eat. Of course, it was drugged as well, the dose very carefully worked out. He wanted her sleepy enough to be easy to abduct, but not so zonked that she could only stagger. Of course, he could have carried her to the van, it wouldn't have been that much of a problem, but the real reason he didn't want her too drugged was that it was her struggles and pleas for mercy that would make his video exciting. No one got turned on by seeing a bunch of men shagging a lump of unconscious flesh.

The chocolate was very bitter, but Charlotte wolfed it down anyway. She hadn't had any chocolate since the morning Tom had appeared at her window, weeks ago. She smiled ruefully to herself. If men only realised just how hooked girls are on chocolate, she thought, there wouldn't be any need for whippings. Tie them up and deprive them of chocolate for a week, they'd suck anybody's dick after that, as long as they got a mars bar in return. Not for the first time it crossed her mind how much happier a place the world would be if semen was chocolate flavoured. Surely the fact it wasn't, was proof that God was not kind, or if he was, he disapproved of fellatio.

She settled down to sleep, snuggling up to the warm, hairy body of the German Shepherd. She felt suddenly very drowsy, and within moments she was fast asleep.

Someone was tugging at her arm. She was trying very hard not to wake up, she felt sozzled with sleep, but they wouldn't leave her alone. She opened her mouth to tell them to sod off, her brain too fogged to remember that she was a slave now, but something was quickly stuffed into it, a thick gagging ball of fabric that tasted of male sweat. Then a sharp spasm of pain shot through her shoulder as her arm was yanked behind her. Rope was being twisted round her wrists, cutting tightly into her flesh. It prickled and scratched, some rough sort of twine. She struggled, but whoever it was dragged her out of the basket, pushed her down on her face and sat himself down on her buttocks, before resuming his binding of her arms.

She twisted her head to look up at him, but it was too dark to see properly. She had the impression he had something over his head, some sort of mask or hood. Charlotte was terrified. Now fully awake, she was instinctively sure that this wasn't just another part of her abuse and manhandling by Carl and his cronies. Oh, why didn't Sheba wake up? Usually the bitch would bark at the slightest disturbance, but not tonight, not the one time she was needed. Charlotte struggled bravely, but the man pinning her to the floor was far stronger, she didn't stand a chance.

He had her arms totally trussed behind her back now, and he'd pulled the twine so tight it really hurt, digging into her and pulling her arms back unnaturally far. Now he tied more twine to her bound wrists and brought two lengths of it down between her legs, then, rolling her over, up between her tits to her collar, threading it through and pulling it, hard. Charlotte squeaked miserably behind the gag as the harsh twine pulled deeply between her fuck lips, scraping against her clitoris and digging into the sensitive meat of her pudenda. The man chuckled. She realised then her assailant was someone she knew, the chuckle was so familiar, but she couldn't quite place it. But, when he stopped binding her, to brutally squeeze her breasts so hard that she started to cry with the pain, she at last recognised his touch. It was Tom.

Charlotte remembered then the occasional looks of resentment he'd given Carl. She'd guessed at the time that he was angry that having found her and manipulated her into compliance it was Carl who had become her master. Tom had wanted to share her with his boss, not hand her over so entirely. So now he was taking her away, God knew where, and God knew what he would do to her. Tom had always been particularly brutal. She was always able to recognise his fuckings, even when she'd been hooded, or taken from behind, because he used his long cock so unkindly, obviously enjoying making her suffer. The thought of him having free rein to abuse her, without the restraining influence of Carl and the other men, was terrifying.

He pulled her to her feet, tugging her not by her neck chain, but by a short loop of cord he'd attached low down, fastening it to the twine which cruelly parted her labia. When he tugged, the twine bit more deeply into her most delicate flesh. Tears of pain trickled down her cheeks. She had to get away. But how?

Tom unbolted the door and led her out into the night. It had been a mild evening after another scorching hot day, but now, in the dull grey hour before dawn, it was cold and damp, and her skin clenched immediately into goosebumps. He gave another cruel, sharp tug on the twine, and as the rough fibres sawed against her tender pussy it hurt so much she almost fainted.

He led her round the side of the house. His window cleaning van was parked on the driveway, and noiselessly he opened the back doors. He'd cleared most of his tools, and in the dim light Charlotte could just make out straps and manacles set into the floor of the van. He pulled her inside, pushed her down, and began strapping her in place. She was as helpless as a collector's butterfly as he pinned her as he wished.

First, a thick, wide collar of leather was strapped around her neck. Again he fastened the buckle so tightly that the edges of the strap cut into her chin. Her head thus immobilised against the cold metal floor of the van, he turned his attention to her legs; first her ankles, then her thighs just above the knee, were buckled down, wide apart. Her bound arms were pressing underneath her, horribly uncomfortable, pushing her buttocks slightly off the floor and scratching her skin with their rough bindings.

She wriggled, whimpering piteously, but only soft squeaks could escape the cloth gag which was now bunched, sodden with saliva, in her mouth. She was entirely helpless, he had her in his power, and could do whatever he wanted.

Tom stood over her. Even now she wouldn't have recognised his face, his ugly troll-like features more hideous than ever behind a stocking mask, but she was almost certain she had guessed his identity correctly. He started to undo his flies, and when his cock sprang out above her she knew for sure it was him, the long, curved length of him, the way his weapon was fatter at the tip than at the root.

He pulled again upon the twine that cut between her lips, yanking it repeatedly as he stroked his cock and as she moaned and wriggled in pain he showed his pleasure by splattering his thick sour semen all over her face and tits. Then he hurriedly zipped up his flies, scrambled to the front of the van and started the engine. Belatedly he had realised he was being foolish wasting time on sex when he needed to get away.

The van bumped under Charlotte's naked body as it rocketed down the driveway. A plumper woman would not have been in so much discomfort, but lithe Charlotte only carried fat where it appealed to male eyes; a little on her buttocks and plenty forming her tits, so her little body felt every judder of Tom's old van.

Suddenly they screeched to a halt, Charlotte's stiff collar cutting into her shoulders they stopped so suddenly. She heard Tom's door open and his footfalls on the gravel, then his voice, low and furious.

"Fuck, fuck, fuck, fucking arse, fucking cunt gates, fucking open, you fuckers!"

Charlotte almost grinned. Of course, the gates of the drive. They opened and closed automatically in the daytime, but at night they were electronically locked shut, an obvious security measure. Was Tom really so dim-witted that he hadn't thought to check it was possible to get out before he had abducted her? Charlotte thought he very likely was. What would he do now? It was too late to go back to the house and pretend nothing had happened. If he couldn't get the gates open...

"Get up you stupid bitch!"

She could hear the panic in his voice. She couldn't get up anyway, though he was unbuckling straps as he spoke she was still far from free. When he'd undone the last strap he didn't give her a chance to get up, he just pulled the twine, dragging her to her feet. Again Charlotte almost fainted, the white walls of the van going dim and grainy and a rising nausea in her throat...

He must have realised what he'd done, for he grabbed her chain instead, and pulled her out of the van. Abandoning it where it was, in front of the resolutely shut gates, he dragged Charlotte after him into the undergrowth next to the driveway. Brambles scratched at her breasts and thorns pricked at her feet as he pulled her uncaringly after him.

"That's far enough."

The voice was quiet, furious with the cold anger that is more deadly than hot passion. Tom swung around, yanking Charlotte's chain to bring her trembling naked body in front of him.

Carl stood there, a straining Sheba pulling on her leash. The dog was growling and snapping at the air.

"Release the whore." Again that quiet, cold voice.

"You let me be. It was me what found her, You got no right taking her over like that. I just want a little of what is rightfully mine."

"Charlotte, my dear, who do you wish to belong to? Myself? Or this moronic imbecile who doesn't even know how to open a pair of gates without setting off every alarm in the building in his attempt?"

Charlotte couldn't reply, her mouth was still stuffed with

the foul gag, but she pulled towards Carl, even though that made the twine cut again into the soft meat between her fuck lips, to let him know she wanted to be his.

"I don't give a fuck what the bitch wants!"

"So I see. In fact I see you don't show any concern at all for the slave, you ignorant man. Just because she's property doesn't mean you shouldn't treat her with some consideration. You're the sort who'd kick his dog or ride his horse into a sweat then leave it to shiver. A man isn't worthy of the name if he doesn't treat lesser creatures with compassion, whether they be bitch, or horse, or whores. Look at the state of her! I hate to think what she'd be like in a couple of weeks if you had your way. I ask you for the last time: let the girl go!"

"And what if I don't?"

Carl smiled.

"Simple. Either you release that bitch, or I will release this one."

As though she understood, Sheba growled again, a low, menacing sound. She certainly didn't look dopey now; Tom must have given her the wrong dose of the drug. Charlotte could feel the wetness of sweat on Tom's hot hands where they gripped her collar and arms.

"But you can't. If you let her go she'll savage the slut, too, then she'd be no use to either of us. Can't we come to some sort of deal?"

The voice was pathetic, wheedling, all bravado spent.

"We had a deal, Tom. You would have got your share, but you were just too greedy. Now you'll get nothing, and you'll never work for me again. And are you really so stupid you think Sheba would hurt Charlotte? They're bedfellows, you moron, Sheba thinks Charlotte is another bitch, just like her. And she's not far wrong, at that. But no matter, please keep holding her, I'm beginning to think I'd rather enjoy watching Sheba deal with you."

As he spoke he bent to undo the leash. Suddenly Tom

pushed Charlotte away from him, turned and ran.

Carl paused, counting softly under his breath, smiling grimly. Tom was struggling to scramble over the high garden boundary wall, looking quite ludicrous as he made repeated attempts to jump high enough. Carl waited until the man had got one leg up, then let Sheba free. She bounded the short distance and flew at him, just too late to pull him back, but judging by the screams, in plenty of time to give him several nasty bites on his flailing ankle.

If Charlotte had not been in such a piteous state she would probably have been amused to see the bullying Tom receive a taste of his own medicine. As it was she just stood there trembling, watching her assailant as Carl allowed him to flee.

"He'll be out of town by tomorrow night, and out of the county within the week. I don't suffer treachery lightly. In fact, I think I might alert some of my friends amongst the boys in blue to the problem. He's a nasty piece of work." Carl spoke with narrowed eyes, not looking at Charlotte. Perhaps he was talking more to himself than to her. He turned and looked down at her, and his expression told her that she must look as bruised and ill-treated as she felt.

"Get back in the van."

Back in the utility room he turned on the light. Charlotte was still bound with the coarse twine, and the pain between her legs was steadily deepening. If she hadn't been gagged she might have pleaded with her Master to release her, as it was she could only utter impotent little squeaks.

CHAPTER THIRTEEN

As he flicked his eyes over the slut's frail body, Carl felt anger rise in his gut. That bastard Tom had trussed her ridiculously tightly. And what had he used? Looked like some sort of garden twine, but thicker. Totally unsuitable for binding a girl, it had rubbed her skin raw in several places on her arms.

He ordered her up on the table, pressed her thighs apart and looked down at her spread pussy. Now he saw that there were two separate strands of twine passing between her labia. One strand had pulled to either side of her clitoris, and they had evidently rubbed against it when she moved, as well as pinching it between them. Her clit was red and swollen. It must be painful. Her fuck holes were both bisected by the line of twine, and here the two strands ran together. Each orifice showed signs of where the coarse fibres had rubbed. Poor slut!

Carl fetched a knife and carefully cut the cords, then the gag, pulling the sodden fabric from the girl's mouth. She was shaking, trembling like a leaf.

"Are you alright?"

"Yes. I'm a bit sore, though."

Her voice was steady. He fetched ice and wrapped it in a clean cloth and handed it to her. Charlotte perched on the edge of the table, pressing the icepack to her pussy. She was trembling less now, gradually calming down. Carl felt a renewed wave of fury at the troglodyte Tom. As a slave trainer he was used to having absolute power over the girls he seduced, and with that power came an acceptance of responsibility. That the submissives he enslaved were nowhere near his equals he took for granted, but that didn't mean they shouldn't be treated kindly, within the limits of the game. Lowlifes like Tom gave the trade a bad name. But still, he thought with satisfaction, it wouldn't be hard to track him down. He wouldn't get the chance to abduct a woman again.

Carl stroked the girl absent-mindedly. She was relaxing nicely, even sighing a little as he gently petted her breasts. He knew that in cases like this it was important to get a slut back to work as soon as possible, it didn't do to dwell on the 'what ifs' and 'maybes'. And anyway, he was erect already, and her role in life was to service cock.

He gestured for her to lie back on the table. Her pretty head with the long mane of glossy auburn curls rested near the edge, and as he undid his trousers his released cock brushed against her hair. He reached for her shoulders, and pulled her slender body further towards him, so that her head hung over the table edge, unsupported. Her breasts rose like sweet snowy peaks from the undulating plain of her naked body, and he noticed that in places the delicate skin was darkly speckled with red bruising where the cord had bound her, it had been tied so tightly. He lay his burning cock between her breasts, luxuriating in the smooth coolness of her fine flesh.

Slowly he started to thrust between her tits, holding them together, not cruelly, but very firmly. They were rich and ripe and firm, and the sensation of slipping his rod between them was delectable. Tiny pearls of milk appeared on her nipples as she became aroused. Her lips brushed against his testicles and he felt the sudden warmth of her little tongue lap tentatively as though in question.

"Suck my balls."

It was beyond delightful to feel the soft lips immediately open and perform as bidden. It was the first time he had used her totally unbound. Yes, this slut was thoroughly broken in and ready to be sold as planned.

Carl leant forwards, pulling his balls out of her mouth and resting his weight on the girl's slight body, thrusting between her gripped tits as though into another fuck hole. He brought his face down to her parted sex lips and began to lick the swollen nub of her clit that jutted invitingly towards him, spreading her labia wide open with the fingers of one hand so that her throbbing red button rose up to meet his tongue between them, holding her two nipples gripped in his other hand to keep her breasts tightly together around his shaft. He felt her pulsate and quiver underneath him, and when, moments later, she climaxed, she screamed in ecstasy. He thrust even harder, squeezing her tits hard together now, and as one of the most intense orgasms he had ever experienced surged through his body, he splattered the taut smooth belly with his load.

Carl scooped his semen from the slut's front and smeared it carefully over her face. Then he buckled her hands behind her back and fastened her chain to the pipes, gesturing that she should resume her sleep in the bitches' basket.

He came next morning to inspect her. Two of the men held Charlotte down on the lawn, each pinning a wrist to the ground, above her head, their other hands each holding an ankle, which they pulled far apart and up and high, almost level with her shoulders. The fierce sunlight glared down upon her exposed genitals, on what had been her most intimate and private parts, but could now be viewed and touched and probed by any of the men as they saw fit.

Her Master prodded her sore pussy with a smooth, glass rod.

"Hmmm. A little raw in places, but she'll be fine. Sunlight promotes healing, they say. I suggest you strap her like this for the rest of the day, it lets plenty of air get to the damaged skin. If anyone wishes to use her he'd better fuck her mouth or tits. And keep the Alsatian bitch away from her, else she'll no doubt be wanting a lick of that sweet scented pussy herself."

And so Charlotte spent the rest of the day pinned naked and spread on her mother's fine lawn. Around lunchtime she heard voices. It was the old gardener John Pearson and his grandson, Harry. One of Carl's men had stuck a little sign up next to her helpless body. She hadn't been able to see what it said, but now the gnome-like gardener read it aloud.

"Cunt and arsehole temporarily out of bounds. Please feel free to fuck mouth and tits or wank on any part of her."

"That'll do me, I like seeing her wrinkle up her posh little nose when I cover her face in my spunk. She hates it, you can tell, that's why I enjoy it so much. What about you, Harry, me lad?"

Harry quietly agreed that plastering the pretty slut's face with come was an 'ace' way to use her. The two men knelt by her head, beating themselves off till they splattered thick semen all over Charlotte's face and lips.

A few nights later Carl once again brought Charlotte to his room. Tethered to the four poster by the heavy iron chain, he fucked her ass roughly whilst she knelt on the bed, her hindquarters raised, her face resting on her forearms. Afterwards he held her in his arms, caressing her quite gently, occasionally pinching her nipples or clit for the sheer pleasure of hearing her moan and whimper, and feeling her slight body wriggle in helpless discomfort.

"I'm going to miss you, little Harlotte," his voice was surprisingly soft, but his words alarmed her.

"What do you mean? Are you going away?"

"I'm selling you, my dear slave. You're thoroughly broken in, you'll do anything your master tells you. We've made hours of videos of you being tormented and gang fucked, they are already bringing in a very healthy profit. You are no longer of use to me, except to make further profit by your sale, and so from tomorrow evening you will belong to a different man. I'm quite sure he'll enjoy owning you."

The softness she had thought she had heard in his voice had evaporated, now it was dry and mocking as usual.

"Who is he? My new Master, who is he?"

Carl chuckled.

"Oh, you'll find out soon enough. Tomorrow night, in fact."

Tomorrow night. Charlotte had lost count of the days, each one blurred into the others, one day of fucking and beating followed so hotly on the heels of the next. But she knew her mother and Henry were due home soon. If they arrived back before this new man took possession of her, she might still be freed. But if not, there seemed little chance that she would ever escape, for surely he would take her away, and how would anyone find her then?

In the morning the men packed away their things, setting Charlotte to clean the house on her hands and knees. In a couple of hours there was no sign they had ever been there, using the house as though it was their own. Except, of course, for Charlotte. Carl had told her that she could get dressed, but that, as before, she must not wear any underwear. Indeed, he told her, smiling lasciviously, to make quite certain she abided by this rule he had thrown out all her panties and bras.

He left her alone in her room to dress, and Charlotte checked the drawers. It was true: all her pretty pink and white cotton knickers and broderie anglaise bras had gone, not a single pair of panties remained. But the drawers were not empty. Leather corsets, black rubber suits with obscene holes to display tits and pussy, harnesses and manacles… her chest of drawers was stuffed with gear in which her new master could display, restrain and enjoy her.

"Ah, I see you've found your new clothes." Carl was standing in the doorway, again that amused, mocking tone souring his voice. "Come to think of it, why don't we pick out something for you to wear under your everyday clothes, I'm sure he'd find that most agreeable."

Carl rooted in amongst the fragrant heap of leather and rubberwear, finally selecting a leather harness. It looked oddly familiar, and Charlotte realised that it was identical to those worn by the Sinclair pony girls: leather straps framed the naked breasts, then went up, halter-style, to a deep leather collar, in the front of which was set a thick, steel ring. Another wide strap encircled the hips, finer straps reaching down from it to pull either side of her labia. It was like the black edging of a pair of panties with none of the fabric that covers the genitals. In this way, the wearer's fuck holes were both displayed and readily accessible.

He buckled her into it, then pushed her in front of the mirror. She blushed to see herself, for the leather supported her milk-heavy breasts just enough to push them up and forwards in a most provocative fashion, and her naked labia were equally enticing in their frame of narrow leather. She looked so obviously a sex slave, and even more so when he told her to gloss her lips with the scarlet lipstick.

Carl pulled out some ordinary clothes for her to wear on top; a tan suedette halter-neck top that neatly hid the leather harness collar, and a short black skirt.

She pulled them on, and looked in the mirror again. Her erect nipples showed through the fine suedette, she had again that look of high class whore. Carl reached up under her skirt and fingered her naked pussy lips, slipping his finger between them to assess her wetness.

"God, you are *such* a slut, you're *always* ready for a fuck," he drawled.

She flushed more deeply as his probing fingers jabbed into her cunt and anus.

"Lift up your skirt."

She did as he told her, and he pointed at the fine leather straps that lay tightly in the crease where her labia met her thigh.

"When you wait for him tonight, in this room, you must stand facing the door, naked except for this harness. Your legs should be about three feet apart, bent at the knee, so that your genitals lie open and ready for his inspection. You should pull your fuck lips under these leather straps, that will pin them back out of the way so that he can see your clitoris and cunt. Open and available. You should aim at all times to be as open and available as possible. Your body must be utterly accessible, always vulnerable to penetration. And so: no underwear. Legs never crossed, always a little apart. Hands behind you, out of the way. Nothing to impede to progress of cock into your owned flesh. Do you understand? You are nothing now, nothing but a collection of fuck holes, just a body to be enjoyed by whoever owns you. Your whole purpose in life is simply this: you are a sex toy, you exist to be penetrated."

As he spoke he pinned her labia behind the straps as he had described, and rubbed her clitoris in steady circles. Charlotte couldn't help but moan with arousal, and he laughed openly at her.

"Stupid little whore," he said. "I'm going now. You may leave this room, but not the house. Disobey at your peril… it might be amusing to hand you over to Tom, after all. Give my regards to your mother, we have known each other for many years. And, of course, give my regards also to Mr. Withers."

With that he left. Charlotte's mind was in turmoil. Carl knew her mother. And more, he knew Henry. She had a dreadful feeling that she understood at long last what was really going on, but the thought was too black to bear examination.

She wandered out into the garden, and carefully picked a bunch of flowers for her mother's room. Sweet English roses, their petals beginning to drop as soon as they were out of the bud, leaves of fern and tall stems of foxglove. Mr. Pearson saw her, and for a moment Charlotte stiffened, expecting him to come over and force her to her knees, so that she could once again taste his sour old cock. But he merely smirked at her and ogled her nipples, as they jutted against her top, and her bare thighs where they disappeared under her skirt.

"Nice and cool that way, innit?" he said when he drew

near to her, leering disgustingly, his eyes flicking over her body like a snake's tongue, tasting her through the air. She flushed as she realised he was referring to her lack of underwear. So he knows, she thought. And does he also know to whom I now belong? It seemed more than likely. But she was glad that things had changed, that the old man apparently no longer had the right to touch her. She was sold, and the staff were not permitted to finger the goods, or at least, not without the owner's express permission.

She walked back into the house, opening windows in all the rooms. The air was still, too still, she felt stifled. The heat wave had lasted the whole of the last month and she was beginning to find it oppressive. Something in her was longing for autumn, for gusting breezes, for falling yellow leaves, and the chill steady soak of rain. But what would these things mean to her, now? Would she still be allowed to walk in the woods? Would she be allowed out of doors at all? It was no longer up to her, she was property. All she could hope for was that her owner was a kind man. Perhaps it was strange that she did not even consider running away, for she knew Carl's threat was probably idle. She was staying because she wanted to stay. Why she wanted to stay, why she was so accepting of her new role in life, she would have found hard to say, but it had something to do with resonance, she thought.

In America there was once a bridge, built without due regard for resonance. It's gone down in history now with the name 'Galloping Gertie'. All was fine until one day the wind blew with just the right force and speed to set the bridge reverberating like a plucked string. Wilder and wilder grew its arcing movements until finally the structure could stand no more, it collapsed into a heap of rock and steel and cement.

Always inside herself had been this black desire for humiliation, pain and restraint. Her earliest pre-sexual fantasies had involved men pinning her out naked in the sun, or strapping her inside a barrel that they rolled along. Once Carl had come into her life, taking control of her, pulling her strings, she had begun to reverberate under the force of his will, like the bridge in the wind. And the blackness of it fed something in her soul, some dark need beyond understanding, and as it was fed, so it grew. And now she was wild, her desires and needs out of control, and without the guiding hand of a man, a firm, cruel hand to keep her in balance, she would be lost.

The sound of gravel under wheels in the driveway, and she looked out to see Mummy and Henry getting out of the car. Henry looked straight at her, up at her bedroom window. Their eyes met, and she felt as though liquid ice had been poured into her through her open pupils; a deadening chill ran through her veins, and she knew that her guess had been correct.

She made herself go down to meet them, made herself smile at Mummy and listen to her happy chatter about the holiday. They had had a nice time, it seemed. Her mother didn't seem to notice that she was rather sluttishly dressed for a day at home, and as they settled down with a cup of tea she even remarked,

"It's nice to see you making the best of yourself, dear," smiling warmly.

Henry was standing behind her as she spoke. He did not speak but he looked right at Charlotte, into her eyes, his mouth turned up in the slightest of smiles. The satisfied smile of a man when something he owns is praised in his hearing, thought Charlotte, and again her blood ran cold.

Everyone was tired, or said they were, so after dinner they went their separate ways, to bed.

Charlotte undressed and washed, still wearing the harness. It looked bizarre on her body now, against the bland normality of her mother's return. But with a shiver she knew that it would soon seem all too appropriate.

She didn't question what she was about to do. She made

up her face very carefully, in the way Carl had taught her. Dark kohl around the eyes, long false lashes and the red whore mouth. She picked out some thick gold hoop earrings, and poked the wires through her pierced earlobes. Yes, they looked quite fitting.

Wrapping herself in her robe she made her way back to her room. The house was dark, silent. She hung her robe on the back of the bedroom door, and went to her window, naked apart from the harness. The sweet scent of summer night was pouring in through the open window, the trees black against a turquoise sky already glittering with stars.

She drew the curtains, and then turned on the lamps. There were several of them, around the walls. They lit her harnessed body with a soft glow that looked somehow very ancient. She knew then, as she pulled her fuck lips separate under the restraining straps, pinning them against her thighs the way she had been instructed, that what was happening to her was part of something very old, very traditional; that men had been enslaving girls to use them as pleasure toys for millennia stretching back, uncounted and uncountable. She was not the first girl to be used thus, nor would she be the last, she was just one of a multitude of females, born of Adam's rib, accepting their fate as cast.

She assumed the position as instructed, facing the door, her feet placed wide apart, her knees bent, her hands gently clasped behind her buttocks. She felt overwhelmingly sexual standing so displayed, and she felt a huge peace spreading over her in the knowledge that females had stood in exactly this pose, naked and accessible, for so many thousands of years. The leather pushed against her breasts, offering them to whoever should come to take possession of them.

He opened the door.

He didn't knock, of course, for a knock is a way of asking permission, and he had no need to do that. He saw her standing, waiting for him, naked and harnessed and ready to be used, and he smiled.

"Hello Charlotte."

"Hello… Uncle Henry."

She wasn't sure whether using his name might earn her a slap. Carl had always insisted she call him 'Master', any other form of address brought a swift cuff to her ears. But she had guessed that part of her appeal to this man was that she was his wife's daughter. He was in a position of power over her, and he was delighting in abusing that power. His smile broadened and she knew she had guessed right.

He walked right up to her and let his eyes wander slowly all over her body. She burnt with pleasure to see how delighted he was with what he saw. She knew she was beautiful, and she had never before been so fiercely glad of her beauty. It was wonderful to see his total approval of every inch of her flesh.

"Lovely," he breathed, "quite lovely. You are even more delicious than I could have hoped. I am so very glad your father was a gambling man."

What did he mean? She didn't understand.

"You see, my dear Charlotte…" as he spoke he began to touch her, trailing his fingers lightly over her jutting breasts and silken belly. It was as though a spasm of sexual electricity vibrated from his touch directly to the core of her, her throbbing clitoris. Her vagina clenched almost violently in an ache of pure need. "… your darling Daddy left your poor mother very deeply in debt. She didn't want to marry again, but she was on the brink of losing everything, including this lovely house. Rather than sell the house she sold the occupants," he tittered at his own joke, "sold herself… and you, too."

Charlotte's blood beat in terrible waves in her ears. What was he saying? That her mother knew about this, had actually helped arrange it?

"Of course, your mother isn't the sort of woman to be able to face such a situation directly, with no pretence, no veneer that things are all perfectly normal. She knows that

I married her to enjoy not just her body, fine though it undoubtedly still is, but also your own. Yes, she knows, because I spelt it out to her. But immediately afterwards she pretended that we had never had such a sordid conversation. Poor Charlotte, your mother is a madam, your home a brothel, you the tart and I the customer. But your mother's sensibilities are such that we must never acknowledge this reality. And besides, it isn't an entirely accurate analogy. For you are not really a tart, you are only a holster."

As he said the last word he poked two fingers hard into her anus. She whimpered a little; he had done it so suddenly and roughly that he had hurt her. But he began to press a third to join them.

"And so, my arrangement with your mother is this. I am a man with vast sexual needs, she knows this, but she is only capable of accommodating me up to a point. And I hold the dear lady in the deepest respect... do not imagine that I only married her to possess you. Not at all, I wanted her for my wife. But one doesn't fuck one's wife up the arse," here he jabbed the three fingers hard into her tender passage, in repeated vicious thrusts, "one doesn't encourage dozens of men to cover her face with their semen, one doesn't arrange to have her cunt fisted by a... big... strong... powerful... black... man." His thrusting fingers punctuated the words. "All these delights... and they will delight me, oh yes, indeed... I save for you, sweet young Charlotte. Besides, your perfect body is just made for torment."

And now, finally, he pulled her over to the bed.

That night Charlotte was subjected to sexual passions of a more depraved nature than any she had yet had to bear. Henry tied her spread-eagled on the bed, every sinew, every muscle taut, so that she could not shift even one inch to avoid the exploring tongue with which he proceeded to anoint and caress her most intimate parts. Then he squatted above her face, lowered himself towards her and ordered her to lick his anus. Charlotte bit her lips tight shut, but the cruel man responded by pinching and nipping at her clitoris until, utterly defeated, she did as her Master bade her. As she stimulated him he beat himself off, splattering come all over her breasts and belly.

She thought then that he might let her rest, surely he had forced her to enjoy enough perversion for one night? But Henry had waited a long time to possess his beautiful and arrogant step-daughter, and he was not yet sated.

Kneeling over her he slipped his index finger into her vagina. She was wonderfully tight, her sex muscles gripped his finger as firmly as though it were a large penis. He slipped in a second finger to join it, and then a third. When his fourth finger was joined by his thumb, all five digits pressing hard towards her tight opening, Charlotte understood what he was going to do. A few days before she would have struggled bitterly against such an indignity, but now she knew better. There was no point resisting, he had her entirely in his grasp. Besides, nothing he might want her to do, sexually, could be as disgusting or humiliating as what he had already forced from her. So finally she lay passive as he began to force the whole of his rather large fist into her so recently virgin cunt.

For a moment or two Henry thought the girl was just too small and tight to take the whole of his hand. But he kept pressing, pushing hard against her hole, and after a few minutes of resistance her body finally surrendered to his plunder. She looked so lovely, so sweet and beautiful and so impure and depraved with his fist inside her, that the few thrusts of his arm that brought the captive slut to orgasm were enough to spurt his own climax over her already sticky pubic mound. Creamy milk was trickling from her full breasts, and he bent his head and licked the sweetness. It was just another way to devour her, another way to possess her.

"Next time I do this to you, Charlotte, there will be a dozen men in the room, each eager to follow suit. And half of them will be manoeuvring cameras, to record every tear, every penetration and every orgasm that your body can offer."

He untied her, but even then he was not finished; throughout that long night she would doze for a while, only to be awakened by his cock, pushing against her lips, or her cunt, or, most often, her anus. Henry had supplemented his normally excellent staying power with a hefty dose of Viagra; he was confident that their first night of lovemaking was not one young Charlotte would soon forget.

CHAPTER FOURTEEN

The next morning at breakfast Charlotte could hardly bear to look at her mother, knowing the older woman had sold her into slavery just to keep her wealth and status. Charlotte's anus still stung from the brutality of Henry's repeated onslaughts. When she did look at her she glared, furiously, as though challenging Margaret to defend herself. She had expected her mother to look shame-faced and defensive, and was startled to find her gaze met steadily, until it was she, Charlotte, who dropped her eyes back to her uneaten breakfast, whilst her mother still regarded her with equanimity.

"I don't think Henry told you the full extent of our deal."

Her mother's voice was calm and rather cold.

"When I married him I did, indeed, agree that he could have you too, and use you as he wished. But only on one condition."

Charlotte looked up, glaring resentfully across the table.

"Well? What condition?"

"He agreed only to claim his rights over you when you made advances towards him. I know about that day in his car, Charlotte. I know how you lifted your skirt to expose your thighs to him, to try and entice him into your bed. I know you wore an even shorter skirt the next day.

"Charlotte, this is all your own doing. You betrayed me; you behaved like a whore by trying to seduce Henry. My *husband*! Your own mother's husband! You behaved like a whore. That was the one condition I laid upon the arrangement when I married: only if you behaved like a whore would you be turned into one. You have reaped your reward.

"And shall I tell you something else? I knew, and Henry knew, that he would get what he wanted. Because every time in the years since your father's death when I've introduced you to a man friend of mine, a man I might have considered wedding, you have flirted, you have batted your eyelids, you have stuck out your tits and bottom like a she-cat wanting a tom to mount her. And Charlotte, I was so very sick and tired of it. You have finally got your just deserts."

She relaxed back into her chair, smiling a little grimly. Charlotte did not know what to say; everything her mother said was true. Swallowing her pride she blurted out,

"Mummy... I'm sorry...I..."

"Oh, you *will* be sorry, Charlotte. I have no doubt Henry will make you very sorry indeed."

With that, her mother picked up the paper and began to read, disappearing from view and effectively ending the conversation.

"But Mummy... I don't understand. If this was all worked out between you and Henry, what about that man, Tom, who saw me in my room... and Carl... how does he come into it?"

Her mother didn't bother to lower the paper, she spoke from behind it in a rather bored tone.

"Tom just chanced upon you masturbating because you're such a slut, you do it all the time, after all, don't you? Henry had already employed Carl to break you in, that's why Tom was cleaning the windows in the first place, though Carl hadn't explained to him, he's very discreet, that's why we employed him. If Tom hadn't called Carl up, Carl would have thought of another way to trap you. And if we needed any further proof that you're a slut and deserve to be treated like one, we certainly got it that day, didn't we?" She lowered her paper and looked at her daughter in disgust, rather as one might regard a particularly revolting invertebrate. "You agreed to have sex with all of them! A whole gang of men! I've seen the video, Charlotte. I would never have believed it. If your dear father had been alive it would have broken his heart. You dirty little whore!"

And with this her mother rose, and left the room.

Later that day Henry announced that she would be accompanying him on a visit to the Sinclairs. Charlotte's stomach tightened in dread, but if truth be told, she would at any rate be glad to leave the house. The atmosphere between her and her mother was intolerable.

Henry must have been aware of this, for on the drive up he said,

"You won't be returning to Beeches. I don't think it would be fair on your mother to continue to allow you under the same roof. There is a spare office adjoining mine in chambers, I am having it converted to house you. You won't get out very much, but no matter, the important thing is you'll be there, ready, available to be beaten and fucked whenever I or my clients should feel like enjoying you. Of course, you'll get worked rather harder there than you would if I kept you at home, but that will do you good, I'm sure. The more cocks use your cunt, the more come on your tits, the better you'll understand that your body is no longer your own and that you only exists for male pleasure."

He didn't speak again until they were sat in a traffic jam, when suddenly he barked, "Pull up your skirt, play with yourself, make yourself come."

Charlotte did as he ordered, trying not to see the lorry driver whom she knew was leering down at her. Henry had dressed her in a short shift of white cotton, through which the dark areolae of her nipples were clearly visible. She tugged it up to her waist and, spreading her lips to expose the glistening sex meat she began to finger her clitoris, rubbing it in little circles with increasing ferocity as her passion mounted. When she came to a shrieking climax the man called out to Henry, "Nice piece of skirt! Wouldn't mind some of it myself!"

"If you'd care to pull in at the next services you can help yourself to her, I like watching her being fucked by other men," Henry called over her.

"Please, no!" Charlotte turned her imploring face to her

master, but he just chuckled.

They didn't even bother to take her inside, just bent her over double between two lorries, pulling her short dress up so that it hung forward over her head, leaving her fuck holes and naked tits accessible to their roving hands. The lorry driver chose her asshole, and stuffed himself brutally inside. He squeezed her tits as he fucked her, holding onto them like reins, his belly skin slap slapping against her buttocks as he drove into her, hard and fast.

"Cheers mate, you sure you don't want me to give you anything for the ride?"

"No, it was my pleasure. Before you put your cock away could you just wipe it on her face? Thankyou. I like to make sure she knows her place, you see."

Charlotte and Henry continued their journey in silence. The lorry driver had filled her ass with a big gift of his come, and it slowly trickled out of Charlotte's anus, making a damp, sticky patch on her skirt where it pressed against the leather upholstery.

As they drove up in front of the dark, daunting manor, Jonathan Sinclair came out to greet them.

"Ah Henry, how good to see you again! And you've brought the cock holster Carl was training for you. I must say, for an amateur Carl does a very good job, a very good job indeed. I'd rather like him to work for me, but he prefers to be his own man and I can understand that. He was turning her into a milker for you, I believe?"

"Great to see you too, Jon. Yes, she's full of milk, see for yourself," and Henry unbuttoned Charlotte's dress, pulling it open to reveal her heavy breasts. Sir Jonathan reached and squeezed her tits and Charlotte felt that familiar painful tingling as her milk let down. The old man started to pull on both her breasts, as though she was a cow with ready udders, and milk jetted from her nipples, down over her dress.

"Mmm, plenty there. Nice and creamy too, by the looks of it. Would you like to see the barn where I keep my milk slaves, she could perhaps join them, they are due to be milked about now?"

"Excellent, please do show me."

Sir Jonathan led them round the side of the house to the farm buildings. As they approached the lovely old barn, Charlotte could hear muffled moans and whimpers. Sir Jonathan opened the door.

A dozen girls were crouched on all fours in straw lined stalls, each girl facing the wall and tethered in place by a short chain that reached to her heavy iron collar, and also by manacles that held her wrists and ankles to the ground. But their faces were hidden by a wooden partition akin to mediaeval stocks, their necks disappearing through a hole so that, unless one leant over, all that could be seen of each hapless girl was her body from the neck down. Charlotte's vagina clenched in shameful arousal at this forceful reminder that these girls were just bodies to please the men who owned them. Then her eyes widened as she saw that each pair of breasts was covered by narrow transparent plastic cups, attached to tubing. As she watched, the imprisoned breasts were lengthened into ridiculous cones by the force of suction, then released back to their normal shape, before being tugged into cones once more. The action endlessly repeated, accompanied by squirting noises as the milk spurted out of the udders, and low moans from the girls who sounded as though they were in considerable discomfort.

"Fasten her here, Henry."

Charlotte looked up to see Sir Jonathan standing in an empty stall, holding out an iron collar... Totally panic-stricken, she turned to flee, but her Master was too quick for her. Although she struggled as best she might the two men were stronger by far, and she was soon kneeling on the straw, sobbing and tugging futilely at her bound wrists and ankles as a stable boy pushed and tugged plastic cups over her own breasts. Both Sir Jonathan and Henry had evidently been aroused by her pathetic attempt at escape, for now they were rubbing their long, hard cocks. Her neck rested against the smooth old wood that formed the lower half of the partition, nestled in the well-worn semi-circle cut out to receive it, and now the stable lad brought the hinged upper half down to imprison her, and she was suddenly divorced from her body, able to feel the indignities they would force upon it but see only the wooden wall of the stall, where there were two empty bottles clipped securely in place, waiting to receive her milk.

The stable lad turned on the milking machine. Charlotte yelped in surprise and pain as the invisible power of the suction tugged her breasts roughly forward, squeezing them as though crude hands were upon them. Again. And again. Now her milk began to flow, and she flushed with humiliation as a creamy white stream jetted along the tubing to the bottles in front of her. At the same moment she felt the heat of a cock against her fuck lips, and knew that she was to be enjoyed whilst they milked her. Charlotte felt quite desperately humiliated. She didn't even know which of the two men was inside her. Not that it mattered much, for as soon as one had finished another cock took possession, pounding into her in time with the sucking tugs of the milking machine.

After enjoying her, the men left the whore being milked and made their way back to the house. They settled in the library to enjoy a glass of brandy before luncheon.

"I've just taken delivery of a new statue, Henry. It's based on Michelangelo's 'David'... but with a few amusing alterations."

Henry raised his eyebrows, smiling enquiringly.

"I think you have to see it to appreciate it, really. I've had it erected in the great dining room. Come..."

He led Henry through the doors at the other end of the library, and smilingly gestured at the new work of art. Monumentally huge, carved from snow white marble, the statue was indeed a modern version of 'David'. But this David was looking down towards his own penis, which jutted in a monstrous erection.

Henry chuckled, "How witty!"

"I was inspired by the phallic fragments from Grecian statues that my great grandfather brought back from his grand tour of Europe. They make excellent dildos."

Sir Jonathan gestured towards 'David', "He hasn't been christened, yet."

Henry chuckled again, "Christened? You mean you will actually impale a slave girl on that monster dick? Oh, excellent, you never cease to amaze me, Jon, you're so inventive."

"Why thank you, Henry. I do try to continually come up with new ways to humiliate and punish the whores, it's more entertaining for the guests that way, but one does sometimes get the feeling in this business that it's all been done before. But no matter, the important thing is to do it superlatively well. I was wondering if you'd like to see young Charlotte impaled on David's rod?"

"Oh certainly, I'd be delighted. Carl maintains she's thoroughly broken, but as you saw in the milking shed, she still rebels on occasion. I think a cock of that size up her cunt would be a salutary experience. And she really is exceedingly pretty, she'll make an attractive ornament for your diners. Hogtied, perhaps?"

"Yes, I think so. And with an iron collar and chain... we can loop the leash over David's hand...he'll look as though he's a giant who has caught and rogered a nymph."

Both men laughed.

"More like a nympho if it's Charlotte on his dick," remarked Henry, as they went to lunch.

Charlotte's ordeal in the milking shed lasted over two hours. The stable hands had instructions not to release any of the holsters until the pint bottles were full. Charlotte had not been milked regularly enough to readily lactate sufficiently, and after the initial gushings her flow slowed to a trickle. Her dry tits ached as the machine continued to pump away regardless, pumping her cream drop by drop into the waiting bottles. Time and again she felt hands on her rump and the hot pressure of a shaft against her cunt or asshole, before yet another cock was forcibly rammed into her trembling body. The stable lads were always hungry for new meat, and this particular bit of flesh was of the best quality; they all wanted to enjoy it.

One of them must have decided that using only one of her fuck holes was either insufficient indignity for her or insufficient pleasure for him, for as his penis pushed to enter her cunt she felt a colder, harder pressure at her anus as a strap-on was driven into her pinioned flesh. She whimpered at this, but he carried on regardless and she was soon being brutally ridden in evident enjoyment. After that they must have decided to share the dildo, for each time a spent cock slipped wetly from her dribbling hole there was a few minutes' pause, and then again that pressure at both cunt and anus together.

Doubtless Charlotte would have orgasmed repeatedly as she was ridden, but the hands were under strict instructions to deliver the whore in an aroused state, the better to please the gentlemen, and so each time they sensed her approaching climax they nipped and pinched her clitoris cruelly until the pleasure seeped away from her abused body.

When finally the bottles were brimful of her rich and creamy milk, she was released to pasture with the other milk sluts. Chained to poles in the field there was nothing for the girls to do but lie in the sun and eat the nutritious but disgusting swill that was standard slave fare at the manor, slurping it as best they could from the stone troughs, with their arms firmly fastened behind their backs.

Charlotte was starving, she wolfed down far more than her share of the feed, butting other sluts out of the way with her head in her determination to eat. Then she lay down in the sun, and slept.

They came for her early in the evening. She was hosed down in the yard as before, and her lovely long hair brushed to shining brilliance by one of the other girls. Her hands were strapped together behind her back, and Joe, the groom, told the girl to paint her face. When she had finished she held up a mirror for Charlotte to see herself. Again the dark slutty doe eyes. Again the scarlet whore's mouth. And she saw that her skin was aglow now with health and vitality and emotional ease: she was blooming in her new life as a cock holster.

Joe led her into the house. She could hear the laughter and merriment of the gentlemen in the great hall, but he did not take her there. Instead he led her to the dining room, where the long, narrow, mahogany table set with snow white linen and glittering silver had been moved to one side for a buffet dinner, presided over by the obscenely aroused David. Joe led her up to the statue. Charlotte stared at it, mouth agape, blushing to see the penis so much larger than life. She couldn't help herself, the desire to touch was irresistible; she pressed her cheek against it, and stroked its length. It was cold, and so smooth it felt like satin, or the silken velvet of a real cock. It curved up in a gentle arc, the tip so beautifully carved that it seemed as though it would only take a magic breath from Aslan to stir it to life…

Joe placed his two, big, strong hands either side of her waist, and lifted her up. Surprised, she wriggled, looked at his intent face which was focussed lower down, looked below her… suddenly she understood what he was about to do. She gasped in shock and tried to squirm away, but it was too late. The cold tip of the stone phallus had penetrated

214

her vagina, and as Joe gently took his hands away her own body weight brought her softly down, so that she sank lower and lower until finally she was totally impaled on the huge shaft, facing away from the statue, facing the audience of dinner guests who would soon throng the room.

Charlotte had been penetrated by many cocks and dildos since her enslavement began, but none so huge as the monstrous rod that now stuffed her cunt full with its solid mass. She moaned and tried to shift her weight so as to be less completely stuffed, but she only contrived to sink even lower on the huge artificial organ.

Joe leant round behind her, and pulled her ankles up to meet her wrists, binding them tidily together. He looped the handle of her chain leash around David's hand, and stood back to survey the effect.

The slut looked magnificent, just as they imagined, like an illustration from some myth where the giants have come to rape and enslave the water nymphs. He felt his own cock spring to hardness, just to see the poor girl impaled in such an undignified and brutal fashion. She was whimpering and wriggling, and he hoped she wouldn't slump into total passivity before the guests arrived, because her futile attempts to help herself added a delicious frisson to the obscene amusement.

Her breasts were unbound, and with her arms and legs hogtied behind her they pushed forwards, exhibiting themselves to best advantage. Perfect, snowy orbs, just made for abuse... Quickly he surveyed the racks, and found what he was looking for. Cruel clips that would snap shut on her sweet nipples, gripping with unforgiving steel teeth. From them hung short bars of steel, like pencils, on which could be slotted iron weights. Joe grinned as the slut yelped in pain as he let the clips fall closed, then he slipped a hefty weight onto each bar, enjoying her pathetic moans of distress. He left a basket of weights on the floor between David's feet, so that the gentlemen could increase her torment as they wished.

He stepped back again. The tableau was perfected. The nymph was now obviously suffering, far more clearly a victim of the cruel giant who had taken her by force. The abused breasts, nipples dotted with white milk, would stimulate the appetites of the diners for the entertainment planned for later that evening. Best of all, the unfortunate Charlotte was now in so much discomfort that she simply could not stay still, wriggling on the impaling phallus like a worm on a hook. He looked at her sex lips, spread so far apart by the thick shaft, and was pleased to see they were glistening with fuck juices. Her clitoris was a fat swollen cherry, doubtless she would climax with very little attention.

The gentlemen began to file into the room.

"Oh I say, Jonathan!" drawled an upper-crust voice. "That really is a superb display. I don't recall seeing this cock-holster before?"

"Thank you, Philip. No, she's not one of mine, she's the property of Henry here, his step-daughter, actually. Was a very prim and proper little miss rich bitch until a month ago, a virgin indeed. But Henry employed Carl Bredon to break her in for him, she's an owned slut, now."

"I can see that."

The drawling man was standing right in front of the pinioned Charlotte, leering at her. She again had that feeling of invisibility, for although he was eyeing her closely, eyeing her cunt where the stone penis stuffed it, and her poor, tormented breasts, and even reaching a hand up to inspect her mouth, she, Charlotte, felt unseen. She was just a body to this man, just a pretty collection of sexual parts. She felt almost as though she were viewing the world from behind glass, no longer allowed to interact with it. From now on it seemed, things would always be done to her, she would be the object, not the subject, of whatever occurred.

The room was filling up. The leering man moved to join the other diners at the table, where elegant dishes of all sorts of delicious foods had appeared. Only then did Charlotte notice the unfortunate girl who had been bound to the table, her neck and head flopping unsupported at the wall side, her naked pussy spread and accessible in the centre. Her wrists were tied together and pulled down towards the floor by the weight of a huge ball and chain, which looked, and in fact was, a mediaeval restraint, passed down through the Sinclair family for generations, like so much else of the estate. Her legs were widely spread... so widely spread, in fact, that Charlotte was sure she must be in considerable discomfort... bent at the knee, and fastened to the glossy mahogany with tight leather straps.

But it was the girl's fuck hole that caught Charlotte's attention, mesmerizing her. A series of rings had been pierced through the soft flesh of her labia, and through these leather laces drawn. Presumably her lips could be laced together, chastely. At the moment, however, the laces were wrapped round her thighs, so as to pull her pussy completely open, and render her cunt totally accessible. Watching the bound girl Charlotte could see why the gentleman needed her so open. She caught snatches of the conversation:

"Would you like some sauce on that celery, Sir?"

"Yes, thank you, what do you have?"

" We have hollandaise, mayonnaise and the chef's special, Sir, served in the whore. It's a delicate blend of organic olive oil and balsamic vinegar de Modena, flavoured with honey and given body with egg yolk. Serving it in a slut adds a subtle flavour that makes it really quite unique, Sir," the servant added with a smirk.

Charlotte could hardly believe her eyes as the man took his stick of celery and thrust it into the poor girl, helpless on the table. She didn't believe for a minute the men were actually going to eat the celery, it was just another way to humiliate a female. Her suspicions were confirmed when one of the other men picked up a whole cucumber and pushed it firmly into the bound slut, easing it steadily in and out so that she groaned, a deep guttural noise of pleasure.

"How about some sauce on this then?" he chortled, to loud guffaws.

The men filled their plates, and stood around chatting. Other slaves were crawling meekly around the room on all fours, apparently begging to be allowed to suck cock. As the men were serviced they paid the whores no heed, nonchalantly continuing to talk and eat even as they were sucked off.

A small group gathered around Charlotte. Men prodded and poked at her cunt, or swung the dangling rods so that the weights stretching her nipples became even more painful. Then one of them discovered the basket of extra weights that Joe had so considerately left between David's feet.

"Ho, ho, let's see how she likes these!"

They proceeded to thread more and more iron onto the rods, until tears ran down poor Charlotte's face.

"I'd say she needs whipping now. What do you say, Henry?"

"Oh please do, be my guest, mark her as much as you like."

The men needed no further encouragement. Poor Charlotte flinched and wept as lash after lash curled in stinging triumph all over her delicate frame, patterning her white breasts and belly with fierce red welts. As each blow struck her aching breasts the pain shivered through her, black and overwhelming. When they turned their attentions to her clitoris, whilst still maintaining the torment of her tits, the agony was indescribable. By the time they had finished their meal and were beginning to wander off Charlotte was barely conscious, swimming in a sexual delirium of arousal and pain. For her submissive, masochistic nature was such that even this cruel treatment aroused her.

When he came to remove the dining ornament, Joe took

pity on her. He held a vibrator against her swollen clitoris, and within seconds she orgasmed, screaming in a climax that was as painful as it was pleasurable.

CHAPTER FIFTEEN

They let her rest the next morning, but by evening the men knew she'd be fit to work again. Henry was very keen to see her 'enjoying' a new fuck machine that Sir Jonathan had devised; it was particularly ingenious and quite desperately cruel, and just the thought of fresh-faced Charlotte on The Swing, as it had been nicknamed, was enough to stiffen his cock.

It was night when they fetched her from the stable where she'd been sleeping, nestled into the companionable warmth of a pair of pony girls. The girls had been kind to her. Neither of them had spoken; Charlotte got the impression that they had almost forgotten how, they had been treated like animals for so long; but they had nuzzled against her, blowing cool breath on her burning welts.

It was Joe who came to prepare her. He carried with him a handful of clothes in which she was to be displayed. First on was a stiff, leather corset, hard black hide, constructed to nip the waist as tightly as possible and to leave the tits totally exposed. Joe strung her from a ring in the rafters whilst he laced it so tightly that she whimpered. The two pony girls whimpered too, as though in sympathy. But Charlotte saw how they tried to rub their pudenda against the wooden stall partitions, before Joe stopped them with an angry slap on their arching behinds. One of the reasons the Sinclairs never had any united trouble from the girls was that each submissive was all too happy to see any of the others maltreated; not an atmosphere conducive to building a rebellion.

After the corset came fine rubber stockings, attached by suspenders. Her feet were clad in stilettos so high she could only mince. An inflatable gag was stuffed in her mouth, and then over that a heavy leather hood; buckled tightly at the throat, mouth and eyes; the darkness itself seemed to press in on her. Her arms were pulled roughly behind her back, and wrist strapped to wrist, elbow to elbow. She was desperately conscious of the nakedness of her breasts, of the way the binding of her arms proffered her tits forwards, as though offering them to be devoured. When a hand gently stroked her nipple she shivered, tensely silent, for she knew by now what was likely to happen next. Sure enough her milk let down, with a prickling, tingling sensation, and then a bolt of pain shot through her teat as a clip snapped shut upon the tender flesh. She braced herself for the next clip's bite, but just to tease her Joe held off a while, then when he saw she was again relaxed and undefended he let the clip snap shut, not on her other nipple but on her clitoris. Whilst she was still whimpering from that abuse the third clip snapped into place on her other teat.

Thus blind, displayed and tormented, Joe led her across the cobbled yard, leading her by a chain attached to her collar. She stumbled a little, and once began to fall, but the hefty groom just yanked her back upright, the stiff collar biting unpleasantly into the soft skin of her neck.

Into the manor, down a spiral staircase, her heels clicking sharply on the ancient worn stone. Dimly, as though very far off through thick walls and oaken doors, she can hear laughter, the happy sounds of relaxation. Male voices, always male, the women here have lost their words, for now a cry rings out, cutting clear above the softer sounds of jollity, and the cry comes from a throat so purely female that in this dark place it can only utter sounds of pain, fear and, above all, arousal.

Charlotte teeters along, scared that she might fall and hurt herself, scared of what might be hidden in the darkness around her, scared of what the future holds. If she had known that this was the path that lay ahead, would she still have acquiesced to Carl's demands, so long ago when she lay naked in the wood, seduced by his quick tongue into offering herself so freely? She is no longer sure. Looking back, now,

221

she feels as though Carl was almost kind to her. At any rate, there is a cruel depravity in Henry's makeup that was not there in Carl. It scares her. It excites her too, but maybe now the fear is getting the upper hand. Henry is so predatory, and sometimes she thinks he would actually like to consume her, make her flesh one with his own, control her mind so completely that she becomes nothing more than a sex puppet, acting out his dreams and dark desire for total domination.

They have reached a long, carpeted hallway now, deep under the old house. Their footfalls are almost soundless, not even a creak of floorboard under Joe's heavy weight. She guesses that the carpet is laid over stone.

Suddenly they stop, and she hears, just to her right, the sound of a handle turning, a door creaking open. At the same moment a gush of cold dank air pushes over her.

He leads her into the room. The floor is stone, she hears her heels click against it. One catches in a groove between the slabs, and she knows from that, and from the grainy roughness of the stone under foot, that this floor is not an elegant marble affair like that in the upper hallway, polished and re-polished to glossy perfection, rather it is both crude and ancient. She shivers because she knows where they have brought her, and can guess that many hapless maidens have stood in this very place before her. She is right inside the black heart of the house, the pulsing heart that feeds the Sinclair slave machine, that fills the coffers of the rich men who own her. She is in the dungeons of the Sinclair Manor. The air around her is thick with silence, but she can sense there are men here, watching her. She can even smell them, the warmth of their bodies, an opulent aroma of cigars and leather and fine soap. But there is a darker odour here, too, the dank mouldy smell that is always thick in the deep moist places of the world, laced with the smells of stale sex, and piss.

Strong hands lift her, and mount her on a small, high seat.

A narrow dildo presses somewhat flaccidly into her liquid cunt. She feels rubbery loops tugged around her breasts, and her ankles tied apart, open. Then, nothing. She waits. And waits.

Gradually she becomes aware of a feeling of heat in her genitals. It grows steadily, uncomfortable within minutes, concentrated on her clitoris. Soon it is intolerable. Through the thick leather of the hood she hears muffled chuckles as she begins to pull and twist, desperate to escape the heat. With horror and overwhelming fear she thinks they must have lit a fire close under her open pudenda. In total panic now she pisses herself.

Loud guffaws of laughter.

"Light another one!"

Within a few minutes the heat is back to full intensity. Again Charlotte struggles and wriggles to escape the fierceness of it. The metal seat upon which she is resting is heating up, how can she get away? But now, as she squirms, she feels the seat under her begin to rock slightly. With a few more experimental twists she realises that she is on a swing, and that she can quite easily avoid the heat under her pussy by moving so as to rock herself back and forth. She lets out a long, low sigh of relief. Her skin under the hood is wet with sweat, and fine warm rivulets trickle down her face and over her exposed breasts.

Henry watched the swinging slut with satisfaction. It had been most amusing when she'd been so scared she'd pissed on the candle. No matter, candles were always in plentiful supply at the manor. This one was a monster, a tall church candle, three foot high, three inches wide. They had set it alight just under the metal plate upon which Charlotte was seated, and it soon heated up enough to panic her. It wasn't hot enough to actually hurt her, of course; they were sexual sadists, not psychopaths; but at least part of the excitement came from the fact that the girls could never be quite sure of that. With her nipples abused and the thick hood forcing her into isolation, poor Charlotte would be sufficiently disorientated to experience that total terror which pain and the unknown delivers so effectively.

Poor little Charlotte. Henry's cock was rock hard. He wondered how long it would take the whore to realise what effect the swinging action was having. Not long, he should imagine. Already the rubber tubes surrounding her heavy tits were plumping up with the steady pump of air, so the dildo inside her which had looked such a meagre and unthreatening piece of equipment would also be swelling. Sir Jonathan really did have a particularly inventive mind when it came to devices to sexually torment helplessly masochistic females. It amused Henry greatly to know that it was Charlotte's own swinging movements that were pumping the dildo so that soon it would be quite agonisingly large. Clever use of valves ensured that no air was lost should she stop swinging for a moment, and even the tiniest movements contributed to the puffing up of the pneumatic rubber shaft inside her. Meanwhile, the hoops around those fine tits would tighten as they swelled, and soon her mammaries would be taut and purpling. All the better for whipping, then, as in that engorged state the lash would really, really hurt her. Henry chuckled happily. There was nothing he enjoyed better than abusing a trussed female, and he congratulated himself yet again on managing to procure one over whose lovely flesh he had total and absolute jurisdiction. And so uncomplaining, too! The girl must be quite stupid to suffer such treatment without any protest, but all the better. The less she complained, the further he would degrade her, the harsher would be his punishments. After all, she could always say no... though he had to admit he was getting rather hard of hearing of late. One of the unexpected benefits of age: an excuse to ignore a bound girl's pleas for mercy whilst remaining free of guilt. Henry smiled to himself and looked round at his friends. Most of them had their cocks out and were stroking them in happy, relaxed pleasure, watching the tormented swinging girl. He would enjoy offering her to them afterwards, though after she had pleased this number of cocks he didn't suppose she'd even be able to walk, her pussy and thighs would be so sore.

At first all she feels is a gentle pressure around her breasts, and an increased awareness of the dildo upon which she has been impaled. But gradually the rings around her tits really begin to squeeze, uncomfortably tightly, reminiscent of the milking machine and at the same time the pressure from the invading shaft grows so that it can no longer be ignored. She whimpers and stops rocking. Immediately the heat between her legs builds up to painful levels, and she is forced to resume her swinging. And now she understands what is happening. She's the victim of a diabolical machine, where her only choice is between being stuffed beyond bearing by a huge swollen phallus, or heated beyond bearing by some flame below her. And just to add to her misery her breasts must also face the same barbaric abuse.

She swings, then stops. Swings, then stops. She's whimpering steadily now, and beyond the noise of her own suffering she can hear the chuckles and guffaws of the gentlemen for whose pleasure she is being so cruelly treated. Her vagina is now hugely stretched, and she can bear no more. She stops swinging. To her surprise the fire is out, they must have taken it away, no wonder they were laughing as she proceeded to stuff herself further. She hangs there, overwhelmed by the size of the shaft inside her tender flesh, so tormented by its unyielding presence that she barely notices her suffering breasts. And yet still her clitoris throbs with desire.

Hands upon her genitals, inspecting them, noting how far open she has been forced. The rubber of the shaft becomes transparent when it is so well inflated, so the peering male eyes can see right up inside her. Her most secret intimate places are private no longer, all is open, all is consumable, her flesh is totally owned.

"Your mother was forced wider than that when she bore you, you little whore. Let's swing her some more!"

And to Charlotte's horror Henry begins to rock her steadily back and forth, pumping the monster shaft to even greater size.

Tears are flowing freely down her face now. She has been taken to the point of enough, and now, at last, she would beg them to stop, but her mouth is so securely gagged she can only moan.

Happily for Charlotte, Henry and Sir Jonathan both agreed she had been amply stretched. But that didn't mean they couldn't have a little more fun with her before unplugging her from the force-fuck machine. Whips were handed out, and soon the little body was jerking and writhing as blow after blow landed with stinging precision upon her aching breasts. They laughed as she was repeatedly whipped to orgasm, a true masochist. But after a while she ceased to twitch and spasm as they beat her, she was overwhelmed, and finally truly subjugated.

Charlotte was too exhausted to do more than endure the orgy that followed. When they took her down from the swing it was with the inflated dildo and tit rings still in place, as the cunning design of the equipment meant that the valves could be closed and then the whore removed complete with the section of the hydraulic system that tormented her.

She could barely stand, but Henry didn't want her standing, anyway. He pushed her down on her face on the cold stone floor. The chill of the flags came as small relief to Charlotte's aching, bound breasts, for Henry pushed down hard upon her back, deliberately crushing her against the ground. Inside the hood she was close to delirious, and could only lie limp and passive as he began to force his rock hard penis into her asshole.

Tight at the best of times, Charlotte's rear fuck hole was tiny now, because of the huge intruder in her cunt. And yet Henry pressed on and into her, gradually driving his shaft inch by inch inside her tender flesh. Little squeaks of pain emerged from behind the gag that stuffed her mouth. When he finally succeeded in fully penetrating her he gave a crude bellow of triumph, and rode her like a demon. Someone remarked that it was a pity to let her mouth go to waste; the hood was removed, and Charlotte's white face emerged into the dim candle-lit gloom of the dungeons.

She was dripping with sweat, her hair plastered to her face, breathing hard through her nose like a mare that's been galloped too hard. Someone pulled the gag from her mouth, but before she could moan in response to Henry's cruel thrusts, a cock was stuffed in its place. But the men who controlled her were too impatient to be satisfied with just one cock sliding in and out of that pretty pink mouth; she was yanked onto her hands and knees, and two of the men knelt in front of her, facing each other, their cocks brushing against each other as they jutted up towards her mouth. They started to force themselves inside her and laughed with barbaric cruelty to see how widely stretched her poor mouth was as they drove into it. She was aware of a bright light on her face, and looking up she saw the omnipresent video lens, recording her defeat for the pleasure of men all over the world as the pain and humiliation brought yet another climax crashing through her trembling body.

After a while they pulled the inflated dildo from her body, whilst leaving her tits still bound. Having seen something so large inside her they all wanted to fist her. And so she ended up lying on her back against Henry's body, her legs held apart by two of the men, whilst the others took it in turns to force ever larger hands inside her burning vagina. Finally it was the turn of the largest man amongst them.

Around six foot six, with gleaming ebony skin that contrasted beautifully with her own milky complexion, his cock was ten inches long and his fists built to the same gargantuan scale. Charlotte moaned and whimpered as one finger after another was prodded up her, until at last he pushed all his digits inside her, oblivious to her tears in his pursuit of his own pleasure. When he balled his hand into a fist and her muscles clamped around his thick wrist he only needed a few thrusts of his arm to bring her to the most devastating orgasm she had ever endured. She was racked by simultaneous pleasure and pain, totally humiliated as her pretty face was drenched yet again in spunk by the men now kneeling over her.

Henry smiled, and shifted his feet where they rested on the naked whore. It had been an excellent move, taking her to the Sinclair mansion for a second time. No one would have guessed that the meek, obedient, keen-to-please slut who so gratefully accepted the benediction of his come and the privilege of his whippings was once an arrogant little rich bitch. Why, now she even *thanked* him when he permitted her to lick his anus! He had been angered by her obvious reluctance to perform the first time he'd commanded her to pleasure him that way, she had not at that point fully learnt the lesson that she only existed to give him sexual enjoyment. Now she had, and it really was a great improvement.

He shifted his feet again, deliberately bruising her with the heel of his boot. She didn't whimper. She made a good piece of furniture, he reflected, he must try her out as a mattress, soon, use one of those rubber jobbies where the slave is imprisoned under the rubber sheet, a fuckable bump in the bed. So much fun to turn a helpless, highly sexed female into nothing more than an object!

And what a good idea it had been to install her in this spare room at work, kept permanently naked unless he ordered her to dress for his pleasure, the thick iron collar attached by heavy chain to a massive iron ball ensuring that there was no possibility of her escape. Whenever his job got stressful she was here to aid his relaxation, either by shagging her or by beating her; both were excellent forms of release. Furthermore, she provided endless entertainment for his clients, crawling around under the table sucking them off during meetings or stripping to order to amuse foreign visitors. That was the only time he allowed her to dress in normal clothes: when he wanted to see her humiliation as she was forced to take them off in front of his laughing clients. And how they enjoyed it when he showed them how to milk her into their coffee!

With a grin Henry recalled her embarrassment when he had forced her to strip for a client who had been an old friend of her father's. He supposed it was the juxtaposition of her old life with her new that had caused her such obvious shame. She'd had been so overcome with blushes that in the end the elderly man had lost patience and ripped the flimsy clothes from her slender body himself, egged on by Henry, of course. Just the thought of her chastened and tearful face as the wrinkled hands had proceeded to prod and poke her pretty tits, delighting in their new freedom to enjoy her, made Henry's shaft rock hard.

A very worthwhile investment. A very worthwhile investment indeed. Need to sort out some regular exercise for her, he mused, she'd lose her looks if she was shut up all day with nothing to do but suck cock. Probably best to take her for a walk each day, like any other bitch. Or maybe a run.

Henry trotted his stallion along the drove road on the Duke's estate. How delightful to be out in the fresh air on private land, none of the hoi polloi within sight or even earshot! The naked slut ran helplessly along, tied behind the horse. Glancing over his shoulder he saw that she was dripping with sweat, her cheeks flushed, her breathing heavy. She was certainly getting a good workout. So generous of the Duke to let him use his land, in return for the occasional loan of the cock holster. Somewhere in the distance he heard the whine of a motorbike, as irritating as a tsetse fly. He scanned the horizon but he couldn't see it. Probably the sound was carried by the wind, and the bike was miles away on land to which the public had rights. They certainly had no rights here.

He brought his horse to a halt and looked at the girl again. She was gasping, quite out of breath, perhaps he'd trotted her a little too fast. Seeing her panting with the sweat trickling over her fine breasts, her arms tied behind her as always, the better to display her tits, he felt his cock twitch. But he needed a crap before he had her. Dismounting he walked behind a nearby boulder and squatted down behind the rocks.

The noise of the motorbike was growing louder. Suddenly he realised that it was very close indeed, it must be someone trespassing on the Duke's land! A wave of outraged fury piled in Henry's breast, combined with a sour taste of alarm; the rider might see his whore, that would never do. He struggled to finish defecating, the sound of the bike now so large in his ears that he knew his horse and his whore must have been seen. Fumbling to pull up his pants he looked over the rock.

Charlotte watched, bemused, as the leathered rider sped along the trail towards her. When he reached her he stopped, hopped from his machine and took out a knife.

She was naked and bound, her Master out of sight, she could do nothing to defend herself; she stood there shaking with fear, wondering what he was about to do. But the man just bent and severed the rope that bound her to the horse, then cut the rope that bound her wrists. Suddenly, unexpectedly, she was free. He looked at her face, really at her face, into her eyes, and smiled. She gazed back at him, uncertain. Then suddenly a flash of memory: all those weeks ago, the man on the motorbike as Carl had taken her to the Sinclair mansion, the man who had watched her being abused and then frowned, as though in disapproval, whilst all the other onlookers had leered and jeered.

"Who are you?" she breathed.

"Perhaps I'm your knight in shining armour," he replied, grinning. "Come on."

He was climbing back onto the bike. Charlotte hesitated. This man was not her Master, but she had become so very used to doing exactly what she was told, there was no resistance left in her. So she clambered on behind him, wrapping her arms around his warm body. Her naked breasts pressed against his broad, leather-clad back, her bare thighs, spread wide either side of the bike, pressed against his leather-clad thighs. He felt strong, very tough and very male.

He revved the engine and they glided away, Charlotte hanging on tightly, scared stiff she might fall off. Her last glimpse of Henry was as he emerged from behind the rocks, his face purple with anger, bellowing something into the wind, which took his words and blew them this way and that, into total incoherence. He waved his fist in futile fury, his trousers slipped to his ankles and he fell over.

Charlotte laid her head upon the warm, leathery back, giggling guiltily.

They rode for an hour, stopping only briefly then to pick up a bag that turned out to have clothes in it for Charlotte. She pulled them on; no underwear but worn jeans and a tight t-shirt. Her full breasts pressed sexily against the T-shirt, but she didn't notice, she was so used to being totally naked after all. Once she was dressed the man drove the bike down to the road and they sped along country lanes and through quaint villages, then out on to high, forested ground.

Dusk was drawing in and she could smell the sweet scent

of wood smoke wafting through the trees. She wondered where they were, she was completely lost. He drove off the road and down a winding forest track, taking her deep into the heart of the wood. The sky above was transparent blue, clear as a gemstone, and the first stars were coming out.

She wondered where he was taking her, this strange handsome man who would shortly be her lover. She wondered what her new life would hold. Free again, no longer a sex slave, no longer bound to serve every cock that wished to use her. The thought filled her with uneasy confusion; she had never loved Henry, in fact looking back she realised now that she rather disliked him, but her life had been very simple, and the lack of choice had made her feel oddly safe, with the same security that any reasonably well-treated pet experiences.

They rode into a clearing and she saw a cabin, bright-lit windows and a plume of wood smoke lazily trailing out of the chimney. Parked by it were twenty or so motorbikes, great black shiny machines like giant beetles, chrome antennae handlebars, helmets strung on them like bulging red eyes.

Her knight in shining armour dismounted and helped her off the bike.

"Come on."

He held both her hands and looked down at her, smiling. Then his eyes slowly travelled over her body, taking in her nipples which were hard now in the evening chill and pressing against the thin cotton shirt, then wandering lower to the jeans that pulled tight around her pussy. Charlotte blushed.

"You won't be needing these any more."

He was pulling at her T-shirt, tugging it up and exposing her breasts.

"What are you doing?" she said, confused and suddenly frightened, but unresisting.

He finished pulling her top off and stood regarding her,

his lips twitching with a wry amusement. He leant forwards, and weighed her heavy breasts in his sinewy, tanned hands, rubbing his thumbs over her nipples, then reached down and began to unfasten her jeans, all the time surveying her face with the same quizzical expression.

"You're surprised? What did you think I was stealing you away for? Didn't you realise I wanted to have you, to own you? If I see something I want, girl, I usually take it. I saw you in that car and you looked so pretty and so meek and you were doing such a good job sucking cock; I decided I'd rather like you for myself. In my line of work it was simple enough to track down where you were housed, and the foolishness of that old fart Henry in exercising you on the moors made it ridiculously easy to capture you."

He was pulling her jeans down now, and the sweet rise of her naked lips came into view. Charlotte didn't know what to say. She just stood there, meek, trembling and aroused. Her new Master slipped a finger between her fuck lips and grinned with pleasure and triumph to find that she was already wet for him.

"Little whore," he said, rubbing her clit so that she moaned and shivered, "I think you'd better suck me off right now, before we go inside and I show the gang their new plaything."

He pushed her to her knees amongst the fallen pine needles and unzipped his leathers, pulling out a large bulbous cock. Charlotte dutifully started to fellate him, daintily licking the huge, red head, but he just forced himself deep into her throat, and holding her little head between his two, large hands, thrust deeply into her. Maybe it was a while since he had used a woman, for he came in moments, spurting her throat and mouth over-flowingly full with a huge load of sour semen.

"Come on, slut," he said, pulling her roughly to her feet, trickles of semen still dripping from her mouth, "You're a biker's girl now, and there are two dozen men in there you're going to please."

He marched her down the path, pinning her arms behind her, and kicked open the cabin door.

"Here you go, lads, I got you another little sex slave to satisfy your every desire. There's nothing this whore won't happily do to please a man."

Charlotte looked around the room with scared eyes. Two dozen beefy men, dressed in leathers and drinking beer, tattoos on their bulging muscled arms, leering at her with delight. Beyond them she saw a cage of iron, where two naked girls dangled helplessly from iron rings. A third iron ring was empty.

Enlaving Anna

Giselle Lorimer

Anna is one of the most unforgettable of Silver Moon heroines. From the moment she reports for work at Sinclair Precision Components; pure, innocent and trusting her employers recognise that she has hidden depths and set about bringing them to light.

She rapidly finds herself in the hands of a centuries old slave dealing concern and is ruthlessly trained for a life of sexual servitude.

Giselle Lorimer's first book for Silver Moon vividly traces the progression of the sweet natured Anna from innocence to self-discovery with a concentrated eroticism we have seldom published before. Giselle brings her own understanding of female submissiveness to bear with devastating effect and the final acts of submission rank very high in Silver Moon's firmament.

Naked Truth

Nicole Dere

Vee finds herself confused and disturbed by her husband's sexual tastes. She had never considered that she might have a submissive side to her nature!

But when, after her husband has been posted to Africa, she is captured on a trip up country by the sadistic General Mavumbi, she is brought face to face with some uncomfortable truths.

In the company of the Danish girl Katya, Vee experiences things she had never dreamed of: things which would change her forever.

SLAVE CORP.

ALEX GEIGER

'"Here we see President Carlson negotiating with the UN just before the Slave Laws were passed. She was, of course, a vocal opponent of such a measure."

Julie looked up and saw a conventional picture of the United Nations Security Council Chamber with all the delegates sat around their desks in a huge circle.

"And here we see one of her negotiating just after."

This time the shot was of an orgy. Valerie Carlson was on her knees, collared and chained, and servicing all the other male leaders.'

Slave Corp, the world's most powerful enterprise, in the wake of the passing of the Slave Laws, controls the female half of the world's population.

Julie, a beautiful nubile eighteen year-old, has just graduated from school as a fully trained submissive – but is she? The flame of something dangerously close to rebellion burns inside her as she sets off on a journey through a devilishly perverted London in pursuit of her true identity and nature, but first she must first pass through the most depraved instruments of pleasure and pain ever conceived. The da Vinci Chamber and Slave Corp's most monstrously perverted creation yet – The Diablo Device.

Silver Moon have over a hundred titles of erotic domination and submission in their catalogue. If you would like to find out more and join our readers' club absolutely free, then write to;

Silver Moon Readers' Services
The Shadowline Building
Wembley Street
Gainsborough
Lincs DN21 2AJ

Tel: 01427 816710 (during office hours)

You will receive a free quarterly magazine with features, interviews, news, views and special offers plus the chance to order titles which are only available to club members.

Alternatively you can log onto www.adultbookshops.com to order books, electronic downloads and much more.